Just the Way You Are

Aaron & Jane
The Adlers

Anita
Louise

Anita Louise
The Adler Family Series

Bad Case of Lovin' You
Brooke & Zack

A House is Not a Home
Michael & Analese

Should I Stay or Should I Go
Connor & Gina

You Light Up My Life
Olivia & Tyler

Candlelite Publishing, LLC

Copyright © 2015 by Anita Louise

Cover Art by Angie Crawford
www.mapsbyangie.etsy.com
www.signsbyangie.etsy.com

Library of Congress Control Number: 2015959069

ISBN-13: 978-0692589304
ISBN-10: 0692589309

Dedication

To my sister Nancy

without whom

The Adler Family Series

would not have been possible.

I love you, Sis.

Meet the Adler family.

What do you get when you combine sexy and smart with kind and considerate?
~ The Adlers.

John and Juliette Adler have done a wonderful job of raising their nine children. Now those children are adults, and Juliette would like to be a grandmother. Besides, she and her husband want their children to experience what it's like to fall head-over-heels like they did over forty years ago. Enjoy the journey as each of the Adler's finds their one true love.

Dear Reader,

Romance novels are my obsession. I've devoured them almost all my life! Getting to know and care about the people I read about is great, but I'd often wonder what happened to them next. Consequently, I've always especially loved reading series. That was one of the big reasons I decided to write about a large family. The Adlers are similar in some ways to the family my husband grew up with—*nine children.* That's a bunch!

I'm thrilled to introduce you to John and Juliette Adler along with Michael, Phillip, Gabriella, Brooke, Aaron, Olivia, Luke, Whitney and Connor. Five boys and four girls with two sets of twins ... Gabriella and Brooke are identical—Olivia and Luke are fraternal. They're all different, but they have one thing in common ... an unconditional love for each other.

Aaron Adler is the "middle child" and channeled his childhood angst into becoming a psychologist turned successful author and speaker. His life is perfect ... except when it comes to love. He's been married—and divorced. He figures ... been there, done that. No need to make the same mistake twice. His ex is trying to win him back, and some sort of déjà vu thing happens when he meets Jane Barloc.

I sure had a great time writing Aaron and Jane's story. Have fun reading about the ups, downs as well as the sizzling romance that takes place along Aaron and Jane's journey to finding true love.

Enjoy!

Anita

P.S. I'd love to hear from you. Please give me your feedback, by writing your review at http://amzn.to/1Q7OBI7. Thanks!

Chapter One

The February wind howled. Aaron Adler's windshield wipers were having a hard time keeping up with the snow falling in large, wet flakes. It was a good thing he was still a loyal Jeep guy despite the fact he could now afford just about any vehicle he wanted. Even though it was only a little after six o'clock, the sun had already disappeared from the Colorado sky, and the clouds made it even darker.

He'd thrown his phone on the passenger seat when he left his house to navigate the winding road up the mountain to his parents' home. The glow from his cell grabbed his attention as it lit up the inside of the car. His iron man ring tone filled the air. Glancing at the phone, his caller ID showed the name Sharon Demasi. He immediately turned his attention back

Anita Louise

to the road, his hands never leaving the steering wheel. Even if he wasn't in the habit of not answering his cell while driving, especially when conditions were as treacherous as they were this evening, he wouldn't have taken her call. This was the third time his ex-wife's name showed up on his phone in the same number of days.

What in the world does she want from me now? Regardless of what it is you have in mind, I'm not interested. Even though Sharon was a very attractive woman, and he had to admit sexy as hell, she was his ex for a reason. Aaron, a highly successful writer and speaker in the area of personal development, often encouraged people to step outside their comfort zone. However, Sharon liked to consider herself a "free spirit," and some of her ideas stretched the outer limits of his own comfort zone a little too far.

Pulling into his parents' driveway, he sat in the warm car and picked up his phone. *Might as well see why she called this time*. He listened to Sharon's slightly deep and sultry voice.

"Hello, Aaron. It's Sharon. Remember me? The woman you were madly in love with? Come on, handsome. Give me a call back. I've got a surprise for you, and I think you're *really* going to like it. Ciao."

A surprise, huh? I'm not sure I'll ever be ready for another one of your surprises. He recalled how she'd surprised him with a visit to a

Just the Way You Are

nudist resort only a few months after they were married.

"There's a lot more to the naturist lifestyle than people think," Sharon told him once they arrived. "It's about freeing yourself from your inhibitions ... learning to accept yourself and others."

After being greeted in the reception area by a half-naked yet very cordial woman, they'd been ushered to the co-ed locker room. Sharon had no inhibitions about showing off every inch of her hourglass figure. She quickly stripped off her clothes and put them into a small cubby conveniently provided for "newbies."

"Come on, Aaron. You've got nothing to hide. Flaunt it if you've got it," she said. Looking pointedly at the front of his jeans, she gave him a suggestive wink.

After he finally disrobed, she led him into the hot tub area. It didn't take long for him to figure out that Chalet in the Pines, the resort she chose for them to visit, went well beyond nudity. In addition to being clothes free, this club condoned, as well as facilitated, the "swinging lifestyle." It had been a *very memorable* experience to say the least. He shook his head as if to erase the memory.

Finally, he stepped out of the car onto the driveway filled with his siblings' vehicles. The moisture from his lungs formed billowy puffs in front of him. Snow was still falling. As it landed on the trees blanketing the mountainside, the skeletal outlines of the bare limbs were softened by the white flakes. Looking down at the lights of Boulder below, the scene was as picturesque as a postcard.

The room was buzzing and filled with people when Aaron walked in. As he looked around the spacious area he smiled. He was surrounded by the one group of people in whom he could trust and therefore, be completely relaxed ... his family. It was forty years earlier, on Valentine's Day, when his parents, John and Juliette Adler, had married. Everyone who knew the couple was gathered together to celebrate the special occasion. The big house on High View Drive in the mountains was filled to capacity.

Aaron was the fifth of nine children between the ages of thirty-eight and twenty-four. As he was growing up, he was alternately babied and tortured by his older siblings, idolized and feared by the younger ones. His spot of "middle child" in the birth order was one of the main reasons he'd become a psychologist. Because he was a gifted communicator, it didn't take long for him to become a super successful author and speaker in the field of personal development.

Aaron's brother Michael, a sought after architect and the eldest of the Adler clan, called everyone together to wish their parents "Happy Anniversary." An enormous cake made especially

Just the Way You Are

for the occasion, sat on the large island dividing the kitchen from the living room.

"It's not a birthday cake," said Michael, "but I think it would still be appropriate for you two to make a wish. After all, this *is* a very significant occasion."

Both parents looked at him indulgently. "We'd love to make a wish, Son, but what could we possibly wish for?" John Adler said in his unmistakable baritone voice. "All we've ever wanted has already been given to us. You and your brothers and sisters are our most treasured blessing and have been all our lives."

"Wellll." Juliette drew the word out dramatically. "There is *something* we can wish for."

Aaron had a good idea what his mother had in mind. "What's that, Mom?" he asked.

"Everyone knows we love our children," she stated. "We deliberately had a large family because we've always loved nurturing and watching our little ones grow. Now *all* of you are adults, but Phillip is the only one who's even married. My darling daughter-in-law Rachel is finally going to make me a *grandmother*, and I'm absolutely delighted." Juliette beamed as she hugged the smiling couple standing next to her. "This child will be the first of many. My wish is for lots and lots of grandchildren from each and every one of you."

Anita Louise

"Honey," said her husband, "don't you think the rest of the kids ought to get *married* before they start having children?"

"Oh, John, you know what I mean. Of course, they're going to get married. I just don't understand what's taking them so long. The moment I first saw you, I *knew* you were the one for me." She pressed a kiss to her husband's cheek.

John Adler smiled. "Jules, you know not everyone is as lucky as you and me."

"Our children are." She stomped her foot in emphasis. "Just like Phillip and Rachel, every single one of the Adler children is going to meet the perfect person and fall madly in love. And then they're going to give us so many grandchildren, we'll have a hard time fitting them all in the house."

"Okay, Mom and Dad," Aaron said. "This isn't the time or place for this kind of discussion. Let's just cut this beautiful cake and enjoy the rest of the evening."

Family and friends smiled and cheered as John and Juliette cut the cake. Standing next to him, Aaron's older twin sisters, Gabriella and Brooke looked like mirror images. Beside them stood Whitney, the youngest of the Adler girls. She was also the tallest, and some would say, the most beautiful, which was probably why she'd become a super model. The younger twins Luke and Olivia were on opposite sides of the room

Just the Way You Are

and were also opposite in appearance. Olivia had the nickname "Tinker Bell" because she was so tiny and petite. Luke, on the other hand, was tall, dark, and muscular, and nicknamed "Bruiser."

All of Aaron's siblings were in attendance except Connor. *So what else is new?* Aaron thought. His mother liked to say Connor had been late since the day he was born. Juliette Adler was well into the third week past her due date when her last child, her "baby," finally decided to make his way into the world. Ever since then, it seemed the family was always waiting for Connor.

Aaron knew it was possible his youngest sibling might not show up at all. But hoped, for his parents' sake, that his baby brother would think of someone besides himself for once and join in the celebration. Suddenly there was a commotion at the front door. Who else could it be but Connor? When he entered the room, the youngest was dressed appropriately, but his walk seemed a bit unsteady and his eyes a little too bright. *Oh, no!* Aaron thought. *Please tell me he's not on drugs again.*

"Come on in!" Connor shouted to an unseen person standing just outside. "Come on," he said again. "You brought me here. The least you can do is come in and meet the family. Join the party! Everyone's welcome in the Adler house!"

It was obvious whoever was standing outside had no intention of barging in on a private gathering, but Connor was insistent. He practically dragged the woman from the porch into the house. Aaron's heart almost skipped a beat. The most uniquely stunning woman he'd ever seen stepped into the room. He felt an instant connection. Had they met before? She was dressed in a business suit, but even the crisp lines of her jacket and skirt couldn't hide her lush curves. The top half of her hair was pulled back from her face and pinned to keep it in place. The rest of her golden locks fell in soft waves around her shoulders. Her eyes, a startling shade of blue, held his only for a moment as if to say, *I'm so sorry about this*. She was clearly embarrassed at having captured the attention of everyone at the party. Aaron was feeling something too, and it wasn't anything he welcomed. He hadn't allowed himself to feel anything more than a good, healthy lust for an attractive woman since his breakup with Sharon.

"Mom! Dad! Everyone! This is Jane!" Connor exclaimed. "If it wasn't for Jane, there's no way I would've made it here tonight."

Aaron had always been the one who could best handle Connor. He'd promised his mother years earlier he would watch over his baby brother. Aaron told himself he was only honoring that promise as he made his way through the crowd to the door. Of course, the fact his youngest brother was standing next to the most mesmerizing woman Aaron had ever seen

Just the Way You Are

in his life had nothing at all to do with it. Absolutely nothing!

Aaron realized he'd been looking at the woman standing next to Connor much like a man lost in the desert looks at an oasis. Steeling himself, Aaron did his best to make his voice sound completely normal as he spoke for the first time to the beauty standing in the doorway. "Won't you please come in?" he asked.

"Oh no, really, it's not necessary. Connor needed a ride and I was more than happy to help him out. I really should go," she said. Stepping back, she tried to ease her way out the door.

"*Please*, Jane," begged Connor. "At least let me introduce you to my parents. It's their fortieth wedding anniversary. That's why all these people are here. It's a *big deal*. C'mon, *please*?"

For some unexplainable reason, Aaron didn't want her to leave either ... at least not before he found out more about her. Of course, he told himself, he only wanted to know how she'd come to know Connor and why she agreed to drive him all the way up to the house on High View Drive. The road up the mountain was full of twists and turns, and those who were familiar with it knew to be cautious. Even though the view from the top of the mountain was breathtaking during the day, there was little to be seen at night (other than stars and the lights flickering in the city below). And it certainly wasn't the kind of drive anyone would want to make twice in a single hour. "Yes, Jane. Please stay for a while." Aaron told himself he was only being polite. "It was so kind of you to bring my kid brother all the way up here. At least let us repay your kindness with a little Adler hospitality. I'm Aaron Adler, by the way." He stretched out his hand to her.

"Happy to meet you, Mr. Adler. I'm Jane Barloc."

When their hands touched it was as if a jolt of energy passed from her body to his. He quickly pulled his hand back. His heart was beating fast in his chest, and he noticed a slight blush color her cheeks. "Have we met before?" he asked. *There's something familiar about this woman.*

Shrugging noncommittally she said, "I'm sure if we had, I would remember." She looked down at the floor, appearing almost shy.

He felt an immediate reaction that included an unwanted tug of attraction to the stunning creature before him. *What's going on?* he wondered. He felt an odd and unwarranted anger surge through him. *I don't even know this woman. She waltzes in here with my derelict brother and expects me to ... expects me to WHAT?* As a psychologist, he was well aware the lovely Ms. Barloc had neither asked for nor did she expect anything from him. He understood it was his own defense mechanisms at work, but it didn't make it any easier. He found himself attracted to this woman, and he didn't like it one bit. Clearing his throat while at the same time doing his best to clear his head, Aaron asked the question he'd meant to ask in the first place. "How do you and Connor know each other, Ms. Barloc?"

"Oh please, call me Jane."

What an ordinary name for such an extraordinary woman, came the unwanted thought. "That would be a pleasure, Jane, if you'll also please call me Aaron."

"Of course ... Aaron."

"And how is it you know the youngest of the Adler siblings ... Jane?"

"We've been, uh ... working together," she replied.

What's she trying to hide? What does she mean they're "working together?" Last I heard, Connor was between jobs ... again. "In what capacity would that be, Ms. Barloc?"

"Jane, please. Well, actually it's somewhat confidential. I'd rather not say. Perhaps you should speak with your brother about it."

Just then, Connor pushed in between them, grabbed her hand and dragged Jane with him across the room to introduce her to his parents.

Chapter Two

Jane did a good job of skirting Aaron's question regarding whether or not they'd met before. They had, but she wasn't about to admit it. If he didn't remember her, it was just as well. Had she realized Connor Adler was related to the famous author, she'd never have agreed to give him a ride to his parents' house. But she had no idea Aaron Adler would be in attendance, and she hadn't known there was a big party going on.

If truth be told, she probably wouldn't have agreed to drive him if she'd known Connor's parents' house sat high in the mountains above Boulder. Jane was a good driver, but she didn't particularly like being behind the wheel at night. And she *really* didn't enjoy navigating the twists and turns of a snowy road carved through the tree covered mountain, especially in the dark.

Just the Way You Are

As much as she didn't want to crash the Adler's fortieth wedding anniversary party, she was glad to have an excuse to at least relax for a little while before making the risky drive back down the mountain. It would also give her time to regroup after being face to face with Aaron Adler for the second time.

Her mind drifted back to their first meeting. She'd been anxious to go to the symposium for clinical psychologists, social workers, and counselors where Aaron Adler was the guest speaker. Every one of his books held an honored position on her bookshelf. She'd watched with admiration as his popularity grew, and his success made him a regular guest on everything from Oprah to the Tonight Show. Of course, she knew nothing about his personal life except what was written in the tabloids. Just like everyone else, she knew the gossip "rags" often exaggerated or told outright lies about their targeted celebrities. Jane Barloc wasn't in the habit of reading the tabloids anyway. But somehow, every time she'd see the name Aaron Adler on the front cover along with some grainy picture, she couldn't seem to stop herself from buying it. There was no doubt about it. Aaron Adler was an absolutely gorgeous man. It was no wonder she found herself attracted to him.

Jane chose a career as a social worker because she wanted to help people. After her mother passed away when she was only eleven, a school social worker helped her adjust to the loss. Nothing could bring back her mother, but knowing there was

Anita Louise

another woman who cared enough to check on her, ask questions about how she was feeling, and how she was dealing with those emotions helped a great deal. It was Jane's only experience with a social worker, yet that interaction made her want to be there for others. She primarily wanted to give advice and support to those in need. However, when she learned social workers are also taught how to challenge social injustice and work to change unfair systems of care, her passion for her field grew even stronger.

Jane was one of the first to arrive at the auditorium where Aaron Adler was speaking. It was open seating, and due to her early arrival, she was able to get a seat right in the middle of the front row. When he stepped on the stage, she was captivated. She listened carefully and took notes as fast as possible. Her only problem was taking her eyes off him long enough to write. It was difficult because everything about him mesmerized her. She wanted to drink him in. Not only was he tall, dark and handsome; he was intelligent, articulate and compassionate. He seemed to really *care.*

When he talked about relationships however, she noticed something was different. What was it? She wasn't sure, but somehow she felt he'd been deeply hurt and had never truly gotten over it. As she listened to his words and watched him walk across the stage during his talk, she thought to herself, *You can trust me. I would never hurt you.* It was just then ... just as that very thought was in her mind, their eyes met. To her, it felt like an eternity was held in those few seconds. It was as if their souls were connected. Time stood still. He'd stopped completely, stopped speaking, stopped moving. There seemed to be no one else in the auditorium except the two of them. Surely, he felt it too!

Later that evening she'd looked for him at the reception being held in his honor, hoping to see if what she'd felt was real or just a figment of her sometimes overly active imagination. When she saw him across the room, her heart leapt at the sight of him. However, he was surrounded by a bevy of beautiful women. One of them even had her hand possessively on his shoulder, and his hand lay casually on the woman's hip.

Who was she trying to kid? What was she thinking? There was no magical connection. He didn't even seem to know or care if she was in the room or not. So she left … never expecting to see him again.

Now here she was once again in the same room with Aaron Adler. This time she was close enough to notice how good he smelled. It was a masculine, woodsy scent. How was it possible? The same powerful attraction she felt the first time she saw him seemed to have grown even stronger. She looked around the room to see who his date might be. However, no one accompanied him as he walked beside her and Connor up to the heads of the Adler family.

Jane began working with Connor Adler several months earlier. He was a nice kid. Maybe a

Anita Louise

little immature for his age, but he was only twenty-four. He'd told her he was the youngest of nine children. Her studies had taught her about some of the typical attributes of the last-born child. As the baby of the family, it was fairly common for the youngest to shirk responsibility and expect others to take care of things for them … especially in a family of nine children. Another trait often seen in the youngest child was to become a "revolutionary" and choose a completely different path than the older siblings. Although he hadn't shared specifics, he'd told her all of his older siblings were either established in their careers or were, at least, well on their way. Connor, on the other hand, was adrift, like a ship without a rudder.

Both of those attributes associated with the youngest child were apparent in Connor. Jane was working with him to help him learn to be more responsible and grow into a mature adult. As far as she knew, Connor was not currently taking any of the antidepressants he'd been on the verge of becoming addicted to. He'd also professed to have given up the propensity of his younger years to "self- medicate" with street drugs. However, his behavior this evening had her a bit concerned, as it was more erratic than she'd seen before. Jane was willing to give him the benefit of the doubt and attribute it to the big family gathering she'd unwittingly agreed to take him to.

"Mom! Dad! This is my friend Jane," Connor said.

Both Mr. and Mrs. Adler greeted her cordially.

Just the Way You Are

"It's so nice to meet you, Jane," said Juliette. The beautiful older woman held and warmly patted Jane's hand.

John Adler chimed in. "Welcome to our home. Please make yourself comfortable and have a bite to eat. There's lots to choose from."

Jane sensed both Juliette and John Adler were sincere in their comments. There wasn't even a hint of disdain for her having shown up so late along with their youngest. In addition, she sensed something in their demeanor indicating to her how much they appreciated Jane seeing to it that Connor arrived at their celebration safely.

Everything Connor shared with her about his parents had been positive. There was no indication of any form of parental neglect or abuse. If anything, Connor's parents had given him too much ... done too much for him. After all, he *was* the youngest of nine children, and there were plenty of family members who could and *did* do more for Connor than was necessary.

Connor told her how, as a kindergartener, he'd been embarrassed because he was the only one in his class who didn't know how to tie his shoes. Whenever the big family was rushing out the door for some activity, it was always easier and faster for someone else to do it for him. When the family realized their mistake, according to Connor, everyone wanted to spend what seemed like *hours* working with him to teach him the simple task. After that experience, Connor confided to Jane, he did his best

Anita Louise

to keep his parents and siblings from discovering anything they were doing that might appear to be "too much."

"So what if one of my older brothers did most of my math homework for me!" he'd said. The grin on his face showed no remorse, even perhaps a sense of pride. "I could usually get one of my sisters to write the majority of the stupid reports they made me do in school too. It wasn't like I *couldn't* do it for myself. It was just so much easier and faster to let one of *them* do it for me. Besides, they *wanted* to do it. It made them feel good to be helping me, so I let them. Nothing wrong with that, right?"

Part of Jane's work with Connor was to help him discover how doing things for himself also helped him develop competence and mastery in his life. Jane was pleased. Connor was making good progress. She could see he was getting better at setting and achieving goals. Even though the goals they set together were fairly small and relatively insignificant, Connor was learning to be more responsible and learning how to handle his emotions more effectively. Jane did, however, understand she had to be careful. She didn't want Connor to simply move his dependence from his family to her, and she was confident he understood the parameters of their counselor/client relationship.

Being at this event where not only were Connor's parents in attendance, but the rest of his siblings as well, might be the perfect opportunity to learn more about the dynamics of the Adler family.

Just the Way You Are

She told herself that wanting to learn more about the individual members of the Adler clan had *nothing* to do with wanting to know more about Aaron Adler specifically. It was purely research to help her client.

Her thoughts were disrupted by the close proximity of Aaron Adler. What was it about this man? She was practically *vibrating* with desire just because she was standing next to him, and the scent of the subtle, yet masculine, fragrance was driving her senses crazy.

"May I get you something, Ms. Barloc? ... I mean, Jane."

Aaron was a polite and attentive host. He must have taken her silence as assent and placed his hand lightly on her shoulder. His touch was almost like a jolt of electricity, causing her to suck in her breath. The attraction she'd felt when seeing him from a distance at the symposium was increased exponentially by his touch. In addition, her body's reaction included an incredible amount of heat. Hopefully, with all of the activity going on in the room, he didn't notice the strong magnetism that seemed to be drawing her to him. "Why, thank you, Mr. Adler," she heard herself say. "Sparkling water with lemon would be perfect. As you know, I'm driving. The road up the mountain required all of my attention, and I'm sure going back down will be just as demanding, if not more so."

She admired his athletic grace as she watched him walk across the room to the kitchen. If truth be told, the drive down the mountain wasn't the

Anita Louise

only reason she didn't need anything alcoholic to drink. She could easily get drunk by simply watching him. When she looked into his eyes she sensed a surprising intensity, but it was his touch that sent her hormones racing into overdrive.

The scandal sheets didn't even come close to giving Aaron Adler the credit he deserved. To call him "tall, dark and handsome" was the understatement of the year! Magnificent, drop-dead gorgeous ... even those words didn't come close to describing him. He wasn't a male model, but he certainly could have been. His body was the perfect combination of muscular and lean, and a camera would love his high cheekbones and chiseled jawline. Gray-green eyes showed intelligence and humor. Did she also see desire in their depths? Probably only wishful thinking, she told herself. It was time for her to rein in her lascivious thoughts and remember she was only a guest – and an uninvited one, at that – in the Adler home.

Taking a few moments to survey her surroundings, she could see John and Juliette Adler had a truly remarkable dwelling. The setting overlooking the city of Boulder was spectacular, and the house itself was an architectural masterpiece. Inside, the home was warm, welcoming, and included lots of wood and stone accents. The floorplan was obviously designed with large groups of people in mind, and allowed plenty of room for the exceptional and exceptionally large family.

Just the Way You Are

As she continued to study the faces in the room, it was apparent not only was this family an extremely good-looking bunch … there was also a close bond knitting them tightly together. Everyone was laughing and smiling. Everyone that is, except one of the younger couples standing across the room near the picture window overlooking the city below. It looked as if they were having some sort of disagreement. From her perspective as a counselor and therapist, it looked more like a lover's spat as opposed to a significant argument. Her career had taught her that in some relationships, fighting could be a way the couple showed how much they "cared" about each other. She suspected this might be one of those situations.

Just then, Aaron arrived with two crystal goblets filled with sparkling water and fresh lemon and lime. It looked delicious, and she expressed her appreciation to her unofficial host. After taking a refreshing sip, she asked about the couple she'd been observing.

"Oh, that's my younger sister Olivia, and Tyler, her brother Luke's best friend. Tyler's been hanging around with Luke since they were in pre-school, and since Olivia and Luke are twins, she's known Tyler the same length of time. For some reason, the two of them are always finding something to bicker about. I think they secretly have a crush on one another and arguing is easier for them to deal with than facing their true feelings. Luke and Tyler enlisted in the Navy at the same time. Tyler stuck with it longer than Luke, and ended up being deployed to the Middle East. Olivia was the only one in the family who kept a steady stream of correspondence going with him the whole time he was away.

They chatted for several minutes more before Connor apparently remembered he'd brought Jane as his guest. It actually looked as if one of Connor's siblings suggested that courtesy dictated he at least check in on her.

"Hey, Jane! Looks like my brother Aaron here is taking good care of you. He's got you all set up with a drink and everything. Is there anything else you need? Anything I can do?"

"No, thank you very much for asking, Connor, but I really can't stay. I agreed to bring you because you said it was important for you to be here this evening, and your car is in the shop. If I'd known there was a big family event going on, I would've simply dropped you off. I really should be going."

Aaron looked like he was going to say something ... perhaps encourage her to stay a little longer? But the words he spoke revealed nothing of the sort.

"Of course, Ms. Barloc, I understand." Looking between her and Connor, Aaron asked, "May I walk you out?"

With Connor's approval, Aaron looked at Jane and then nodded toward the exit. Jane noticed not only did he keep his distance, he kept his hands in his pockets as well. Even though he appeared to be uncomfortable, it seemed to her there was something more going on. Was it her imagination, or was the attraction she was feeling reflected in his eyes as they walked together toward the door?

Jane started her VW Beetle. She was doing her best to regain her equilibrium before driving back down the steep, winding road from the mountaintop home to her condo in Boulder. Her hands were on the steering wheel, but her mind was more focused on Aaron Adler than it was on the road in front of her. What was it about Aaron that turned her into a quivering mass of Jell-O?

She was a confident, competent woman ... not some teenager with a crush. In fact, she was *far* from a teenager. Her thirtieth birthday had just passed. And she'd celebrated it - alone. Well, not completely alone. Henry was with her. Henry, her big, orange tabby cat was her closest companion.

So she had a cat! There was nothing wrong with that, was there? Henry was her only pet. It wasn't like she had a dozen cats running around her house. Just because she had a cat, it *didn't* make her an "old maid, crazy cat lady" ... did it?

"Of course not!" she heard herself say aloud. *OMG! Maybe I am turning into a crazy cat lady.*

Regardless, it was time to get home to Henry. Who was she trying to kid? As long as there was ample food and water in his dishes, and there always

Anita Louise

was, Henry could care less when, or even if, she came home.

Maybe it was because it'd been quite some time since her last serious relationship that home just didn't sound quite so homey. She and Henry had been living in Boulder for almost eight months, and it'd been about ten months since she'd stopped seeing William (not Bill). They'd dated for almost three years. William was a great guy: fairly good looking, decent job, nice, sweet, and considerate. Everything a girl could possibly want in a husband.

Of course, they had sex – every Saturday night after their dinner and a movie - like clockwork. Sex with William was like oatmeal. It was good, but kind of bland. He did his best; he tried hard. He offered to do "things" she knew he was uncomfortable with, but he said he'd try them … if she *really* wanted him to. And as much as she might like to try those "things," she didn't want to try them with William.

William was an accountant. William was an only child who loved his mother maybe a little too much. William was *boring.* And William had asked her to marry him.

Maybe she should have seen it coming. Maybe she should have broken it off before it got that far. Maybe she'd led him on - let him believe their relationship was going someplace - like to the altar. But, as much as she cared for William, she just didn't love him. She hadn't meant to hurt him.

Just the Way You Are

Jane *tried* to love him. She'd done her best to feel something when he kissed her or made love to her, but she just *didn't*. Maybe the reason she'd ignored the signs William was getting way more serious about where their relationship was going than she'd ever wanted was because it was easy. She had a "boyfriend" when she needed one. She didn't have to stress out over the dating scene. If a client should begin to get ideas about having anything more than a friendship with her, she could always point out the fact she and William were together.

Oh well, she'd always believed things tend to work out for the best. Her move from New Orleans to Boulder made it clear to William their break-up was irrevocably final. Just recently, she'd heard through the grapevine he'd gotten engaged to a girl who worked in his office building. Evidently, his fiancée had been worshiping William from afar the whole time he'd been dating Jane. By turning down his proposal and putting him back on the market, Jane opened the door for William to find true love.

True love. *Will I ever find true love?* An image of Aaron Adler appeared before her eyes just as she missed the turn.

As soon as she realized what was happening, she turned the wheel sharply to the left. Her headlight beams illuminated the trees along the side of the mountain that were now directly ahead of her. The car fishtailed, lost traction, spun around and slid off the road. Branches smashed into the windshield which quickly became a spider web of shattered glass. She heard the crunching of hard metal collapsing against the strong trees lining the paved surface.

Oh God, help me ... please! she thought just before she passed out.

Not long after Jane Barloc left the party, Aaron decided it was time for him to head home as well. He'd purchased a home in Boulder specifically for times like this. Of course, he was welcome to stay in the spacious Adler home up on the mountain. There were five bedrooms with comfortable beds, plus blow-up mattresses and pull out couches were available for just such occasions. But as much as he loved being around his family, he also enjoyed his solitude. And tonight he needed some alone time. He needed to do some thinking.

There was something about that Jane Barloc woman. He'd *felt* something. After Sharon, he'd convinced himself that hot sex and short term relationships suited him just fine. But Connor's beautiful companion had, somehow, started to open the heart he thought was sealed shut permanently.

As he rounded one of the sharper turns, he saw the headlights. They were shooting out from a strange angle ... and from the wrong side of the road. Another accident. It wasn't all that uncommon on this stretch. People drove too fast, talked on their cell phones, or worse yet, tried to text and drive, and as a result, ended up missing a curve. Well, this one had gotten lucky. Two large trees were keeping the car from plummeting down the mountainside.

He pulled his Jeep carefully to the side of the road, put on his flashers and dialed 9-1-1. Once he knew the emergency vehicle and tow truck were on the way, he got out of his SUV to see how many people were inside the car, and how badly they were injured.

Making his way carefully down the steep hill to the vehicle, he was glad he always kept a flashlight handy in his glovebox. Luckily, the Volkswagen bug was wedged securely against the trees ... no chance the little sedan would come loose and do any further damage to its occupants.

As he approached, the vehicle looked to be in pretty rough shape ... probably totaled. The windows were broken out, and he could see the driver was the only one inside. It was a woman. She lay across the deployed airbag looking like a broken rag doll, her head hanging loosely, hair covering her face.

Suddenly, his heart started beating out of his chest. Even though he couldn't clearly see her face, he knew immediately it was Jane! He tugged furiously on the door handle and wrenched the passenger door open. Sliding into the car, he carefully touched her chin. Warmth. Her skin was warm. He brushed her hair back. There was no blood, no visible signs of trauma. She was alive. Thank God, she was alive.

Aaron sat in the car with her, holding her hand, murmuring words of encouragement until the ambulance arrived. He explained to the officers and EMTs what he knew. Her name was Jane Barloc. She'd been at the party at his parents' home earlier in the evening. No, she hadn't been drinking. He'd left the party about fifteen minutes after her, saw the headlights of her vehicle off the embankment and dialed 9-1-1.

He would have gone in the ambulance with her, but he couldn't leave his Jeep at the side of the road. Consequently, he followed the rescue vehicle to the emergency room at Foothills Hospital. They must have assumed he was someone significant in her life as they allowed him to stay with her until the doctors could see her.

As he sat next to her bedside, holding her hand, he looked at her sleeping visage. Some might not consider her to be a classic beauty, but he found her enchanting. Her face was a little more round than oval. The arch of her eyebrows was relaxed above her long eyelashes that lay unmoving above her high cheekbones. Her hair, even though it was tangled and mussed from the accident was thick and a lovely, burnished golden color. He remembered clearly that her eyes were a remarkable shade of blue. He couldn't help but notice them when Connor first introduced him to her. And even in sleep there seemed to be a sweet, gentleness about her. She'd been so protective of her relationship to Connor. What *was* she doing with his younger brother? Surely there wasn't any sort of romantic involvement. He felt a flash of unexpected jealousy at the thought.

Just the Way You Are

Now it was six hours since the accident, and Jane was still unconscious. They'd taken her in for a CT scan, an MRI, and an EEG, and the results showed no signs of any severe brain injury. Almost imperceptibly, her eyes fluttered.

"You're here," she whispered. Then she squeezed his hand, before immediately closing her eyes once more.

With that slight pressure of her soft hand, something ran through his body he hadn't felt in a very long time. Even with her hair a snarled mess, and wearing a rumpled hospital gown, she was gorgeous. He found himself staring at her mouth – a mouth made to be kissed. Her lips were full, and even in sleep she looked as if she knew some sweet secret that kept a semi-smile in place.

What's wrong with me? he thought. *This woman's been in a serious accident … has just barely come out of a coma, and all I can think about is wanting to kiss her. Besides that, I hardly even know her.* Giving himself a mental shake, he called out, "Nurse, she's awake. Can you please get the doctor to come in and see her now?"

When Aaron let go of her hand and stepped away, he thought he heard a small sound of displeasure escape her lips, and her bottom lip was protruding slightly. Was she pouting? He felt an unexpected glow of pleasure at the idea that even in her semi-conscious state she would be perturbed by his releasing her hand.

Aaron stepped out of the room while the doctor checked his patient over thoroughly. The badge on his white coat read *Dr. Zackary Carter*. In Aaron's opinion, Doctor Carter looked more like a surfer than a doctor with his spiky dark hair and bronzed skin. However, the man carried himself with a distinct air of authority in spite of his youthful demeanor. When the physician emerged from the room, he looked around. Noticing Aaron, he cocked his head toward the door.

"I think she's asking for you. You're Aaron, right?"

"Yes, I am. She's asking for me?"

"Aren't you her husband?" asked Dr. Carter.

"Oh, n-n-no, no," Aaron stuttered. "We're not married."

"That's okay. A lot of people aren't these days," he responded easily. "We're going to have to keep her overnight for observation, but she'll be ready to go home tomorrow. She's suffered a fairly severe concussion and has quite a number of bruises and some small lacerations. She'll likely be experiencing quite a bit of discomfort, and we'll have her on some pretty strong pain-killers. She shouldn't be left alone, so make sure to have someone stay with her if you have to leave your home. You'll get complete instructions tomorrow before she's discharged. She's going to be just fine."

With that the doctor briefly shook Aaron's hand and walked away.

Chapter Three

*T*ake her home? What was the doctor talking about? As beautiful as she was, and as helpless as she might be at the present moment, Aaron Adler wasn't responsible for Jane Barloc. Why, he barely even knew her! Surely, she had family or friends in the area who'd be willing to help her. He'd just have to talk with Jane and figure this out. With that, he squared his shoulders and walked back into her hospital room.

The lights were dim, and she appeared to be sleeping. He didn't say a word ... just stood there watching the soft rise and fall of her chest under the hospital coverings. The blanket molded to the outline of her breasts. They were obviously quite large for a woman of her relatively small stature. He felt a hot rush of desire at the thought

Anita Louise

of touching and caressing not only her breasts, but other, even more sensitive parts of her body.

Take her home. The thought held an entirely different connotation than it had a moment earlier. What would it be like to have her in his bed, healthy, naked and wanting?

"Aaron?" The sweet sound of her voice calling his name had him cursing himself for his wanton thoughts.

"Yes, Jane. I'm here," he said softly, as he walked to her bedside. "How are you feeling?"

"Grateful. I'm feeling very, very grateful," she replied.

"Grateful? You're in the hospital with a concussion and multiple bruises. How in the world could you be feeling grateful?" Gratitude was the last thing he expected her to express.

"You're here. You saved me. I'm grateful you came and rescued me. How could I *not* be grateful?"

He thought, *I saved you? Not really. Anyone would have done what I did under the same circumstances, wouldn't they? Well, everything except staying here at the hospital with you, and of course, taking you home.* Instead he said, "Jane, as much as I appreciate your gratitude, I didn't do anything special. It could've been anyone who drove by and found you. Your headlights were shining from the opposite side of the road. Whoever drove by would've seen them and done exactly what I did."

Just the Way You Are

He could feel himself pulling away, erecting once again the wall he'd built against the pain of Sharon's betrayal. What was he doing here … holding hands with a woman he'd just met only a few hours before? For all he knew, his brother Connor could be Jane's "boy toy." He knew absolutely nothing about her.

All the while his mind was telling him these things, his heart was speaking another language, the language of love. Oh, no! He'd made that mistake before, falling for someone he barely knew. He'd fallen in love with Sharon, and look where that had gotten him.

Did you really love Sharon, or did you love the idea of Sharon … the idea of being married? came the unbidden thought.

He'd been so much younger and a bit naïve when he and Sharon first met. She was his real estate agent and helped him find his first small home near the CU-Boulder campus. He could have continued to live with his parents, but he was the oldest son still at home, and felt it was time to strike out on his own. He wanted to be a little more independent of his loving, yet sometimes overly involved family.

Sharon was a few years older than Aaron, but that was inconsequential to him. Her confidence and maturity actually had a lot to do with the initial attraction he felt for her. Not that he wanted, or needed her to take care of him.

Nevertheless, he liked that she obviously neither wanted nor needed *him* to take care of her.

He liked her independence. He appreciated that even though she had a successful career as a realtor, Sharon was also taking classes to better herself. After a whirlwind courtship, she'd ended up moving in with him when he closed on the purchase of the little bungalow she'd helped him find.

It wasn't that Aaron was so much a traditionalist. But knowing what a wonderful marriage and family his folks built together after their *own* whirlwind romance, made him comfortable. Even if he wasn't totally confident in formalizing his and Sharon's arrangement with a wedding, living together just seemed to be the most logical next step.

From the minute Sharon moved in with him, she'd begun talking about what a money saver marriage was ... emphasizing the benefits, the benefits, the benefits.

"Did you know that there are 1,138 federal benefits to a legally recognized marriage?" If he hadn't known it before, he sure did by the time he'd heard her say it for the fifteenth, or fiftieth, time.

Even though Sharon spent more than forty hours a week on her real estate career, she'd told him she was taking classes because she really wanted to earn her bachelor's degree in public relations. She thought that particular

Just the Way You Are

diploma would help her to enhance and build upon the fast-paced lifestyle she preferred. As a bonus, she anticipated it would give her access to a few special events, and might even provide her with the opportunity to meet a celebrity or two.

"Who knows," he remembered her saying, "maybe I'll have the inside track on all those multi-million dollar homes the rich and famous are always buying around here. The commission on just one of those a year would put me on track to be one of the top agents in the company!" When the PR classes she started taking turned out to be less about the rich and famous and more about writing, writing and more writing, he often heard her complain, "This sucks. If I wanted to write this much, I'd have gone into journalism."

If he was truthful with himself, he'd known his marriage to Sharon was a mistake almost from the beginning. At her insistence, they'd gone to Las Vegas for a weekend getaway. While they were there, she'd talked him into getting married. He may have had one too many cocktails, but at the time, he couldn't seem to think of a reason why *not*. So they went to the Shalimar Wedding Chapel where they got their "Fremont Street Experience" wedding for only $129.00 (plus tax). No friends, no family, just two "crazy kids" tying the knot.

Looking back, he often asked himself, *What in the world was I thinking?*

Anita Louise

Their wedding was more like a joke, and not a very good one. His family had been totally disappointed. Not only were they not invited, but they knew absolutely nothing about it. Had they been given even a small amount of advance notice, they'd have dropped everything and made arrangements to be there. But Sharon insisted they'd have a "real wedding" with family and friends later. In the meantime, they'd be enjoying all those tax advantages while planning for their formal ceremony with the family. If truth be told, she probably never had any intention of a second wedding.

Of course, sex had a *lot* to do with his and Sharon's relationship. Ah, yes. Whatever might have been lacking in the other areas of their relationship, sex with Sharon had been hot … blazing hot. She was adventurous and liked to "try different things." Her naughty drawer was filled with vibrators, dildos and more. She'd had a sex swing installed in the basement of their little bungalow shortly after she moved in with him.

He probably shouldn't have been shocked when she'd taken him to the nudist resort. The minute they arrived, Sharon could hardly wait to shed her clothes and "relax" by the pool. She'd enlarged her rather small breasts with implants shortly after their wedding, and walking around naked gave her the opportunity to show off her now exceptionally large breasts. Aaron had tried to talk her out of the cosmetic surgery, assuring

Just the Way You Are

her that, to him, her small and perky breasts were perfect. He'd expected her to increase her size from her "A" cup to a moderate "C" and was totally shocked when she revealed her generous "D" implants.

Since he was tall and muscular, Aaron had no reason to hide his masculine physique. However, he had no desire to show it off either. He wasn't a "gym rat," but he did enjoy the benefits of regular workouts, and as a result, had a nicely toned body. In addition, he was well endowed where it was, perhaps, most important when it came to a nudist resort. Rather than being relaxed, Aaron felt like he was on display, and he was very uncomfortable. However, he had to admit, after a few drinks while sitting in the overly warm pool area, his inhibitions began to subside.

He noticed several couples seemed to know each other extremely well. He wasn't positive, but he was pretty sure when two couples left the room, the men and women had switched partners. When he asked Sharon about it, she smiled slyly and asked, "Why? Are you interested in doing something like that?"

He'd quickly responded that taking his clothes off in front of complete strangers was almost more than he could handle. Anything more was incomprehensible. *Oh my God, was she actually thinking about having sex with other people?*

Anita Louise

She'd brushed off his concerns with a laugh, and they'd gone back to their room which was furnished with a fireplace, carefully positioned mirrors, and "special erotic channels" on the TV. They enjoyed an exceptionally vigorous night of sex. After that, Sharon suggested on multiple occasions they go back to Chalet in the Pines, but it was not an experience Aaron had any interest in repeating.

When Aaron told Sharon he wanted to sell the little bungalow in Boulder, and move to California so he could further his education, she readily agreed to list it. She'd also happily helped him stage the home perfectly for a quick sale.

He couldn't help but notice as they were packing things away to be put into storage, she was careful to put her things in separate boxes from his and label them with the appropriate name. Therefore, it really wasn't much of a shock when she announced she wouldn't be moving with him to Stanford. However, when he asked her where she would be going and if she'd like some help moving her possessions, she simply stated, "No, that won't be necessary. Lance and I have everything taken care of. I've already consulted a divorce attorney. You'll be receiving the papers soon."

Lance? Divorce?

He'd known things were not the best, but hadn't realized how badly things had deteriorated. In total, their excuse for a marriage only lasted a little over a year.

Thankfully, Jane had drifted back to sleep while Aaron ruminated on his less than stellar marriage. Maybe he just wasn't cut out to be a husband ... a father. No! That couldn't be true. He'd grown up in a family filled with love and laughter. His mother and father were a team. They'd worked together to raise nine children and each and every one of them turned out just fine.

Just look at Phillip and Rachel. They'd been married for almost three years now and were soon to have their first child. One look at those two and you knew for sure that true love and a happy marriage were still possible, despite what any of the statistics about divorce had to say.

Oh sure, Connor was still struggling a little, but he was only twenty-four ... just a kid.

Hmph! I was only twenty-two when I met and married Sharon. Maybe I should give myself a break. Just because I made some foolish choices nine years ago, doesn't mean I'm doomed, does it?

It was at that moment Jane turned her head and opened her eyes. Looking at him, she smiled almost shyly. "You're still here. You must have so many other more important things to do besides sit here with me. Thank you so much for

Anita Louise

everything, Aaron, but it's okay ... you can go now. I'll be fine."

Yes, there were other things he could be doing. He'd promised his publisher the draft of his next book by the end of summer. But it was only February. There was still plenty of time. That was one of the beauties of being a self-employed, successful author and speaker. He could, for the most part, set his own schedule. He loved his work, and he felt certain the writing and speaking he was doing were having a positive impact on the lives of many people.

Whenever he went on a book tour or gave talks, men and women, young and old, came up to him and sincerely thanked him ... told him how his books helped them to change their thoughts and their lives for the better. In addition, he received letters and emails almost every day from appreciative fans sharing their personal stories of positive change. He did his best to read each one and respond to those where he felt he could add support or advice to further inspire his reader's self-improvement. Often, he'd send a copy of one of his other books, encouraging them to continue to read and make personal growth and development a permanent part of their daily lives.

"Yes, Jane, you *will* be fine. I've spoken with the doctor, and they're ready to release you, but you can't be by yourself. Who do you have to come and stay with you for a while?"

Just the Way You Are

She furrowed her lovely brow for a moment. "Well, there's Henry, but I don't really think he counts."

Henry? Then why was she with Connor? No matter. What was he thinking? Of course there's a man in her life. Just look at her. She's absolutely gorgeous. He should have known!

"Well, can you call Henry and have him come and pick you up?" he asked. He did his best to keep his voice as calm as possible.

She started to giggle and then quickly grimaced in pain. "Oh, my gosh! It *hurts* to laugh," she noted rather uncomfortably. "No, Henry won't be able to pick me up. Henry's my *cat*." The look on her face bespoke both playfulness and embarrassment.

"Your *cat?*" he said with a mixture of humor and relief. His mind went instantly back to his youngest brother. "What about Connor? Would you like to call Connor?"

"Oh no, Connor's my …." She cut off her sentence, cleared her throat and started to speak once again. "I appreciate you asking, Aaron, but there's really no one in the area who can come and stay with me. I moved to Boulder less than a year ago and haven't met that many people yet. My father and his wife live over a thousand miles away in New Orleans. My sister's there too, but she's busy with her new baby. It's her first, so as you might expect, she's over the moon in love.

Anita Louise

There's no way I'd even ask her to come here right now."

"Surely there must be *someone*." Aaron was almost desperate. He knew she couldn't be left by herself and the thought of being alone with her ... just the two of them. Well, it just wasn't possible, that's all, simply impossible.

Chapter Four

"Aaron, really, you don't have to do this," Jane repeated for the tenth time.

"I know," he replied as he helped her from the wheelchair. Hospital policy dictated she use it to depart from their premises to Aaron's waiting Jeep. "I *want* to. Really, Jane, it's my pleasure to help you out."

"I know they wouldn't let me go home alone, but I could have hired a nurse. There are services out there specifically for situations like this," she stated once again.

He'd heard this argument several times over as well. He wasn't quite sure himself why he'd been so insistent she come to his house and recuperate upon her release from the hospital. He decided to try a different tactic. "Well, if you'd *rather* have a nurse than be stuck with me for a few days, I guess it's up to you." He did his best to look sad ... forlorn ... hurt.

"Aaron, *please*, you know I don't mean it like that. It's just that you've done so much for me already, going to my house, feeding Henry. As much as I appreciate everything, I don't want to take advantage of your kindness."

"Speaking of Henry, I have a little surprise for you when we get home," he said with a twinkle in his eye.

Henry was a *gigantic* cat! Aaron's first look at the tabby made him wonder if Henry had been the inspiration for the Garfield cartoon character. Not only was Jane's cat Garfield orange, it had to weigh close to thirty pounds. In addition, Henry's attitude seemed to be that humans were only there to take care of his needs. With Jane still in the hospital, the cat had been left alone for over twenty-four hours. As soon as Aaron put the key in the lock of Jane's condo, the disgruntled animal could be heard howling. Apparently, Henry was hungry and the feline wasn't too happy about it. It didn't seem to matter even a little bit that it was Aaron and not Jane who walked through the door.

Jane's home was a tiny 850 square foot, two-bedroom condo near the campus of Colorado University – Boulder. It was clean and neat, but Henry seemed to take up an awful lot of space.

Just the Way You Are

The cat led Aaron to the kitchen and quickly pointed out his empty dishes. It took a little searching, but Aaron found both dry and wet cat food. He put some of each in two of the three pet dishes on the floor, and then added fresh water to the third. It was no real surprise when Aaron noted the mat on which the cat's food and water was placed prominently displayed a picture of Garfield stating "Feed Me" in bold letters.

It just made sense to bring the Garfield look alike back to his house across town. After all, Aaron lived there all by himself and he had plenty of room ... over 4,000 square feet and in addition to his master bedroom retreat, there were three fully furnished additional bedrooms just waiting for someone to use them.

That is, unless Jane was occupying my bedroom ... in my bed ... with me, came the unbidden thought. He shook his head in an attempt to keep his mind from further straying to what could possibly happen in his bed with Jane. Just the thought of those startling blue eyes and soft curves had his body heating up and it took some effort to shove the thought aside.

With a loud "meow" Henry made his presence known once more. The animal then proceeded to rub his substantial body against Aaron's legs. The rumble coming from the cat's body must have been a purr, but sounded more like a distant locomotive. Obviously, the feline was used to human companionship so it only made sense to take Henry, his dishes and his Garfield placemat to the same place his recuperating owner would be ... Aaron's house. Besides, he reasoned, having her beloved pet nearby might help speed Jane's recovery.

It was late afternoon when they pulled up to the front entrance of his home, and Aaron noticed Jane's eyes light up with what looked like appreciation for his abode. Secluded among the trees, the landscaping was carefully groomed yet made the spacious house look warm and inviting. Beyond the roof line you could see Colorado's Rocky Mountains in the distance. She looked directly into his eyes, smiled and said, "Aaron, you have a beautiful home. Thank you so much for allowing me to share it with you for a few days."

Aaron genuinely appreciated her complimentary words regarding his house. Why was it when she said "for a few days," he felt a sense of disappointment? Some part of him, a part buried for years, wanted it to be more ... much more.

This was the second house he'd owned in Boulder, the first being the one Sharon helped him find. His eldest brother Michael was a renowned architect, and Aaron was in a financial position where he could afford to get exactly what he wanted. He'd hired his brother to design and build his home. Aaron wanted his new home to be nothing like the first.

Aaron had let his then realtor and now ex-wife make most of the decisions regarding the location and amenities of the first little bungalow. It turned out to be a complete disaster. With this house, he was involved in every aspect of the home design and building process. The location had to be perfect ... close enough to his parents without being too close. He was also adamant about characteristics regarding the size of the home, number and dimensions of bedrooms and other living spaces. Both indoor and outdoor areas needed to be conducive to family gatherings. Almost without realizing it, he'd been looking for a house that would also become a *home*. Somewhere, hidden beneath the scars left by his ex-wife there was a part of him that longed for what he'd grown up with; a family that cared for and supported each other unconditionally, and a home filled with love.

Suddenly, he realized that Jane Barloc was the first woman outside of his family members he'd ever invited into his home. All of his sexual encounters over the past several years had taken place either in hotel rooms or in the bedroom of whatever woman he happened to be seeing. Besides, Jane's being here had absolutely nothing to do with sex.

He offered to have her as a guest in his home *purely* because of his instincts as a

Anita Louise

gentleman. He'd been reared by a loving mother and had four sisters, and the girls had been known to get into situations where a little male assistance came in handy. There were times when it came to a woman in need, you just had to step up and do the right thing. He was simply doing what anyone with his upbringing would have done ... wasn't he?

His home was his haven, the one place he could totally be himself. He liked to read, work out, spend time in his yard, or do the research and writing necessary for his best-selling manuscripts. When he wasn't on a book tour, he spent as much time with his family as was reasonable. A very "open door" policy was adhered to when it came to family members, and it wasn't uncommon to have one of his siblings drop by unexpectedly.

When he divorced and moved to Stanford, he made friends with several faculty members and others in the area. However, since building his house in Boulder, he hadn't really taken the time to develop any new relationships outside of his family in his home town. Perhaps, up until now, it just reminded him too much of the fact his failed marriage had begun and ended right here in Boulder.

He couldn't quite put his finger on it, but something about Jane Barloc was different than any other woman he'd ever known. Perhaps part of it was that she was one of the few women he'd

Just the Way You Are

met in recent years who hadn't thrown herself at him. If truth be told, he was the one who stayed with her to the point where the doctor assumed the two of them were a couple. It hadn't really been necessary for him to even *go* to the hospital, let alone sit by her bedside all that time. Simply calling the rescue vehicles and seeing to it that she was moved from her totaled VW to the ambulance would have been enough.

Aaron was totally puzzled by his behavior regarding Jane. Yes, he was drawn to her physically. After all, she was stunningly beautiful, although she did nothing to flaunt it. In fact, he remembered she'd hidden her lush curves under the business suit she wore to his parents' anniversary celebration.

Why was it that even just thinking of her could cause a flare of desire to shoot through him? His mind wandered further. *What would she look like with nothing but the soft, cotton sheet on his bed to cover those lush breasts and wonderfully rounded hips?* His attraction to her took him by surprise. Not only was it powerful, but it happened so quickly. He'd met her less than thirty-six hours ago. Actually, he barely knew her. Now he wanted to use this time with her to explore these feelings he was having. He needed to get to know her better and find out if what he felt was real or a figment of his imagination.

Aaron walked around, opened the car door and offered her his hand to assist her from

Anita Louise

the Jeep into his home. Once again, the energy he felt from merely her touch was palpable. This time when he felt it, he drank it in rather than trying to escape it as he had upon their first meeting in his parents' home.

Her golden locks shone in the light of the setting sun. Up until now he'd only seen her in the artificial light of his parents' home, and in the hospital, where she wasn't exactly looking her best. He noticed her silky hair was thick and held a natural wave. *What would it be like to run my fingers through her beautiful, shining hair and look deeply into her gorgeous blue eyes before bringing my mouth down upon hers for a long, slow kiss?*

Once again, he found his thoughts were on the *wrong* track. He must remember. She was here because she needed his help to recuperate after her accident, not so he could help her into his bed.

Escorting her up the walk to his front door, he stood aside leaving the door open for her to pass through in front of him. Evidently, he was standing a little too close to the opening because not only did the scent of her fill his nostrils, but her hip brushed the front of his trousers as she moved through the door. Without even a modicum of effort, she exuded such potent sensuality, he could hardly keep himself from groaning out loud.

Just the Way You Are

He paused, shook his head to clear his thoughts, and kept his voice as steady as possible as he said, "Welcome home."

Jane still couldn't believe she was actually standing in Aaron Adler's absolutely stunning and undoubtedly very expensive home. When she woke up in the hospital after her accident, she was surprised to see him sitting next to her bed, and even more shocked when she realized he was holding her hand. She was both appreciative and confused by his presence.

Why had he stayed there, next to her hospital bed? As hard as she tried, she couldn't think of a logical explanation. It just didn't make sense. She remembered the accident ... remembered losing control of the car while making her way down the steep and winding road from the party at the home of Connor's parents.

Did Aaron feel some strange sense of duty or responsibility because he found her in the car after the accident? What else could possibly account for the fact he not only stayed with her while she was hospitalized, but brought her to his home when the doctor insisted she not be left unattended?

Obviously, her benefactor had been raised right ... by kind and loving parents. She could see it clearly in only the few minutes she'd spent in their home, but kindness and consideration only went so far. Right now, it was all just too much for her to try and figure out. She'd suffered a concussion and had multiple large bruises to attest to her accident. Her fun little Beetle was a total wreck, and she hadn't been able to see any of her clients for several days. All in all, her already tenuous financial stability was now seriously shaken.

Jane didn't come from a poor family, but they wouldn't be considered rich by any standards. After her mother died, she and her sister were allowed to finish out the year at the school she'd attended since kindergarten. The school social worker had spent only a few short months with Jane, but had helped her a great deal to adjust to the loss of her parent. A tragic event was made more tolerable. In addition, the dream of following in the footsteps of the woman who'd counseled Jane through the most challenging time in her young life was born.

When the middle of June rolled around and school closed for the year, Jane and her sister were sent to live with an aunt and uncle who never had children of their own. The home of Aunt Emily and Uncle Jim held plenty of rules and very little affection. Jane learned at an early age to take care of herself. Expecting others to be there for you was a luxury reserved for other people, not for her. She knew she'd have to work hard for anything she wanted. After finishing high school, she paid her own way through college with a combination of loans, scholarships and lots of hard work.

As much as she appreciated Aaron's hospitality, she knew she needed to be practical. Allowing herself to read anything into being here would be foolish. *Wouldn't it?*

"Jane? Are you all right? Do you need to rest?" His voice brought her back to the present.

Oh my gosh, every time I hear him say my name in that low, powerful voice I practically melt. The aches in her body from the accident were suddenly mixed with a pleasant tingle of desire. There was no way she should be feeling anything outside of the residual pain from her serious car crash. It shouldn't be happening, but it was.

She gave her head a slight shake to clear it. He must've taken the movement as some sort of response to his question, and he seemed to be having difficulty understanding her response.

"Would you like a cup of tea? Coffee?" he asked. "I bought a few muffins from the bakery in case you wanted a little something to nibble on. How does that sound?"

Every word from his mouth sounded delicious, and she was in no condition to deal with her overactive female hormones. "Thank you, Aaron. Right now, I think I should lie down for a while if you don't mind." Actually, what she needed was to escape from the emotions he seemed to be stirring up inside her … emotions she wasn't ready to deal with at the moment.

Anita Louise

Standing in the entrance to his home, Jane closed her eyes and took a deep, calming breath. It was then she heard a loud *"MEOW."* Thinking Aaron had a pet he'd neglected to tell her about, a smile lit up her face.

"Oh, you have a ... *Henry!*"

Her swift movement of bending down and attempting to scoop up her pet caused her to lose her balance. The next thing she knew she was being held gently, but firmly in Aaron's arms. Jane looked into the gray-green eyes of the man who'd just protected her once more, this time from what could've been a painful fall onto the marble tile of his foyer.

It struck her that not only was this man absolutely gorgeous, he was also one of, if not *the* most caring and thoughtful person she'd ever had the good fortune to meet. She closed her eyes once again, this time to try to control the combination of pleasure and lust that had her heart racing. She gave Aaron the strongest hug she could manage and kissed him soundly on the cheek.

"You brought Henry." Those simple words could in no way express the gratitude she felt. Having her pet with her alleviated any concern she had about the big tabby being alone and lonely, plus it helped Jane feel more at home in her current quarters.

As good as it felt to be held in his strong arms, Jane knew her presence in Aaron Adler's home was only temporary. Henry broke whatever spell she'd been under by pushing his head between the couple's legs in an effort to pry them apart. The tabby was used to being the total focus of her attention. Somehow, in spite of his weight, it was easier to scoop up her pet, than it was to move out of Aaron's embrace.

She cradled her oversized kitty as she took in the main living area of her benefactor's home. The exterior of Aaron's house was definitely impressive with its natural stone surfaces and breathtaking view of the mountains. However, the interior of his home was not meant to impress, but to welcome. The large open rooms were filled with comfortable and inviting furnishings. Light from the setting sun poured in from the abundance of windows, and the mountains were a spectacular focal point through the wall of glass across the rear of the home.

Jane thought of her condo near the campus of CU-Boulder. It'd taken her quite some time to save up a down payment, and there was very little left for furnishings. She'd been very frugal and combed through dozens of thrift shops to make her home cozy and comfortable. Even though it was on a much grander scale, she could see similar care and thought had been put into Aaron's home.

"Once again, Aaron, your home is lovely. Did you have a designer help you with it?"

"Well, my brother Phillip's wife Rachel is an excellent interior designer, and I must admit I did ask for her expert opinion from time to time. But it was really important to me for this place to look and feel like *my* home, not some designer showroom. So I did the vast majority of it myself."

He was surprised at the next thought that came to his mind. *The only thing that would've made the whole experience better would be if you'd have been there with me when I was doing all this.*

As she gazed appreciatively around the room, Jane's only comment was, "I wouldn't change a thing!"

"Thank you, Jane. That's good to know."

Not quite knowing what to do or say next, Jane used the best excuse she could think of to find the time she needed to gather her thoughts.

"Would you mind terribly if I rest for a little while?"

"Of course. Please, follow me. I think you'll find the accommodations to be adequate." She followed him down the hall to the master suite. "I decided to give you this room, Jane, as the other bedrooms are on the upper level, and I thought it'd be easier for you if you didn't have to climb stairs."

"Thank you, Aaron, but no … please. You've done so much for me already. Walking up a few stairs will probably be good for me. I've barely gotten out of bed in days." *Besides that,*

Just the Way You Are

she thought, *I only want to sleep in your bed if you're in it with me.*

"Really, Jane, I insist. If you don't want to do it for yourself, do it for me. Please allow me to feel like a proper host and take this room. I guarantee I won't bother you. Besides, I've already moved my things into one of the guest suites, so you staying in this room actually makes it *easier* for me. Please?" He spoke the last word almost in a whisper with a look of utmost sincerity.

"Of course, Aaron, if you insist. You've already gone to so much trouble, how could I possibly refuse?" *I'd do just about anything you asked me to anyway.*

"Great then ... that's settled. I had one of my sisters get the things together you wanted from your condo, and I took the liberty of bringing your bags over here yesterday. Everything's over there on or next to the luggage rack. There are a couple of empty drawers in this dresser right here, and there's plenty of room in the closet if you'd like to hang any of your things up. Anything you need, just ask. I'll leave you alone now, so you can get some rest."

As Aaron left the room, Jane let out the breath she hadn't realized she'd been holding. As much as she was grateful for his hospitality, his solicitousness left her both pleased and confused. If she was honest with herself, Aaron

Anita Louise

was everything she'd ever wanted in a man ... kind, educated, successful and drop dead gorgeous! The question was, what did he see in her?

She certainly wasn't *ugly*, but the poor self-esteem of her youth had followed her into adulthood. She'd been called "Plain Jane" frequently while growing up. As a child she'd been painfully thin and very bookish, and as a result was quite shy. Her body had also been slow to develop from the straight lines of a little girl to the curves of a woman. Even though she'd been assured by those closest to her that maturity had transformed her from an ugly duckling to a beautiful swan, she still found their words difficult to accept.

Looking back on her relationship with William, she could understand how *he* was attracted to her. If there was a male equivalent to a "Plain Jane," William would be the poster child. But Aaron Adler was a whole different story.

It must've been his watchful attentiveness, and the memory of how fabulous it felt to be held in Aaron's arms for those few moments, that made her begin to see herself in a different light. There was something about the way Aaron looked at her when he practically insisted she stay in his enormous master bedroom suite that made her feel not only cared for, but beautiful.

Right now, she needed to do something to relax and relieve some of the pain and stiffness

Just the Way You Are

left from her accident. She considered lying down on the oversized king bed, but the thought of Aaron having slept there only the night before made her more tense than relaxed.

She'd noticed the large whirlpool tub with powerful jets when Aaron first showed her to his suite. The idea of soaking in warm water and having her body massaged from head to toe practically had her moaning out loud. *Yes. That's exactly what I need,* she thought.

Opening her suitcase, she removed a pair of pajamas and a fluffy robe. She chuckled to herself. *Flannel pj's aren't exactly the accoutrements of the kind of beautiful, sexy woman Aaron Adler would have in his bedroom.* They were, however, exactly what Jane Barloc would be most comfortable in for the rest of the afternoon and evening.

As the tub filled with warm water, she hung some of her things in the huge walk-in closet and put the rest back in her suitcase. Empty drawers or not, there was no way she was going to put her things into Aaron Adler's dresser.

After removing her clothes, she stepped into the oversized tub. Jane immediately felt her body begin to relax. Once fully submerged, she rested her head on the rim of the bathtub where she'd carefully folded one of the plush hand towels into a makeshift pillow. It was a pleasant surprise to note from her *very* comfortable position that she could watch the puffy, white

Anita Louise

clouds move slowly across the blue expanse through the large skylight above.

In spite of her recent accident, lying there looking up at the sky with the water bubbling all around her, she felt more feminine ... sexier, than she'd probably ever felt before. Even though she didn't understand it, apparently Aaron Adler, a man who could very likely have just about any woman he wanted, was attracted to *her*. Her breasts throbbed as the Jacuzzi sent jets of water across her chest. She became conscious of the heat and moisture between her thighs which came from the inside rather than her environment.

Was she being foolish? Was her desire to have a husband, a family, to have a relationship built on mutual trust, love and respect too much to ask? Not in her wildest dreams had she dared to believe she would have the opportunity to even *meet* a man like Aaron Adler. She'd had a "schoolgirl crush" on him almost since the first time she saw his picture on the dust jacket of his first book. Surely only fate or the hand of some unseen power had to be at work here. Now she was not only in his house, but in the fabulously warm and soothing Jacuzzi in his master bedroom.

The aches and pains seemed to disappear as Jane experienced the thrill of her own sensuality. She'd always had a strong libido and enjoyed the kissing and caressing leading to

Just the Way You Are

a sexual encounter. Even though sex with William had been pretty bland, she used her imagination to make the experience much more arousing than it would have been otherwise. And the current fantasies she was having involving Aaron Adler turned her on more than anything else ever had.

There was a bar of beautifully scented soap on the edge of the tub. She picked it up and inhaled deeply of the fragrance. It smelled like Aaron. She could see clearly those gray-green eyes, his slender yet muscular frame.

Her mind seemed to take control of her body. Almost without realizing it, she began to move the soap slowly across her breasts. She felt her heartbeat quicken as she pictured Aaron's hands caressing and massaging the swollen tips. Desire was racing through her. She realized unless she did something to sate these incredible feelings, she was likely to behave in a totally inappropriate way when she next encountered her handsome host.

It'd been quite some time since she'd indulged in the type of needs her body was now craving, and she was somewhat shocked by the thought of what she was about to do. Shouldn't she be feeling more of the residual pain from the accident and less of the enjoyment coming from her natural sensuality?

Jane closed her eyes and allowed herself to relax even more into the massaging warmth of the tub. As her hands continued to move slowly across her own body, a moan escaped her lips at the exceedingly pleasurable sensations coursing through her. Her hand moved down her stomach, then lower to the clump of soft curls between her thighs, and she saw once again the gorgeous face and gray-green eyes of her imaginary lover. She could feel the silky wetness caused by her arousal, and her breath quickened as she remembered how good it felt to be held in Aaron's strong arms.

As her fingers swirled in the most intimate way, her fantasy consumed her. Somewhere in the back of her mind, she heard herself call out her lover's name as she felt her muscles spasm, and her body exploded in one of the most delicious orgasms she'd had in a very long time. Moments later she released a long sigh as she felt the languid calm flow through her now satisfied body.

Her relaxation quickly turned to panic when she heard and saw Aaron rush through the bathroom door saying, "Jane! Are you all right?" His look of concern quickly turned to surprise, and lust, when he realized the sounds he'd heard were cries of pleasure ... not pain.

Holy smokes! Aaron could hardly believe what was happening. His eyes were glued to Jane's gorgeous and obviously sensual body covered only by the water in the Jacuzzi. This was a sight he would *not* soon forget. The look of surprise and embarrassment on her face did nothing to hide her beauty ... her big, blue eyes and soft, full lips. He'd have liked nothing more than to strip down and join her in the tub and make their own heat.

His head was spinning. He was having a hard time wrapping his mind around the fact a woman who only recently left the hospital after being involved in a serious automobile accident, could also be so sexual. He felt like a man with a schoolboy crush.

He quickly flashed back to the warm kiss she placed on his cheek after she realized he'd brought her cat Henry to his home as well. The feel of her arms wrapped around his neck, her full breasts pushed up against his chest ... everything about her body pressed tightly to his felt so *right*. But, that was *nothing* compared to what he was feeling now.

He knew instinctively she possessed a sensuality that could keep him in an almost continual state of arousal, and he wished the kiss they'd shared could have been *more*. He imagined his mouth covering hers ... exploring the contours behind those soft, full lips. He did his best to rein in his wayward thoughts. Now was not the time to be thinking about sizzling, hot sex.

Here he was standing in his own bathroom with a rock hard erection, staring at her beautiful, nude body. When he heard her call his name, he assumed she was in need of his help. Now, however, he was quite certain the reason she'd just shouted his name was because she'd been in the throes of ecstasy.

Their eyes locked for a moment ... Aaron didn't quite know what to do and it appeared neither did Jane.

"I'm so sorry, Jane, I thought you needed me." *And it would've been my* <u>pleasure</u> *to be of assistance.*

Jane's skin turned an even brighter red than it already was from being in the hot water of the Jacuzzi. She continued to stare at him as she moved her hands in an attempt to cover her nakedness.

"It wasn't your fault. I'm the one who should be apologizing. I don't know what to say. I just ...." She gulped and looked away.

It was obvious she was thoroughly embarrassed. A true gentleman would've quietly left the room and allowed her to recover her composure and have her privacy, but he found taking his eyes off her to be an impossibility at the moment.

His appreciative gaze moved quickly up and down her body as he said, "My God, Jane, you're a stunningly beautiful woman." He paused and allowed his eyes to take her in once more. "I should've turned around and walked out of this room as soon as I realized you were in no danger. And now, rather than debating who should be apologizing, why don't I force myself to leave you alone and, if you'd like, we can pretend this never happened."

"Thank you, Aaron," she said softly as she looked shyly up at him.

"Oh no, it's my pleasure to sincerely thank *you*, Jane," he said with a twinkle in his eye as he turned and left the room.

As she sat in the hot tub that was now barely warm, Jane did her best to examine her feelings. Of course, she was embarrassed at having Aaron walk in just after she'd experienced one of her most pleasurable orgasms *ever* while practically shouting his name. But the fact was, she was also feeling a certain sense of female pride from the look of admiration and *more* in his eyes before he'd (somewhat reluctantly) left the room.

Jane no longer had the boyish figure of her childhood. In fact, her body had developed into one most men seemed to find attractive. However, she didn't see herself that way. Even though her outward appearance had changed, altering the self-image she'd accepted as a child proved to be more challenging. What was most important to her was that she be treated as a professional by her colleagues and clients, both male and female. Therefore, she dressed so as to downplay her voluptuous figure. All her

Anita Louise

business suits were cut in such a way as to hide her curves as much as possible. Her casual clothes and night wear tended to be loose and comfortable as well.

Her relationship with William hadn't exactly been the kind to warrant Victoria's Secret type lingerie, but her move to Boulder had her rethinking the type of relationship she wanted in the future, *and* her undergarments. One of the first things she'd done to give her femininity a boost after her breakup with William, was to purchase some of the most gorgeous and sexy silk and lace undergarments she could find. Her conservative exterior now hid a very different and newly developing side of Jane Barloc. She couldn't help but grin when she thought, *Well, even though he's seen me naked, I wonder how Aaron would react to seeing what I wear <u>under</u> all the prim and proper clothing the rest of the world gets to see?*

As she stepped out of the tub and pulled a thick, plush towel off the heated rack, she remembered the look of admiration in Aaron's eyes before he left the room. No one ever looked at her like that before, like she was something special ... some*one* special. An emotion she was totally unfamiliar with seemed to hit her in the center of her chest, right where her heart was. *Love.* The truth was she'd fallen head over heels in love the moment she'd first locked eyes with him from her front row seat in the audience all those years ago.

Jane Barloc understood it was an accident ... or perhaps a better word would be *fate* that brought her into Aaron Adler's home. However, she'd read all of Aaron Adler's books, and he always encouraged his readers to "visualize the future you desire and take the steps necessary to make your dreams become a reality." Jane could clearly see some unseen power had given her a helping hand. Her future, her dreams were right here ... with Aaron Adler.

Being with Aaron felt *right.* Even when he walked in on her unexpectedly, she hadn't really wanted him to leave. His eyes on her had made her feel warm, appreciated ... loved. Now it was up to her to *somehow* win the heart of the man of her dreams.

Chapter Five

Jane awoke the next morning feeling refreshed. The only thing affecting her sleep was the dream of gray-green eyes gazing at her full of love. She relaxed into the soft pillows and enjoyed the feel of the luxurious sheets and fluffy duvet covering her pajama clad body. Stretching her arms above her head made her aware that she was not yet completely healed, but there was also a feeling of contentment knowing where she was … in the home and in the bed of the man she loved.

Too bad he's not in this wonderful bed with me. The thought was accompanied by a wave of pleasure at the idea of sharing a bed with Aaron.

Although there was, of course, a degree of embarrassment associated with what had taken place in Aaron's master bath yesterday, she couldn't help but remember the look of desire on his face when he'd walked into the room. She'd keep her thoughts focused on not only rekindling that desire, but doing everything in her power to turn it into something more.

The clean lines and fresh colors of the master suite made it feel relaxing and serene. As she peeled back the covers and stepped onto the plush carpet, she smiled to herself and sang softly, "Don't go changing hmm, hmm, hmm, hm, hm ... just the way you are. She continued to hum as she took a closer look at the beautiful view and furnishings surrounding her. *This room is perfect just the way it is ... just like Aaron. I wouldn't change a thing,* she thought.

She smoothed out the bed and walked back into the master bath, grinning foolishly when she passed by the Jacuzzi as she remembered the previous evening's experience. This time she stepped into the shower, continuing to hum as she soaped up her body and washed her hair. A delightfully wicked thought popped into her head. *The only thing that would make this experience better, would be if Aaron was enjoying this warm, soft spray with me.*

After drying off, she selected a comfortable pair of slacks and a sweater. Surveying herself critically in the mirror, she took a little extra time to make sure her hair and make-up looked as good as possible. The thought of

Anita Louise

seeing Aaron again, fully clothed this time, had her heart beating a little faster than normal.

Squaring her shoulders, she allowed the words of the old Billy Joel tune, *Just the Way You Are,* to continue to play in her head as she put a smile on her face and walked into the main living area of Aaron's beautiful home.

"Good morning!" she said cheerily as she entered the kitchen. Aaron's back was to her as he stood facing the spectacular view of the mountains. When he turned and smiled, her heart practically skipped a beat. He was so incredibly handsome it took her breath away.

"Did you sleep well?" he asked.

Suddenly, all the confidence she had only moments earlier seemed to disappear completely. She felt a blush creep over her cheeks. Unable to speak, she only managed to nod her head. *How in the world did I imagine a man like this could ever fall in love with a 'Plain Jane' like me?*

A look of concern clouded Aaron's gaze. "Are you all right? Do you need anything? What can I get for you?"

"I'm fine. It's just that ...," Her voice trailed off. The only real discomfort she felt was emotional, not physical.

"If it's about last night ... I mean, it was ... Um, I uh...," he stammered.

It seemed as if the world famous speaker and author was, for once, at a loss for words. His lack of bravado seemed to restore her confidence.

"Oh, you mean that thing we're trying to pretend never happened," she managed to say with a slight grin and only a bit of a blush.

Her candor seemed to break the thin ice they'd been attempting to walk across. He grinned unabashedly and said, "I can try and pretend all I want, but I'm sure I'll *never* forget last night."

With that, he gestured toward the counter, "Would you like coffee, or do you prefer tea?" After a moment's hesitation, he continued. "It seems there's quite a bit we need to learn about one another."

"Yes, it seems there is. And I'm very much looking forward to it … almost as much as I'm looking forward to a cup of that delicious smelling coffee."

She watched as he poured two cups, put cream into his own and looked at her while still holding the creamer. After she nodded, he added cream to her cup.

"Sugar?" he asked.

Her response of, "Perfect," held more meaning than just the simple little word. It didn't seem to matter where they were or what they were doing. To Jane, everything about being with Aaron Adler was perfect. Even the casual dialogue that came with sharing an ordinary cup

Anita Louise

of coffee seemed extraordinary. It felt to her, that the air between them crackled with electricity.

They took their coffee to the table in the breakfast nook overlooking the panoramic view behind his home. She noticed a small plate of muffins had been placed there earlier.

"I hope these are all right," Aaron said. "I consider myself a pretty good cook, but with only myself to feed the vast majority of the time, I tend to keep things quite simple here at home. It also means I either eat out a lot or order in. Of course, my folks take pity on the old bachelor from time to time and invite me over for dinner. But now that I think about it, the rest of my brothers and sisters are usually also invited, so I guess I'm not so special after all." He shrugged sheepishly.

Finding it difficult to keep her thoughts to herself, she whispered, "Oh yes you are ... very special." Not wanting to appear too forward, she quickly stated in her normal voice, "This is wonderful. I'm not a big breakfast person anyway. Thank you."

They both reached for a muffin at the same time.

Their hands touched ... and stilled.

Her breath stopped.

A simple touch had never affected her this way before. She looked up and their eyes locked, much the same as they had in the master bath the night before.

Just the Way You Are

She heard him catch his breath, and when he spoke it was only her name. "Jane."

It was all she could do to stay in her chair. In spite of the fact they barely knew each other … in spite of the fact she knew she was only a guest in his home because of his gallantry and generosity, she wanted to wrap her arms around his neck and kiss him until they were both senseless. She could hardly breathe as her eyes took in every inch of his face. Finally, she was able to speak. "I can see you're enjoying your breakfast," she said teasingly. "You're wearing a little bit of your blueberry muffin as evidence. It's right here."

She felt him still as she leaned forward to carefully touch the area next to his mouth gently with her thumb and brush the tiny crumb away. Oh, how she wished she could run her thumb slowly across his full lower lip … move her hands to caress his handsome face. What would it be like to have him capture her hand to lick and then suck on her thumb, followed by one delicious finger after another, and then move on to other more sensitive parts of her body? Her heart was racing at the thought of what it would be like to be held in his arms and to feel the press of his lips against hers.

What am I doing? Why can't I seem to control myself when I'm around this man?

It was almost a relief when Aaron broke the ever growing sexual tension between them, by asking, "Do you feel up to taking a walk after we finish our breakfast? There's a nice trail just a short distance from the edge of my property. Of course, we'll stay away from anything too strenuous. How does that sound?"

Getting some fresh air to help clear her wayward thoughts was just what she needed. "That's a great idea, Aaron. I'd like that very much."

"We're only taking a walk. It's not like we're going on a date or anything." Jane stroked her pet's fur and spoke calmly to Henry while she put on an extra sweater in preparation for her walk with Aaron. Of course, it wouldn't hurt to take a few extra minutes to check her hair and makeup as long as she was in the powder room. *Who am I trying to kid? I don't care where we're going or what we're doing. Anything done with Aaron Adler is like a dream come true.* Giving herself a final peek in the mirror and squaring her shoulders for an added boost of confidence, she joined him on the back patio where he was waiting for her outside.

"There you are," he said with a smile that lit his face and eyes. "You look like you're dressed warm enough. This isn't going to be too much for you, is it?" The appraising look he gave her made her feel both cared for and appreciated.

Just the Way You Are

"Thanks for asking, Aaron. I'm very much looking forward to a little fresh air and exercise. This is the first opportunity I've had to get outside since the accident. I'm more than ready. Let's go," she said as she smiled at her handsome host.

After the intense feelings exploding in the breakfast area, the serenity of the outdoors, walking beside Aaron in companionable silence for several minutes, was helping her regain her equilibrium. Hopefully, the raging hormones she'd been experiencing weren't giving Aaron the wrong idea. There was no doubt a wealthy, attractive man like Aaron Adler could have his pick from the throngs of adoring women fans, and as much as Jane *was* a fan of Aaron's, she wanted her relationship with him to be so much more.

Jane Barloc knew what she wanted, and a short term fling with the gorgeous, sexy author was not it. With the sparks zinging between them every time they were together, she knew he'd be happy to take, and she'd be totally willing to give, her body to him completely. But she needed to make sure he understood it was a package deal. When Jane gave her body to Aaron, she'd happily give him her heart and soul as well.

Her train of thought was interrupted by his query. "What made you decide to move to Boulder?"

"Oh, I needed to make a change, and after doing some research, Boulder seemed like the perfect choice. I was able to get a position at UC-Boulder, plus I'm starting my own ... pract, uh ... business." *Oh, darn it! How could I have forgotten about Connor? I can't break my client's trust, even to one of his family members.*

In spite of wanting to be completely open with Aaron, her code of ethics required her to keep some things to herself. Unless and until Connor gave his permission to share the real reason they knew each other, her profession as a counselor and social worker would have to remain a secret.

"There were certainly a lot of people at your parents' house the other night. Tell me again. How many are there in your family?" she asked to shift the conversation away from herself.

"Two wonderful parents and nine children, five boys and four girls, two sets of twins, one identical and one fraternal."

"Wow! That's a *big* family. And where do you fall in there, Aaron?"

"Smack dab in the middle. Two older brothers and sisters, two younger brothers and sisters. And, on top of that, I was born right between the two sets of twins. I think that had a lot to do with my becoming a psychologist."

"Yes, I'm sure it did. Being 'stuck in the middle' so to speak, of such a large family must have been challenging for you as a child. It's

Just the Way You Are

funny, isn't it, how things that happen in our young lives affect the choices we make?" Jane commented.

Somewhat surprised at her insightful remark, he turned to look at her. Once again, he was shocked by the jolt of energy that passed through his body when their eyes connected. Her cerulean blue eyes, held such incredible beauty and sincerity they seemed to stop him in his tracks.

"Figuring out how people relate to one another ... trying to understand my brothers and sisters was a big part of the reason I became a psychologist. It took me a while, but I finally realized that the better I understood myself, the better I was at understanding my siblings. After that I started writing about how working on yourself and becoming the best person *you* can be is what makes all your other relationships work even better."

Thinking about his failed marriage, he added, "But, the truth is, sometimes it seems to be a lot easier to write about than it is to live it."

"I'm not an author or a psychologist," Jane said, "but I *have* had some experience with less than wonderful relationships, so I understand what you mean." Hoping to keep the conversation on a more positive note, and to keep the questions about her background to a minimum, she asked, "Do I remember correctly? It was an anniversary celebration for your parents, right?"

"Yes, it was ... forty years. I don't know if you remember, but my mother's name is Juliette, and even though my dad's name is John, she likes to say that she 'found her *Romeo*' the first time she laid eyes on him. They fell madly in love way back then and still look at each other like it was only yesterday."

She thought she heard a note of wistfulness in his voice. "Finding a relationship that lives up to one like theirs must be quite a challenge for you and your siblings."

"Well, my brother Phillip, and his wife Rachel, sure seem to have found the key. They had a few rough patches at the beginning, but it's obvious they're crazy in love. Most of the time, they can hardly take their eyes off one another. It's almost like there's nobody else in the room even when it's filled with people. And now Rachel's going to have a baby, and they're ready to expand that circle of love."

"What a beautiful description, Aaron. It sounds like they *have* followed in your parents' footsteps," she said with a sigh. Without thinking she blurted, "What about you? Are you looking for a relationship like your parents?"

The look Aaron gave her let her know he wasn't entirely pleased with her question, but after a moment's thought he replied, "I'd be lying if I said I didn't. I think just about everyone *wants* to be with someone they can love and trust completely, but what you *want* isn't always that easy to find."

Doing her best to quote material from one of his own books, she responded. "If I remember correctly, an excellent author I've read extensively, says you shouldn't dwell on the negative things from the past and instead keep your focus on what you *want,* and if you do so long enough, it must come to you … it's inevitable."

Looking a little shocked as well as a bit pleased by her obvious knowledge of his work he replied, "Why, Ms. Barloc, you make a very good point. And just because something isn't easy to find, doesn't mean it isn't worth looking for, right?"

"Right, Mr. Adler," she said with a satisfied grin.

They'd walked only a few steps farther along the path when they heard a sing-song, high pitched voice calling, "Helloooo. Dr. Adler? Is that you?"

Giving Jane a grin accompanied by a slight eye roll, he replied, "Yes, Mrs. Worthton. It's me. How are you today?"

Just then a petite, older woman dressed in designer jeans and a leather jacket stepped onto the path next to them. Noticing Jane for the first time, her face broke into a delighted smile. "Hello, Dr. Adler. And who is this lovely lady?"

Anita Louise

"Mrs. Worthton, this is Jane, Jane Barloc. She's a friend of my younger brother's and was in a serious automobile accident. She's staying with me for a few days while she recovers."

"Ohhh, no! Are you all right? You look just fine ... very pretty, in fact."

"Why thank you, Mrs. Worthton," Jane said, extending her hand to the woman.

Clasping Jane's hand while covering it with her own, the woman briefly acknowledged Jane's comment with a nod. "Staying with Dr. Adler, are you? Why that's lovely ... just lovely. He's such a wonderful man. I'd marry him myself if I was thirty years younger! I was just getting ready to take my afternoon stroll. How wonderful to have the pleasure of sharing it with the two of you. Now, you've got to tell me all about it. What happened? How did you get into that terrible automobile accident, Jane? You don't mind if I call you Jane, do you? You may call me Millie, if you like." With a nod and a wink toward Aaron, she continued. "I always call him *Dr.* Adler. I think it shows respect. And I guess that's why he calls me *Mrs.* Worthton. He really doesn't have to. I prefer Millie. Since we're both girls, it's all right if we call each other Jane and Millie, isn't it?"

Millie Worthton tucked her hand into Jane's elbow and proceeded to walk down the trail, asking questions without waiting for answers ... chattering on about the scenery, her dear departed husband and many other of the

Just the Way You Are

abundance of thoughts that obviously filled her quick mind.

Jane looked back over her shoulder at Aaron, and was not surprised to find him chuckling quietly with an amused look on his face. Twenty minutes later they'd walked Millie's entire route. They were back to the pathway leading to her home which, Jane had learned, was adjacent to Aaron's property.

Leaning her pixie cut blonde head closer to Jane's ear, Millie Worthton whispered conspiratorially, "You know, you're the *only* woman Dr. Adler has *ever* had come to his house … except for those beautiful sisters of his, of course. Such a handsome young man, and so nice too. He's a great catch! You make sure you hang on to this one. Let me know if there's anything I can do to help." With a wave and a "See you later" to Aaron, she disappeared back into the shrubbery dividing her yard from the pathway.

Jane agreed with Millie, Aaron Adler was *extremely* handsome … better looking than any man she could remember. However, he didn't seem to even be aware of how utterly gorgeous he was, and that made him even more appealing to her. The glimmer in his eyes along with the little smirk on his lips tugged at Jane's heartstrings.

"How'd you enjoy meeting Mrs. Worthton, Jane?"

Anita Louise

"*Millie* is absolutely delightful ... and a bit exhausting."

"Oh, Jane! I'm so sorry. Have I kept you out here too long? I don't know what I was thinking. I guess I *wasn't* thinking. Like Mrs. Worthton said, you don't look like you've just recently left the hospital. In fact, you look lovely."

Suddenly the cold air was filled once again with the heat of desire. His eyes seemed to devour her with a look of hunger and longing. She noticed the hint of his enticing male scent as a breeze ruffled her hair. *God, he smells good!*

He reached over and brushed a lock of hair that had caught on the corner of her mouth back over her ear. Her skin tingled where his finger had brushed her cheek. She could feel her skin turn hot ... burning with desire.

Her shaky reply of, "I'm okay," must not have sounded very convincing, because the next thing she knew, she was being scooped up into his arms.

As he walked purposefully into the house, he muttered, "What was I thinking?
"

Chapter Six

When Aaron walked through the French doors into his home, he was surprised to see his brother Michael standing in the middle of the living room. Michael was the oldest of the Adler children, and the only one that Aaron still hadn't quite "figured out." Consequently, Michael was the lone sibling who had the power to unnerve Aaron's normally quiet, but definitely *in charge* demeanor. Realizing he was still holding Jane in his arms and not knowing quite how to handle the situation, Aaron quickly, yet carefully, stood Jane up next to him as his brother looked on.

"Michael. When did you get here? If I'd known you were coming, I would've been sure to be here when you arrived," Aaron said somewhat apologetically.

"Just got here. I didn't know you had company, or I'd have let you know ahead of time I was stopping by." The look he gave his brother clearly asked, *What's going on here?*

"Michael, this is Jane, Jane Barloc. You met her at Mom and Dad's anniversary party. Jane, this is my brother Michael."

Being a successful business owner, as well as the oldest of nine siblings, Michael had dealt with a myriad of unusual circumstances, especially where his siblings were concerned. Michael extended his hand and smiled pleasantly. "Oh, yes. Hello, Ms. Barloc. Nice to see you again."

After shaking his hand politely, Jane nodded toward Aaron and said to Michael, "It's nice to see you too, Mr. Adler. I hope you don't mind, but I'm going to excuse myself."

As Jane walked into the master bedroom suite, Michael raised his eyebrows with a questioning look toward his brother.

"Mike ... really, it's not what it looks like." Aaron only felt a twinge of guilt when his mind flashed back to how stunningly beautiful Jane looked last night when he walked in on her in the bathtub after she called out his name. How could he possibly explain to his brother the strange sequence of events leading to Jane Barloc not only being in his house, but his *bedroom?*

Just the Way You Are

"Hey, Brother, what you do in the privacy of your own home is none of my business. You don't owe me any explanations. In fact, I'm glad to see you're finally moving forward after that last fiasco of a relationship you were involved in. I *am* just a little curious, though. Is this serious, or are you two just shacking up for fun?"

"Hey! Wait a minute, Bro." Aaron found himself strangely hot under the collar over Michael's remark. "First of all, I'd appreciate it if you showed Jane a little more respect. We are *definitely not* 'shacking up' as you so crudely put it. The truth is I *don't* owe you any explanations, and it really *is* none of your business. However, because you're my brother, and I want to continue to have a great relationship with you, I'll do my best to give you the short version of a very unusual set of circumstances."

Aaron proceeded to tell his brother about leaving their parents' anniversary party and coming upon Jane's wrecked car. He went on to explain about following the ambulance to the hospital. Justifying why he stayed long enough for the young doctor to assume they were a couple was a little more difficult. The fact was Aaron didn't fully understand it himself.

"What's up with her and Connor?" Michael asked. "There's got to be some sort of a relationship there, or she wouldn't have been with him at Mom and Dad's party."

Anita Louise

The logic in his brother's statement was not lost on Aaron. "Well, I'm pretty sure there's nothing romantic going on between them. He's too young and a little too screwed up for a woman like her. But, she's been very elusive when it comes to talking about Connor *and* what she does for a living."

"You don't think she's into something, uh … kinky, do you?"

"Come on, Mike!" Aaron practically jumped out of his chair. He and his oldest brother had certainly gotten into fights over the years, but it'd been a long time since Aaron wanted to punch his brother in the face. Right now he was having a hard time restraining himself.

"Okay. Okay. I get it. You've really got a thing for Jane. It's cool. I understand, but I *do* think you should find out a little more about her before you get yourself in too deep. You remember how fast you got involved with Sharon, don't you? And you know how that turned out."

Michael was right. Aaron had jumped into his relationship with Sharon too quickly and he knew exactly what that had gotten him … an ugly divorce and a distrust of women. Just because Jane was beautiful and had a body any man would love to take the time to explore in wonderfully minute detail wasn't everything. He was looking for more than just good looks … more than someone who was good, or even great, in bed. He'd had both of those things with

Just the Way You Are

Sharon and knew from experience, as important as physical appearance and hot sex were, they weren't enough. He needed more.

In addition, his marriage to his ex-wife taught him what he was looking for was *not* something he could hope to see develop over time as the person and/or the relationship matured. No, she needed to have those traits to begin with. There was no way he was going to try to change someone into the person he wanted them to be.

I want someone I can love just the way they are, he thought.

Mentally he went over the list of characteristics he was looking for in a mate. First of all, he wanted someone who was kind and intelligent, with a great sense of humor ... a joie de vivre. Someone who was mature enough to be open and honest, yet still be sensitive to the needs and feelings of others. He wasn't sure if he'd ever be ready to marry again, but he *was* looking for a lifelong friend and companion to share his dreams and goals. But that person also needed to be independent enough to have ideas and interests of her own, so she could offer him a fresh perspective. And, of course, he'd only commit to someone who'd be faithful to him, and to whom he was so utterly and completely in love with that even the *idea* of being with someone else would be totally ludicrous. He could see some of those things in Jane already. Was it

Anita Louise

possible she possessed the other traits he was seeking as well?

After talking with his brother, he realized his feelings for Jane were developing stronger and faster than he was totally comfortable with. If this relationship was going to go any further, he knew he needed to take some time to find out more about Jane Barloc.

"Thanks for stopping by, Mike. You're a good brother, and I appreciate this conversation. You've given me a lot to think about."

"Well, Aaron, except for that time with Sharon, you've always been one of the most level-headed of all of us kids when it comes to relationships. I love you, and I just don't want to see you get messed up like you did back then."

"I know, Mike. I love you too, Bro. Don't worry. I'm not going to make the same mistake twice. That's for sure."

"Hey, I have an idea," Mike said. "Why don't I throw a little impromptu party on Friday night? You can bring Jane, and we'll put her through the 'Adler Test.' You know, let the other brothers and sisters check her out. History has shown that before any of us get serious about someone, we're all better off if the family approves *first*. Maybe if you'd done that with Sharon ..." Michael's voice trailed off.

"Now that you mention it, Mike, that's not a bad idea. In fact, I kind of like it. Okay, let's do it. You rally the troops and I'll bring Jane as my date. In the meantime, I'm going to see what else I can find out about Ms. Jane Barloc."

Jane was both pleased and surprised when Aaron gallantly swooped her up because he thought she'd overtired herself with their walk. Being held in his arms made her feel safe and protected. It felt only natural to lay her head on his shoulder and snuggle into his neck. The only thing better would've been to lace her fingers through his hair and draw his face down to hers for a long, slow, passionate kiss.

Walking into the house and seeing the handsome man standing in Aaron's living room quickly erased any possibility of following through on her lascivious thoughts. Once Aaron carefully placed her feet on the floor, and introduced her to his brother, she could clearly see the family resemblance. Michael was dressed casually, but it was apparent he was a man who was successful and used to being in charge. Of course, *her* Adler brother Aaron was successful and used to being in charge too.

Her Adler brother? Come on! Who was she trying to kid? Aaron was no more "hers" than was the beautiful house she was staying in temporarily.

Knowing there was nothing she could say to explain her presence or the fact Aaron carried her into the house, Jane took the easy way out

Anita Louise

and excused herself as quickly as possible. As she made her way to Aaron's bedroom, she could almost *feel* Michael watching her go. Perhaps she should've stayed put. No doubt, her heading into Aaron's bedroom was going to open up a great big "can of worms."

Oh well, Aaron's a psychologist, and as such, I'm sure he's had to explain 'stuff' to his brother before. He can handle it much better than I possibly could.

Once she closed the door to Aaron's bedroom, Jane released the breath she hadn't even known she'd been holding. Now that she had a few minutes alone, she needed to think. She'd learned a long time ago how to take care of herself. As much as she'd love to believe a couple of idyllic days with Aaron Adler could lead to something more, she needed to be practical.

Dr. Carter told her she must take at least a full week off work. While still in the hospital, she'd called the college and the secretarial staff manning the office space she shared with the other counselors and therapists to set things up. Her classes and appointments were being covered by highly competent and qualified professionals until the beginning of next week.

There was only one patient she felt she needed to contact personally … Connor Adler. What if, instead of seeing Michael standing in the living room, it'd been Connor? She needed to talk

Just the Way You Are

with him and explain where she was and why she was staying in his brother's home.

Why *was* she here? A good upbringing, and a perhaps misplaced sense of guilt or responsibility for her accident couldn't really explain Aaron's bringing her to his home, could it?

No matter, now was not the time to think about that. She had other things to do. Now *another* Adler brother was about to be brought into this rather confusing situation. With a sense of determination to do what she knew was the right thing, she picked up her cell phone and dialed the number for Connor Adler.

Connor answered almost immediately. "Hello? Jane? Oh, my gosh, Jane! Where are you? I came in for my appointment and you weren't there."

"Hello, Connor. I'm glad to hear you came for your session. You're doing so well, and continued support is very important in helping you to reach your goals. Did you work with Mr. Caplin?"

"Yeah, he's okay, but I miss *you*, Jane," he whined.

Jane had been working with the youngest of the Adler family for several months, and he was making very good progress on taking responsibility for himself. He was finally starting to understand that being responsible also meant being empowered. Rather than running to his

Anita Louise

family to bail him out of situations caused by making hasty and sometimes unwise choices, he was learning to become aware of his thoughts and discard those that didn't serve him. He was learning to act upon only those that would move him closer to his goals.

He was a sweet kid … very attractive, just like his older brothers, and the rest of the family for that matter. Of course, she liked him, but she had absolutely no interest in anything beyond their professional relationship and possibly an ongoing friendship. She often remained friends with her clients after they were no longer counselor and patient. However, it was also fairly common for patients to develop some type of a "crush" on their counselor or therapist, and she'd been trained to handle these exact types of situations.

"Connor, you know we've talked about this. We will always be friends, but the time is coming very quickly where you won't need me or anyone else to help you make the best decisions for yourself and your life."

"I know, but …,"

"No buts, Connor. It was only one session, and I'll be back next week. Tell me about your time with Mr. Caplin." Connor shared the highlights of his counseling session with her substitute. Jane would, of course, speak directly to Dave Caplin for the details and professional opinion of the session when she returned to work

Just the Way You Are

the next week. When the professional part of the discussion was finished, Jane knew it was time to let Connor know what had happened and where she was. "Connor, you remember when I dropped you off at your parents' house the other night, don't you?"

"Of course, I do, Jane. I really wish you'd stuck around longer. You'd really like my family, especially when you get to know them better. They're a super great bunch of people."

"Yes, I'm sure they are. In fact, I *know* that about at least one of your siblings."

"Huh? What do you mean? What sibling? What's going on, Jane? Where are you?"

Jane did her best to answer all of Connor's questions in a calm and professional manner. "I was in a fairly serious automobile accident on my way down the mountain from your parents' house. Fortunately, your brother Aaron saw my car off in the trees along the road and called the police and an ambulance."

"Oh, my God, Jane! Are you all right?"

"Yes, Connor, I'll be just fine, but the doctor didn't want me to be alone since I did have a fairly serious concussion. The fact is I have no family in the area. Aaron was the one who saw my car after the accident and made sure that the ambulance got me to the hospital. Now he's graciously allowing me to stay at his house and is keeping an eye on me."

"You're at Aaron's house? Now?"

"Yes, Connor, I am."

"Okay. I'll be right there!"

With that he hung up the phone and Jane was left looking at her cell phone thinking to herself, *Oh, my ... this should be interesting.*

Not knowing exactly how long it would take for Connor to arrive, Jane felt it was important for Aaron to know his youngest brother was on his way over. Walking out from the bedroom, her eyes scanned the room. Michael was gone and Aaron was standing with his back to her, gazing at the magnificent view of the mountains.

Just looking at his profile was doing funny things to her stomach. As she remembered the look of hunger in his eyes when he walked into the bathroom the night before, her nipples hardened, and she felt a tingling sensation between her legs. *What would it be like*, she wondered, *to be lying in his bed with him on top of me, filling me, making me moan with pleasure?* So lost in her fantasies, she was barely aware he'd turned to her. Suddenly she realized he was walking purposefully toward her with an intense look on his face. What was he thinking? Of course, he couldn't possibly read her thoughts, but it felt to her like the air surrounding them was electric with sexual tension.

"Who are you and what are you doing to me, Jane Barloc?" he asked more to himself than

Just the Way You Are

to her. He stopped only inches from her ... not touching her, only looking deeply into her eyes.

She didn't move a muscle, waiting for him to come closer ... to hold her, kiss her. The longing she felt must've been apparent in her gaze because the next thing she knew, she was in his arms and his mouth was pressed to hers. She sighed, breathed in the scent of his woodsy cologne, allowed her hands to go to his face, brushing her thumb along his slightly prickly jawline, then lacing her fingers through his hair. Her lips parted and his tongue met hers, wet and willing. Their first kiss was beyond anything she could have possibly imagined. The taste of him was like her own personal ambrosia ... a hint of his morning coffee along with a little mint (a recent breath freshener?). She wanted the kiss to go on forever, but some part of her brain kept nudging her to remember ... something. The doorbell chimed, bringing them both back from the wonderful new world they'd just discovered.

"Aaron ... it's Connor," she said as she dragged herself unwillingly from his embrace.

Apparently confused, Aaron asked, "What? Connor? What in the world would Connor be doing here?"

"I just called him. I told him I was here. I'm sorry. I should've spoken with you about it first. I guess I wasn't thinking clearly." She paused. "Shouldn't we answer the door?"

"Of course. Of course." Aaron seemed just as stunned as she was by the power inherent in their first kiss.

Aaron composed himself as best and as quickly as he could. He opened his front door just as the bell was ringing for the third time. "Hello, Connor, come on in," he said as normally as possible. Aaron was aware that his youngest sibling and the woman he'd just kissed with a passion he'd never before experienced, knew each other. But what he *didn't* know was in exactly what capacity.

"Where's Jane?" Connor asked. Seeing her standing near the sliding glass doors at the back of the home, Connor immediately crossed the room without further acknowledgement of his brother. "I don't understand, Jane. Tell me again. What happened? Why are you here? What's going on?" Connor's questions held both concern and curiosity as he looked between her and his brother.

"Hello, Connor," Jane said calmly. Looking straight at Connor with a slight nod toward Aaron, then moving purposefully toward the seating area in the living room, she went on, "I think we should all sit down and talk. Is that okay with both of you gentlemen?" Once everyone was seated, Jane continued. "As I explained to you on the phone, Connor, I was in an automobile accident. That's what led to my being here. Perhaps now would be a good time to enlighten your brother as to how *we* know one another."

"Yeah, I guess so. I just wanted to make sure you were okay, Jane. I was worried about you!"

"As you can see, Connor, I'm fine. Please go on."

Connor looked at his brother somewhat sheepishly. "Gee, Aaron, I'm sorry about barging in like this. It's just that when Jane wasn't there for our appointment, and then she called and said she was *here*, I kind of freaked out."

"Appointment?" Aaron queried.

"Yeah, well … you remember last year when I got in that little scrape? You remember … when I had to go to court because of the marijuana thing …?"

"Yes, Connor, I *do* remember. Mom and Dad were pretty upset by it all. You're lucky you didn't end up in jail. But what's that got to do with Jane?"

"Well, you see, Jane was assigned to be my counselor … by the court. At first I was required to go in and talk with her every week. Now I don't really *have* to go *every* week. It's just that it's really made a difference … a *lot*, and I feel like it's helping me to stay on track … talking with Jane, that is."

Jane stepped in. "You've made great progress, Connor. I'm very proud of you."

Addressing Aaron, she explained, "Although it certainly wouldn't have been illegal, I felt it would have been unethical for me to share this information with you, Aaron. I thought it was in Connor's best interest to have *him* explain his and my relationship."

"You're right, Jane, and from a professional perspective, I totally agree with you." With a subtle, yet telling look, Aaron continued. "And from a personal perspective this information explains quite a bit."

Looking curiously between Aaron and Jane, Connor burst out, "Are you two ... uh, well, you know ...," He trailed off.

"No!" Jane and Aaron responded in unison.

"Oh, okay. Well, I guess I should be going." Shaking his head, he looked from his brother to his counselor and back again. "All I've got to say is, whatever is going on here ... I don't get it."

Jane thought, *Neither do I.* And from the look on Aaron's face, he was thinking exactly the same thing.

Chapter Seven

"Well, that explains quite a bit," Aaron stated as soon as Connor left.

"Yes, things just got so complicated ... with the accident and my staying here, and all. And Connor *has* made great strides in the last few months. I didn't want to see him lose any ground because of this." Jane waved her hands loosely in the air in an attempt to better explain herself.

THIS ... what is this? Well, whatever it is, I have to figure it out, he thought.

Aaron did his best to look at the circumstances he found himself in with Jane through the educated eyes of the psychologist he was. However, it seemed that just like a lawyer who tries to represent himself has a fool for a client, the same analogy applied to a psychologist. And it didn't take a psychology degree to analyze his attraction to Jane Barloc. Every time she was near him, his reaction to her was immediate. He could feel something inside of him come alive. She was bringing back to the surface deeply buried emotions.

To Aaron, her physical beauty was unique and practically mesmerizing. Yet it seemed as if she had no idea how utterly beautiful she was. And even though most of the time she wore clothing designed to hide her voluptuous figure, it was impossible to hide those gorgeous curves no matter how hard she tried. She possessed an innate sensuality, yet there was a sweetness about her he found almost irresistible.

He'd felt an instantaneous connection with her when she first walked through the door of his parents' house. It was crazy, but somehow it felt as if he recognized her the moment he laid eyes on her. He was aware of those who believed the important people in your life were, very likely, someone you knew before... perhaps in a previous life, but it was not a belief he shared. Yet there was *something* about Jane Barloc that felt so familiar. He was drawn to her like a moth to a flame.

It was late afternoon, and although the happenings of the day did answer some questions, many still remained unanswered in Aaron's mind. An early dinner and a good night's sleep was probably the best thing for both of them.

Just the Way You Are

"How about I throw a couple of steaks on the grill for dinner?" he said. "I know a lot of people only cook outside in the summer, but I enjoy it all year round. If it wasn't February, I'd suggest a fire. I have a great fire pit."

"That sounds great, Aaron. Then, if you wouldn't mind, I'd like to go to bed a little early? It's been quite a day."

She was doing it again! Was she reading his mind? How did she know he needed some space? Maybe she also required some time to reflect on what was taking place between them. He thought of his list of characteristics in the "perfect" woman. He was looking for someone who was kind and who was also sensitive to the needs and feelings of others. The way Jane handled the situation with Connor, by allowing the young man to be the one to explain how they knew one another, met that part of his criteria.

His ideal mate would be someone with a good head on her shoulders ... someone he could converse with on more than just a superficial level. He knew from his own advanced degrees it would've been impossible for Jane to become a counselor and a therapist if she weren't a very intelligent woman. And she'd certainly held up her end of every conversation he'd had with her thus far. He smiled to himself as his thoughts flashed back to their conversation the morning after he walked in on her in the bath tub. Although it was obvious she was embarrassed, she was also clearly teasing him with her little quip about pretending it never happened.

As kind, intelligent and witty as she might be, it was also an undeniable fact she was absolutely beautiful! Remembering how she looked lying naked in his Jacuzzi had him heating up all over again. Oh, how he'd love to stand next to her gorgeous body in a hot shower and soap each other up from head to toe. He felt himself grow hard at the thought of running his hands over those lovely large breasts, teasing and rolling her nipples to firm little peaks.

"Aaron? It's been quite a day for you too. Are you okay?"

The sound of her voice brought him back from his wayward thoughts. He quickly turned and walked to the kitchen, not only to get the steaks, but to hide the obvious bulge in his trousers. A loud "meow" followed him into the kitchen and soon another bulge, the one of Henry's overly large body was rubbing against his legs, reminding Aaron it was dinner time for the Garfield look-alike as well.

"Did our furry friend find you in the kitchen?" Jane asked. "You might as well feed him, because he'll never leave you alone until you do."

Aaron smiled as he looked at Jane's cat. He wasn't much of a pet person, but this critter had a certain charm that was hard to resist.

Just the Way You Are

Reaching down he scratched Henry's ears and was rewarded with a loud, rumbling,"Purrrr."

Dinner seemed like a perfect time to learn a little more about his house guest, so Aaron turned on his psychologist charm to do just that. "As I recall, you got me to do most of the talking on our little walk, so now it's your turn. Please, Jane, tell me a little bit more about yourself. How long have you been in Boulder, and how did you happen to move to our wonderful town?"

"Yes, I did turn the tables on you a bit, didn't I? And, of course, your lovely neighbor, Millie, captured my attention for much of the time," she said with a teasing note in her voice. "And that was before you knew Connor was one of my clients so I did my best to deflect your questions. I did a pretty good job too, if I do say so myself." She grinned as she buffed her nails on the front of her shoulder.

He couldn't help but grin back at her. She did have a pretty good sense of humor … check another one off the list. "Oh, no you don't. You're not getting away with it this time. Spill it! I want to know all about you, Jane Barloc."

"Well, where should I start? Do you want the long story or the shortened version?"

"Your choice. We have plenty of time," Aaron responded.

"To answer your questions, I've been in Boulder for just about a year now. Moved here from New Orleans. I decided on Boulder because you just can't beat 300 sunny days a year. Of course, there were other things. I'm not a snob, but I must admit I thought it was pretty cool when I learned there are more Ph.D.'s per capita in Boulder than any other city in the U.S. Also, I really like the active lifestyle here. I don't think I've ever seen so many people running, jogging, roller blading, biking ... you name it. I've actually gotten to the point where I *enjoy* stuff I used to consider 'exercise'... like biking. That's become one of my most favorite things to do, next to walking, that is. It was so nice to get outside for a while today. Thanks for suggesting it."

Aaron smiled. "You're very welcome. I enjoyed it too. Were you born in New Orleans? I don't detect much of a Southern drawl or Cajun twang in your voice."

"No. My family moved around quite a bit while I was growing up. I only lived in New Orleans for a few years. Although it looks like I'll be going back there to visit on a regular basis. My dad and sister both seem to love it there. They would've preferred it if I'd decided to stay there too, but it just wasn't for me ... too hot and muggy in the summer time, and I missed the change of seasons. I'm not a huge fan of winter, but being born in the north, I must say, in my opinion, Christmas should be *white* or at least cold enough that it *could* snow."

"Yeah, I'd agree with you there. Somehow Christmas and cold weather just seem to go hand in hand. It's probably because, other than the few years I lived in California, I've spent most of my life here in Boulder. And even when I *was* going to school and living in Stanford, I always came home for Christmas."

Jane smiled knowingly, "Your family's very important to you, aren't they, Aaron?"

"Without a doubt," he replied emphatically. "I love my family a great deal. There's always been a lot of love and support for each other. And, as we've all gotten older, everyone's been really great about opening their arms to new or potentially new family members. I mean, we all love Rachel, Phillip's wife, just as much as if she'd been part of the Adler clan since day one."

"That's good to know," she said cryptically.

For some strange reason he wasn't ready to explore, Aaron's desire to know everything there was to know about her seemed insatiable, so he continued his questions. "Where in the north were you born, Jane?"

"Born in Niagara Falls, New York. Have you ever been there? The falls are spectacular … one of the seven natural wonders of the world, you know."

"No, I haven't been there, but I'd love to see them."

"Oh," she enthused, "you really should. It's an absolutely amazing place - summer and winter. When it's warm out you can take a ride on the Maid of the Mist and literally 'soak' in the excitement." She grinned at her own quip and rattled on animatedly. "And in the winter there's ice *everywhere!* They have a Winter Festival of Lights from November through January that turns the place into a true winter wonderland. You'd just *love* it."

He smiled as he watched and listened to her. It was impossible not to notice how Jane's eyes sparkled even more than usual and her tendency to "talk with her hands" was even more pronounced when she was enthusiastic about her topic. As he continued to probe into Jane's past, Aaron found the stories she told of her youth and family members to be both entertaining and insightful. She hadn't had the easiest of childhoods, but explained earnestly to him how she'd learned to "make lemonade from lemons."

"It was pretty rough after our mom died, and Patty and I were sent to live with Aunt Emily and Uncle Jim. They'd never had children, and I think they liked the *idea* of kids a whole lot better than the reality. I remember they had a dog. His name was Taffy, a Welsh Corgi, and when Patty or I would ask for a second helping of meat, Aunt Emily would say, 'No! You can't have any more meat. If you're hungry, have another potato. We cooked that meat for Taffy.'" She chuckled softly

Just the Way You Are

and continued. "I always thought that was pretty interesting ... the dog was more important than my sister and I were to our aunt and uncle. But, then again, I figured Taffy was there before we moved in, and the dog was there long after we moved out. So maybe they were right to give their pet priority over us after all."

"Would you like some more steak, Jane?" Aaron asked, half-jokingly.

Giving him another one of her heart melting smiles, she replied, "No thank you, Aaron, but thanks so *very much* for asking."

They talked non-stop during the rest of the meal. Then after dinner, they companionably cleared the table and worked together to clean up the kitchen. He realized how much he enjoyed just standing next to her, chatting about nothing in particular, doing mundane chores.

He observed her backside as she leaned over to put another plate into the dishwasher, and felt the now familiar surge of lust. How he'd love the luxury of reaching over and caressing her beautifully rounded derriere. He pictured her swatting his hand away and then turning around only to walk straight into his arms. The loving kiss she'd give him would lead straight to the bedroom ... if they made it that far. The thought of just how much fun, and pleasure, *that* could lead to poked its way into Aaron's thoughts.

Once the counters were wiped and the last spoon was in the dishwasher, Jane yawned

Anita Louise

and stretched. "Thank you again, Aaron. I think it's time for me to get some rest. I have my first follow up visit with Dr. Carter tomorrow. I'd be happy to take a cab if it's not convenient for you to drive me. The doctor doesn't want me behind the wheel again until he checks me out once more. Then I'll have to do something about replacing my sweet little car. I sure hope the insurance comes through for me. It took me quite a while to save up for that little beauty."

Aaron stood there, just looking at her. The blush appearing on her cheeks hinted at her distress.

"I'm rambling, aren't I?" she stated more than asked. "I can tell by the way you're looking at me. Oh, my gosh. I've probably been doing it all evening. Okay, that's it. I'm going to bed before I humiliate myself any further."

He gently grabbed her hand as she turned to leave the room. "Don't be embarrassed, Jane. Okay, so you've been rambling a bit. So what? I loved it. You're natural and spontaneous. You're interesting ... and *interested.* You're one of those rare people who look for the good in every situation, and because of that, you tend to find it. You care about people and about a lot of other things. I *like* you, Jane Barloc. I really like you." Her eyes filled with tears. "Jane, what's wrong? I didn't mean to upset you."

"Oh, Aaron, you didn't upset me. These are happy tears. That was one of the nicest things anyone's ever said to me. Thank you. I like you too … a *lot.*" And with that she kissed him lightly on the cheek and left the room.

It was in that moment Aaron realized his desire for Jane went beyond the potent physical attraction he had to her. There was so much more to her than met the eye. When his brother Connor practically dragged her into his parents' house less than a week ago, he'd been immediately captivated by her unique brand of beauty. Her bright and lively intellect was apparent and had increased his interest in her during their rather brief conversation at the party. His esteem for her had only grown stronger the more he got to know her. She'd been reluctant to accept his offer to stay at his home, even though she had no one else to help her out. It was nice to see how grateful she was. Not only was she appreciative of being able to recuperate in his home, but he'd been tickled pink by her almost overwhelming delight when she saw her cat was also there. He'd brought the Garfield look-alike to his house only because of the convenience of taking care of the animal at his home instead of having to drive across town. It had *nothing* to do with wanting to please her, did it? When he looked at his feelings truthfully, he understood Jane Barloc *was* slowly, but surely breaking down the walls he'd built around his heart after Sharon's betrayal.

Anita Louise

It was true. Jane *did* need to get some rest. But just thinking of Aaron was doing crazy things to her insides. Sleep would be impossible, at least for a little while. She recognized her love for Aaron was deepening. His comments touched her heart in a way she'd never experienced before. Even boring old William had wanted her to be someone she wasn't. Whenever she'd gone off on some tangent instead of sticking to whatever subject she'd started talking about, he would look at her disapprovingly. "You're doing it again, Jane," William would chastise. "One subject at a time, please."

Instead of trying to change her, it seemed like Aaron not only *accepted* her, but he actually *liked* her ... just the way she was. She sighed almost blissfully at the thought. Fate had a wonderful way of working things out. She'd learned so much more about her handsome host in the last few days. For the next several minutes, she let her mind review the chain of events that led to her being not only in Aaron Adler's house, but in his bedroom.

Just thinking about him had tingles moving up her spine. She felt sure that in addition to being a wonderfully skilled lover, he would also be conscious of his partner's needs. Learning everything there was to know about him was something she wanted very badly. Her body heated up at the thought of feeling the strength of his arms enfolding her. She remembered the way

Just the Way You Are

his gray-green eyes had gotten dark and smoky when he looked at her in the bathtub that first night. When he walked into the bathroom he was like a knight in shining armor coming to the rescue of his damsel in distress.

She tried to ignore her rapidly beating heart, but the thought of being in his bed ... with him, naked and *hot* had her heating up instead. As much as she wanted to touch herself, to gain release from the desperate need that was building from simply *thinking* about Aaron, she didn't. There was no longer even a shadow of a doubt. Now she was certain. She wanted *more*. She wanted the real thing.

Jane wanted *Aaron's* hands and lips on her. Wanted to hear him speak her name and look at her ... his eyes filled with desire. She wanted him next to her, holding her, caressing every inch of her body. She wanted to touch him, to feel him, to have him inside her. Jane Barloc wanted *more* than she'd ever wanted before. She wanted it all. She wanted Aaron Adler's love.

When Jane first saw Aaron Adler at the symposium in New Orleans, she'd gone because of how much she enjoyed his books. Of course, she knew how handsome he was, and she did have a "schoolgirl crush" on him. Had she been a teenager, there would most likely have been Aaron Adler posters hanging on the wall above her bed. Everything she read about him in the tabloids described him as a real "playboy," and seeing him surrounded by a bevy of beautiful women at the reception after his talk only confirmed that perception.

What if I hadn't seen the announcement of his coming to speak? What if I hadn't been able to get a ticket?

Jane had no idea Aaron lived in Boulder when she'd made her decision to move to the area. In fact, the little she'd learned about him from the gossip magazines had him living in California. She was totally honest when she told him her reasons for moving to Boulder. It truly *was* the abundance of sunny days, healthy lifestyle, and the fact many intellectuals chose Boulder as their home that had positively influenced her choice.

What if I'd chosen to move to some city other than Boulder? She'd had offers in San Diego, Albuquerque and Seattle. What if she'd accepted one of those offers instead?

When the court assigned Connor Adler to work with her, it never occurred to her he might be related to the famous author. Not once did it cross her mind that the young man who was overindulged by his extra-large, and perhaps too "helpful" family was in any way related to the one man she could never seem to completely get out of her thoughts.

What if Connor had been assigned to another counselor?

Just the Way You Are

What if Connor's car hadn't been in the shop, and he hadn't asked me to drive him to the party at his parents' house?

What if Aaron hadn't been able to make it to his parents' party for some reason?

What if I hadn't gotten in the accident?

What if Aaron hadn't been the one to see my car off the side of the mountain?

What if? What if? What if?

Adjusting herself comfortably on Aaron's big bed, she allowed herself to drift off to sleep. Her dreams were of gray-green eyes in the face of a little boy who looked amazingly like his father. The two of them were laughing and smiling ... playing catch in the back yard of the beautiful home overlooking the majestic Colorado Rockies. She sat on the patio watching them, and in her arms, she held an adorable baby, dressed in pink. When the child looked up at Jane, the little girl's smile shone in her big blue eyes, as she said, "Mama."

Chapter Eight

Getting to know more about Jane over dinner the evening before was both enjoyable and enlightening. Aaron *wasn't* totally ready to admit how quickly and how much he'd grown accustomed to having her around. Okay, so he actually liked her company. The problem was, his physical attraction to her was practically out of control. So much so, he was torn between wanting her to get well so she could get the hell out of his house and wanting her to stay forever.

Aaron had been up for over an hour waiting for Jane. He was tired of sleeping in the guest bedroom. He wanted the comfort of the gigantic king-sized bed in his own master suite. The only problem was that he didn't want to sleep there alone. He'd be more than happy for his

Just the Way You Are

house guest to stay right where she was ... in *his* bed ... with *him,* at least for a while longer.

He hadn't had a "nocturnal emission" since he was a teenager ... until last night. His mind drifted back to the sexy dream causing the unusual occurrence. His head was bent over two beautiful, large breasts. As he cupped his hands around their softness and pushed them together, his mouth and tongue went from one firm nipple to the other, sucking and nipping. He could hear her breathing faster, little whimpers of pleasure coming from her full lips. He continued to lick, suck and nibble his way down her torso, giving special attention to her navel ... dipping his tongue in and swirling it around. His hands kept caressing and tweaking the taut peaks on her chest. He could feel her fingers in his hair, pushing his head down to the place of her need. Her whimpers changed to moans of desperation.

"Spread your legs for me," he heard himself say. She did, and the sweet nectar between her thighs was like ambrosia. "Mmmmm, you taste so good."

Her hips were rocking up and down, and he heard her voice, Jane's voice begging him, "Please, Aaron, please. I have to have you inside me. Take me ... please, take me now."

He looked into Jane's amazing blue eyes full of love and wanting. His erection was rock hard. He lifted up and slowly entered her wet and willing opening. Ahh, it felt so good. With the stamina of a teenager, after only a few hard thrusts he had exploded ... all over the sheets of the bed in his guest room.

Enough of this! He was a grown man with a grown man's wants and needs. Even though it'd been a few months since he'd bedded a woman, he hadn't expected his desire to express itself through a *dream*. He wanted Jane Barloc, and he wanted her for real ... *soon*.

Well, today's visit to the doctor would answer any questions he had about whether or not she was healthy enough for ..... He stopped. Healthy enough for what? For sex? Is that all he wanted from Jane Barloc? Was she just another adoring fan to take to his bed for a few pleasurable hours and then send her away, much like a child discards a once favored toy? He was not a child. He was a mature adult. Was he willing to use her ... to hurt her like that?

And what about me. What about Aaron Adler?

The physical needs he'd been thinking about all morning suddenly became less important. What he really wanted was happiness ... joie de vivre, the joy of living. Yes, he wanted a great sex life, but that was only part of what made life joyful. He thought again of how many characteristics he'd already discovered in Jane that he'd hoped to find someday in a mate ... a mate for life ... a soul mate. He'd already admitted to himself that Jane was chipping away

Just the Way You Are

at the barricade he'd built to protect himself from the potential hurt of allowing someone in. He thought of a quote from Socrates he was contemplating using in his next book.

His reverie was interrupted by a cheerful, "Good morning, Aaron. Isn't it a beautiful day?"

He turned to see Jane smiling happily at him, and couldn't help but give her a smile in return. "Looks like *someone* had a good night's sleep," he said.

"Oh, I *did*. And *dreams* ... I had wonderful dreams." With that she did a little pirouette before coming to him and planting a warm kiss on his cheek.

"How about you, Aaron? Did you have sweet dreams?"

Even though he was not one to blush, the thought of the erotic dream in which Jane held the starring role had his cheeks heating up. "Uh, well. I don't tend to remember my dreams much," he muttered.

Oblivious to his embarrassment, she went on. "Neither do I ... usually, but I'm sooo glad that I remembered this one!"

"Would you like to share it with me?"

"Maybe ... someday. Not today, but maybe someday. What's for breakfast? I'm famished!"

"There you go again, changing horses in the middle of the stream. But that's okay. I'm not much in the mood for talking about dreams anyway. How do pancakes sound? I'm practically world famous for my banana walnut pancakes," he said with a grin.

"Sounds yummy. I'll pour us some orange juice. Did you know that orange is the only word in the English language that there's no rhyme for? Oranges, poranges, oranges, poranges .... Ain't no rhyme for oranges!" she sang and giggled.

Feeling the weight of his earlier thoughts float away, he couldn't help but chuckle at her silly song. They were walking out of the kitchen to relax in the living room for a few minutes before it was time to leave for Jane's doctor visit when Jane started speaking.

"Should I take my things with me when we go to see Dr. Carter? I should probably come back and get Henry. He wouldn't like waiting in the car while we're in the doctor's office. Oh, I forgot. I don't have a car yet. Would you mind bringing Henry back to my condo, Aaron?"

Hearing her talk so blithely about leaving took Aaron aback. "Don't you think you should wait and see what the doctor has to say before you start making all these plans? Are you really in such a hurry to leave my humble abode?" he asked in mock dismay.

Looking seriously into his eyes, she replied, "I love it here, Aaron, and so does Henry. Quite honestly, I figured you were probably getting tired of being stuck here with us. You're

Just the Way You Are

single. In fact, I understand you're quite the 'man about town.' Isn't having Henry and me here cramping your style a bit?"

"Man about town, eh? Where in the world did you get that idea?"

"Oh, I have my sources," she said with a wink.

"Whatever. Well, your sources are pretty crumby, Ms. Barloc. And the truth is I've really enjoyed having you and Henry here. In case you haven't noticed, this house is quite large and with only one person here it can get to feeling a little empty. Why don't we wait and see what Dr. Carter has to say before we go making all kinds of plans? Besides that, my brother Michael is having a little shindig at his place on Friday night. I'd really like it if you'd go with *me* this time instead of Connor."

"I'd love to go with you to Michael's party. And, to be accurate, I *didn't* go to your parents' party with Connor. I drove him there because his car was in the shop, and he *insisted* I come in for a few minutes. Of course, I'm glad I did because I wouldn't have met you otherwise."

"Tis true, m'lady," he replied in jest. He lowered his head and chest in a courtly bow.

"Now, Sir Aaron," she quipped, "back to Michael's party. Is it casual or dressy? Since I wasn't planning on going to any 'shindigs' any time soon, I truly don't have *a thing* to wear... as the old saying goes."

Anita Louise

"Mike's not a dressy kind of guy for the most part. And this gig was sort of an impromptu thing, so I have to figure you can pretty much be as casual as you want to be. Wear whatever you want. It's no big deal."

"Typical man!" she snorted. "Now, if I asked one of your sisters or your mother, I'm sure I'd get a much more reasonable answer."

"Do you want me to call Mom and ask her?"

"Of course not!" she said in mock horror. "Your mother doesn't even really *know* me. And if she hears I've been staying in your house, she'll think I'm ... that we're ... Oh, phooey!" She sat down heavily on the sofa with her lower lip sticking out, looking rather forlorn.

"Jane, you've met my mother. I think you could see what kind of person she is. You can bet she already *likes* you, and she's going to *love* you once she *does* really know you. She's not a woman who jumps to conclusions about people ... unless you consider always assuming the best about someone jumping to conclusions."

Her expression brightened. "You always seem to know just the right thing to say to make me feel better. Thank you, Aaron. Can we please stop at my condo after we see Dr. Carter? I'll look in my closet and see if I can find anything appropriate. If not, I guess you'll just have to take me shopping," she said with an irrepressible grin. With that she flounced out of the room, presumably to finish getting ready for her check up with Dr. Carter.

Sharon Demasi was getting a little irritated with her ex-husband. *Why isn't he calling me back?* she wondered. The number of times she'd called him in the last few months was almost too many to count. She'd started keeping tabs on him once he moved back to Boulder.

If I'd had any idea he was going to become some big deal, super successful writer with that personal development stuff he was always talking about, I'd never have divorced him, she told herself for the hundredth time.

Even though her marriage to Aaron Adler was short-lived, it'd been fun. Since he was a couple of years younger than her, she'd been the one who controlled the relationship right from the beginning. In her opinion, that's the way all marriages should be. "Happy wife. Happy life." If more men understood that, there'd be a heck of a lot less divorces.

Well, since he won't call me back, maybe I should just pay a little visit to that big fancy house of his, she thought. A look of displeasure crossed her face. *I can't believe he spent a ton of money on real estate and didn't do it through me. Humph! You'd think the man would show a little gratitude and loyalty for all I've been to him and done for him.*

Anita Louise

She shrugged her shoulders dismissively. *He'll be begging me to take him back once he finds out about the little surprise I have for him. It'll be impossible for him to resist what I'm offering. After all, it IS every man's secret desire.*

Jane sat with her feet propped up on the ottoman of one of the oversized reading chairs placed next to the window of the master suite. Henry was curled up in her lap purring contentedly. Her pet was making himself comfortable in Aaron's beautiful home, and Jane's dream had sparked a vision that had her mind working overtime.

"I think we're getting to him," she said aloud as she absently stroked her pet's fur. *I have to think like a fisherman ... not a hunter.* She was mentally reviewing a relationship lecture she'd attended. The topic was about hunting versus fishing when it came to developing rapport and building a bond with a potential mate. The speaker pointed out that a hunter is *chasing* his prey which is, of course, running in the opposite direction as fast as possible. The fisher, on the other hand, casts out the bait and *waits.* A good fisher knows exactly the kind of bait her "catch" prefers. If the fish is hungry, it *willingly* comes *to* the bait. In the same way, when someone is drawn to you ... when it's their *choice* to be with you, then they will want to stay. *"And, oh, how I*

Just the Way You Are

want _you_ to want _us_ to stay together, Aaron Adler."

Placing Henry carefully on the sunny ottoman, Jane stepped in front of the mirror and quickly finished her final touch ups, before walking back into the living room where Aaron was waiting patiently. Within minutes she was sitting in the passenger seat of Aaron's Jeep.

"Why a Jeep?" she asked. "Why not a Jaguar or Porsche or some other exotic car?"

"I'm not an 'exotic' kind of guy, Jane. Sure, I've done quite well financially with my writing, but it hasn't changed who I am as a _person_. I've always loved the sportiness of a Jeep. In fact, my first car was a wonderful little rag top Jeep Wrangler. Boy, did I love that car. Drove it until the wheels practically fell off."

"There's a lot more to you than meets the eye, Aaron Adler," she said with a look of admiration.

The radio was tuned to one of the local "oldies" stations and each of them would sing a line or two when they recognized a favorite song from their past. When Billie Joel's voice started singing, "Don't go changing ..." they both joined in. As the lyrics continued, Jane couldn't help but look at Aaron when she sang the words, "I love you just the way you are." _If only he knew how much truth there is in those song lyrics,_ she thought.

There was no further conversation in the Jeep until they reached the doctor's office.

Aaron waited in the lobby as Jane went in for her follow up visit. After a thorough physical examination, Dr. Carter asked a few more questions to support his findings.

"Any headaches, dizziness? Ringing in your ears? Nausea or vomiting?"

"No, Doctor. I've really been feeling fine."

"Any confusion at all? Feeling like you're in a fog?"

"No ..." *Not unless you count the way I feel when I get too close or think too much about Aaron.*

"Well, Ms. Barloc, you're doing extremely well considering the severity of your injuries when you were first brought in. It appears you've been following doctor's orders and haven't been over doing it ... getting plenty of rest, right?"

"Yes, I have. The truth is I need to get back to work as soon as possible. Do I have your clearance to start back on Monday?"

"Yes, that's fine, Ms. Barloc. Do you still have help at home?" Dr. Carter asked.

"Actually, I've been staying with a friend. Is it all right for me to be home alone now?"

"Hmm, based on everything I've seen here, I'd say that would be fine. Yes, you should be all right on your own now. Any other questions?"

"No. Thank you, Dr. Carter."

Jane wasn't sure if she was happy or sad. She could go back to work ... get back to her "normal" life. Aaron had asked her to wait until after her follow up exam. Now that the doctor had given her clearance to go back to work, there was no longer any excuse to stay in Aaron's home. A little down in the dumps, she dressed slowly, and thought about how enjoyable the past few days with Aaron had been.

Some little "devil" hopped on her shoulder and whispered in her ear, *What if you told him that the doctor said you needed a few more days of supervised care?*

The "angel" on Jane's other shoulder quickly stepped in. *No ... you can't do that. You've been completely honest with Aaron right from the start and that's never going to change.*

Dressed and ready to face whatever lay ahead, she squared her shoulders and walked into the waiting room.

Aaron looked up from the magazine he'd been casually leafing through, a little grin on his face. "Well? Good news?" he asked.

Putting the best smile on her face she could manage, she replied, "Great news. I can go back to work on Monday, and I no longer need supervised care. So I guess that means it's time

Anita Louise

for me to get back to my condo and let you have your place back to yourself."

Aaron's smile faded. "Oh," he paused for a moment, and then continued. "The fact your health is good is great news. And I'm sure you're ready to get back to work. But what about your car? Don't you need a car to get back and forth?"

"Yes, I do. To be honest, I hadn't really given it much thought."

"Well, I *have*, and I think it would be best if you and Henry stayed with me at least through the weekend. If you'd like, I can help you find your new car. Come to think of it, it's been a while since I've looked at new vehicles. It might be fun. Also, since you've already accepted my invitation to the party at my brother's on Friday, you staying at my house will make it a lot easier for me instead of having to pick you up and take you back to your condo. How does that sound?"

Smiling at him happily, she replied, "That sounds absolutely wonderful, Aaron. Let's go to my condo first so I can see if I have anything that will work for Michael's party. If not, you can add shopping to our list of things to do."

She held out her hand, and he took it without thinking. He'd gotten used to the zing of pleasure that accompanied her touch. But this time there was something more … an added warmth. Her hand felt so soft and small in his much larger palm. It felt good … very good.

Chapter Nine

*H*e *wants me to <u>stay</u>!* Jane's heart leapt with joy. No matter what they were doing, it seemed to her the air around them swirled with the electricity created by the attraction she felt for him. *I'm almost <u>positive</u> he feels it too.* They'd only shared one kiss ... one fabulous, earth shaking kiss, and even that had been cut short by Connor's arrival.

The thought of being alone together in his house for a few more days had her pulse racing and her female hormones doing jumping jacks. It was true. Being this close to Aaron for almost a week was certainly having an effect on her. Obviously, controlling her desire for him was difficult, especially when she was living in his house.

Yes, she wanted Aaron to return to his master bedroom, with her. She wanted the two of them under the covers, naked and hot. There was no doubt in her mind that sex with Aaron would be better than anything she'd ever experienced in her life. And she wanted, needed to touch him and to feel his hands on her ... to see his eyes burning with desire for her, almost as much as she needed air to breathe.

And still, that wasn't all. She knew she wanted more. She was sure Aaron would happily join her in bed and fulfill her dreams of passionate kisses and even more. But was that enough? *If hot sex is all he wants from me, will I be able to pull off an act ... pretending that wonderful, glorious, hot sex is adequate? Will I be able to walk away if need be? Would it be possible to hide a broken heart?*

As soon as she was seated in the passenger seat of his Jeep, he asked, "What should we do first?"

Pushing aside all her unanswered questions, Jane took a moment to think. "Well, you're absolutely correct. I *do* need something to get back and forth to my job, among other things, so getting a vehicle needs to be right up there on the priority list. Why don't we do this? Let's go to my condo. You can do a little research online for a vehicle for me, while I look through my closet to see if there's anything perfect for me to wear to your brother's party. Does that sound all right?"

Just the Way You Are

"Fine with me, Jane, but what kind of car are you looking for? I know you had a nice little Volkswagen. Are you going to get another one?"

"As I said before, I haven't given it a lot of thought, but some of the conversations we've had over the past few days have given me some ideas. Since I've grown to enjoy biking so much, I thought I'd look at something that would make getting my bike to and from some of the local trail heads a little easier. I'm considering either a vehicle that will accommodate a bike rack or even one that will allow me to put my bike inside. What do you think?"

"Funny you should ask," Aaron responded. "My sister Brooke is an avid bicyclist, as well as a teacher, and she bought a mini-van not too long ago. There's lots of room for a bicycle, or more than one if need be. Plus, it works for transporting stuff for the projects she gets into at school. That would be a *major* switch from a VW bug, however."

Jane's thoughts veered off to all the times she'd seen mothers loading and unloading groceries and other items from mini-vans full of children. All of a sudden, the idea of a mini-van sounded better than it ever had before. "You know, Aaron," she said with a smile and a twinkle in her eye, "that might be just the vehicle I need at this time in my life. Yes, a mini-van might be perfect."

Anita Louise

Jane directed Aaron to her assigned parking spot in the condo complex. She'd spent a lot of time finding a home she could afford near the University of Colorado - Boulder campus. Her residence was on the end of the building and backed up to a community park. There was plenty of sunshine pouring in the windows, and a small private patio was located outside her sliding glass door. The outdoor area was just the right size for Jane to sit and relax with a glass of wine after a long day at work. Of course, there was no comparison to the beauty and luxury of Aaron's home, but she was proud of how nicely she'd decorated her place.

"Here we are," she said as she opened the front door. They walked into her cozy little house.

"This is very nice, Jane," he said. "You have a very comfortable home."

"Thanks, Aaron. I'm glad you like it. It's small, but there's plenty of room for me and Henry. Come on upstairs. That's where I have my home office. You can do a little research on the internet while I look through my closet."

At the thought of going up to her bedroom with Aaron, Jane felt a delicious thrill move up her spine. *Oh, what wonderful things we could do in the BEDroom.* She sneaked a peak at him. The look in his gray-green eyes had her body heating up from head to toe with particular emphasis on certain areas. A blush colored her cheeks when

Just the Way You Are

he winked at her ... seeming to read her thoughts.

She was glad she didn't have to take him into the small room where her bed took up most of the space. Luckily there were two bedrooms upstairs. She led him into the one equipped with a small desk, chair, a couple of bookcases, and a reading lamp sitting on a table next to a matching chair and ottoman. While Jane was booting up her computer, Aaron reviewed the titles on the shelves against the wall.

"I see you have a few authors you tend to favor," he said with an amused chuckle.

"If you mean I own every book you've ever written, then yes, I do have *several* authors I 'tend to favor,' and *you* happen to be one of them. In fact, if you'd like to pull out one by Dr. Aaron Adler and write a beautiful inscription to me that would be great."

He paused for a moment, and then said, "I'll be happy to do that for you, Jane."

Jane watched as he selected the first book he'd written from her shelf and looked at the well-worn copy. She didn't know what she could or should say to explain the fact his book had obviously been read multiple times. So she simply shrugged her shoulders, gave him a sweet smile and said, "I liked it." Wanting to escape his insightful gaze, she quickly followed with, "Computer's ready to go. Why don't you sit here while I go take a look through my closet?" With that she got up and left the room.

What will he write? What should I wear to the party? Do I dare ask to read it right away? Will it look like I'm trying too hard if I go out and buy something new? What if he writes something super impersonal ... something he would write to just anyone who showed up at one of his book signings? There must be something in this closet that will work. What if he writes something special ... something meaningful? Her thoughts seemed to be all jumbled up. She plopped down on the bed with a sigh. *Oh, Aaron, if you only knew what you do to me.*

After lying there for a few minutes, she was able to collect her thoughts enough to get up and look through her closet. Even though she'd been living in Aaron's house for several days, she looked at this party as their "first date." She wanted to wear something that would make her feel confident and beautiful ... a little bit flirty and even a tiny bit sexy.

Somehow, the idea of asking Aaron to take her shopping for an outfit to wear to his brother's party just didn't feel right. So, after looking at practically everything in her closet, she chose two outfits, both casual, but one a little more dressy than the other. The first possibility was a lavender silk blouse that brought out her blue eyes. She paired it with her most flattering pair of skinny jeans and heeled boots. Option

Just the Way You Are

number two was a not-too-clingy peach colored sweater with a wide cowl neck, a chunky gold necklace and a black pencil skirt with classic pumps. Putting both outfits in a garment bag, Jane walked back into her office. Aaron was still sitting at her computer.

"How's it going?" she asked. "Have you found the perfect vehicle for me yet?" He looked up at her and smiled, and as usual, her heart practically skipped a beat. Oh, how she wished she were the kind of woman who always knew the perfect thing to say or do to make a man fall for her. Not possible. *Plain Jane* didn't have a perfect bone in her body.

"Well, I've come up with a few options at dealerships nearby. Are you ready to go?" Aaron asked.

Ignoring her impulse to run to the bookshelf and read the inscription he'd written for her, she nodded affirmatively and said, "All set. Let's go buy me a new car."

The rest of the afternoon flew by. After they visited several local auto dealers, Jane finally settled on a dark blue mini-van with rear seats that folded down to easily accommodate multiple bicycles. It would be ready for her to pick up and drive to work on Monday morning.

Once she settled back into Aaron's car, Jane was quickly lost in thought. There was no doubt the chemistry between her and Aaron could lead to some amazing sex, but she wanted more ... so much more. As silly as it might seem to anyone reading her thoughts, the real reason she purchased the mini-van was because she had a very clear picture of children ... Adler children, climbing in and out of the vehicle's roomy interior. She'd even gotten a rear facing video player. She smiled as she visualized the kids ... hers and Aaron's, settling down in the back seat to watch their favorite Disney movie.

The time she and Aaron had spent together so far ... doing average, every day activities was wonderful. It almost felt as if they were a *real* couple. She was certain the two of them could lie around for hours, just laughing and talking ... so wrapped up in each other that nothing else in the world would even matter. She'd always *be there* for him and vice versa, through whatever ups and downs that life might bring. Aaron Adler wasn't perfect. She understood that, but then neither was she. She also knew that in the relationship she wanted, both she and her mate would look *beyond* those imperfections and love each other in spite of them. *I love you just the way you are.* The words and melody continued to play in her mind.

One look into Aaron's eyes could take her breath away, and just his smile did crazy things to her insides. Jane knew she was one of those women who had a very high sex drive. She felt certain that *when* (not *if*), she and Aaron made a commitment to be together, many hours would be spent in bed and other interesting places, making love and pleasing each other in a multitude of ways.

The one kiss they'd shared was *incredible!* The heat with which her body reacted to him was unlike anything else she'd ever experienced. *What might it have led to, had Aaron's brother Connor not arrived at the door just then?* As much as she wanted to make love with Aaron, there was part of her that was so *afraid.* What if sex was all he wanted?

Growing up, her father always told her, as far as boys and men were concerned, the guy's philosophy was, "Why pay for the cow, when you can get the milk for free?" As a result, although she wasn't a virgin, Jane had always been cautious in her relationships. Very few had gone beyond the delight of passionate kissing and some heavy petting.

Even though Jane was a highly intelligent woman, she'd been known to read the tabloids, especially when it came to Aaron Adler. She knew his reputation for being somewhat of a "womanizer." The way she looked at it was, simply because he wrote about personal development, it didn't mean he was a relationship expert.

Although unconfirmed, the story she'd read about Aaron in the gossip columns held a ring of truth. It said that before he became famous, he'd been married to an older woman

Anita Louise

who dumped him. Maybe that accounted for the fact he was rarely, if ever, seen with the same woman more than a few times. There was always a new gorgeous face and spectacular body to replace the previous one. He never stuck with any specific model, movie star or single mom long enough for her to be labeled as his "significant other."

And who do you think you are, <u>Plain Jane</u>, to think you could even qualify to be one of the string of women he's gone through ... let alone be the one to change Aaron Adler's philandering ways?

Chapter Ten

Driving back to his house, Aaron was lost in thought. Being together with Jane for nearly a full week was taking its toll on the almost impenetrable walls he'd built to protect his heart. As much as he wanted to deny it, he was powerfully drawn to Jane Barloc. Being this close to her had his libido clamoring for attention. He needed to do something to distract him from her all too alluring presence.

"Jane, looking at my books in your office reminded me. I really need to get some work done. My publisher has me on a deadline for my latest book, and if I don't get a few more chapters to my editor soon, he's going to send out the troops."

"Of course, Aaron. As you already know from my bookshelf, I've read everything you've ever written. I've been a big fan from the beginning. Do you remember the time you spoke in New Orleans after your first book made the best-seller list?"

"Of course I do. Not only was that one of my first speaking engagements, it was also my first and only visit to New Orleans. What a great city. Were you there?"

"Yep, front row and everything." She grinned.

He stood there for a moment lost in thought. He shook his head. *No, it couldn't possibly be.* "What a coincidence. I wonder what might've happened had we met personally back then?" he mused.

Jane shrugged noncommittally, and changed the subject. "Is there anything I can do to help, or would you prefer I just stay out of your way?"

"Well, since you *are* a fan and have read my other work, perhaps you might be interested in reading what I've written so far and giving me some feedback. Of course, if you don't give me rave reviews, I might have to punish you." He joked. As soon as the offhand remark left his lips, a picture of her beautiful, bare backside lying across his lap appeared in his mind. It wasn't typical for Aaron to use spanking, bondage or other forms of eroticism as a preamble to sex. But, somehow the idea of his hand turning her buttocks pink caused a spike of arousal in him that almost took his breath away. He glanced surreptitiously at Jane and caught a glimpse of a blush color her face. *What are you thinking, my lovely Jane? Did that turn you on as much as it did me?*

The idea of being "punished" ... the vulnerability and almost helpless submission inherent in being bent over Aaron's lap filled her with a delicious, forbidden warmth. She had to fight back the desire that moved through her. As much as she wanted a continuance of their earlier kiss, his insistence on needing to get some work done kept her from voicing the suggestive ideas that ran through her brain.

In an attempt to hide her wayward thoughts and put their conversation back on track, she said, "Aaron, you *deserve* my rave reviews. The generosity you've shown by having me and Henry stay with you, and of course, helping me find my new car, have been more than kind. I want to do whatever I can to repay you. It will be my sincere pleasure to read your work." She paused. "One of the things I've always loved about your books is it doesn't sound like you're writing above your readers' heads. You write so everybody can understand the concepts and put the information to *use.*"

Aaron looked at her with what she assumed was respect for her honest opinion, yet mixed in, she thought she detected a reflection of her own desire in him. Being in such close proximity to him for the last few days was doing crazy things to her. She couldn't remember the last time her sex drive was in high gear like this. *Had it _ever_ been?* And on top of that, both her head and her heart were falling ... fast, for the handsome man sitting only a few feet away from her. In spite of the fact there were many, much more exciting and lascivious endeavors she'd like to pursue with him, she did her best to keep her focus on the idea of helping him with his manuscript. With as much enthusiasm as she could manage, she said, "Well then, I can hardly wait to get started reading your new book. Let's do that as soon as we get back."

Once again, the look on Aaron's face made her think his mind was also veering off toward activities having a lot less to do with writing and editing his work and a lot *more* to do with getting to know each other in much more intimate ways. The sexual tension in the air for the rest of the drive back to his house was palpable, but he made no further comment.

As soon as they were inside the house, he hung up their coats and then moved toward his home office.

"Please follow me, m'lady Jane, and I'll give you my manuscript," he said with a mock bow and a flourish of his hand. She followed him through French doors into his sumptuous home office. The room was large and comfortable with a desk, sofa and cozy seating area for two near the windows. The wall behind his desk was lined with books on psychology, spirituality, personal development and other subjects. His desk was at the back of the room, and his view was of the Colorado mountains. When he noticed her perusal of his study and its contents he commented, "I like to look at the sky and the mountains. It's a great view for giving me inspiration when I need it."

"This space looks to me to be perfect for writing, reviewing *and* for inspiration. It's lovely," Jane said.

"Yes ... lovely." He looked at her with what she thought was undisguised desire.

The sound of his voice practically had her heart beating out of her chest. How was she going to concentrate on reading his manuscript if things continued like this?

It was almost as if he could read her thoughts. Aaron gave his head a brief shake. Was he trying to clear his mind of wayward ideas similar to hers? He then took a deep breath and walked to the credenza beside his desk. After unlocking the cabinet, he reached in and pulled out what looked to be about 150 pages held together with only a large binder clip.

"Here you go," he said as he extended the papers to her. "I think you'll find one of the chairs next to the window to be not only comfortable, but there's also plenty of natural light. If you need it, there's a reading lamp as well."

Following his lead, she did her best to control the high voltage desires and hormones that seemed to be running rampant inside her. Carefully, she took the manuscript from his hand. She made sure there was no physical contact ... certain that one touch could turn the burning embers of her attraction to him into a roaring inferno.

Suddenly she was struck by the fact she was holding the pages of Aaron Adler's next book in her hands. Jane Barloc was going to be one of the first people, outside his inner circle, to read what could once again, end up on best-seller lists all over the globe. She felt both honored and humbled by the privilege. She wasn't sure if the shaking in her limbs was caused by her delight in reading his work or simply because of Aaron's close proximity.

Shortly after sitting down in one of the plush leather chairs near the windows, Henry came in and planted himself on her lap. She petted him absently as she opened the sheaf of precious papers. It was only a few moments after she began to read that her surroundings seemed to disappear. Aaron was venturing further into spirituality with this latest work, and Jane was enjoying it thoroughly. After what seemed like minutes, but was actually several hours, Jane's concentration was broken by Aaron's question.

Just the Way You Are

"What do you like best so far, Jane?"

"Oh, Aaron, *I love it.* The Marcus Aurelius quote you use at the beginning of the first section of the book is wonderful. 'Accept the things to which fate binds you, and love the people with whom fate brings you together, but do so with all your heart.'"

"I'm glad you like it, Jane. The wisdom of ancient philosophers, like Marcus Aurelius, Epictetus and, of course, Socrates and Aristotle, is still so very applicable today. If more people could learn to accept whatever they're experiencing without the anger, frustration or impatience most of us indulge in when things don't go exactly as we'd like, we would all enjoy life so much more."

"That's so true." Jane loved listening to him talk about his work and the philosophies that were part of what made him the man she loved.

"The section of the book you've been reading delves quite a bit into the concept of acceptance ... learning to deal with the things that happen without having to label them as 'good or bad.' Like Shakespeare said, 'there is nothing either good or bad, but thinking makes it so.'" Jane concurred with a nod of her head and he went on, "The section I'm working on now focuses on those 'people with whom fate brings you together.' I feel very fortunate to have grown up in the middle of a larger than average family. Thankfully, ours has many more characteristics of

Anita Louise

a functional rather than dysfunctional household. Consequently, it's been pretty easy for me to love the *siblings* fate has brought into my life, but I can't say the same for all of my other relationships."

Jane considered his statement carefully before speaking. "I can relate to what you're saying. Even though my family is quite small, just my dad and sister, the three of us have always loved each other unconditionally. Dad remarried a couple of times since Mom died, and his choices in mates haven't been exactly perfect. But, because we love our father, my sister and I have always accepted whoever he's with."

"Please. Tell me more about your sister."

Jane's face lit up. "Patty's the greatest. We're only thirteen months apart. A lot of people thought we were twins growing up. No matter what, we've always been there for each other. I think I may have mentioned that Patty recently had a baby girl ... Arianna. My plan is to visit them between Christmas and New Year's."

"What about Arianna's father?"

"Well, the baby daddy that fate brought into my sister's life didn't stick around too long. Patty's track record when it comes to relationships isn't a heck of a lot better than Dad's ... maybe worse. Arianna's father was gone before Patty even knew she was pregnant." Jane shook her head and shrugged, not knowing what else to say.

Just the Way You Are

"What about you, Jane?"

"Me? I've watched Dad make less than stellar choices when it comes to his girlfriends and wives over the years. Even though Patty's only a little older than me, she started dating much earlier than I did. I was more the wallflower type while she was out there 'blooming' as fast as she could. I think the mistakes I've seen those two make have made me super cautious."

"Come on, Jane, you're a beautiful woman. Surely there've been some significant relationships in your life."

"Yes, a couple. There's my best friend Sheila back in New Orleans, but you're probably talking about male female relationships. Oh, I tested the waters, so to speak in college, but nothing super serious ever came from any of my college beaus. The only really significant relationship I've had since then was with William. We dated for almost three years. He even asked me to marry him, but I knew he wasn't the one for me, so I broke it off. I understand he's happily married now."

They sat quietly for a few moments, just looking at one another. There was so much she wanted to know about him. *What experiences ... what relationships made you the man you are today?*

She was totally in love with him. There was no point in trying to deny it. She loved just watching him. The way he looked when he was

Anita Louise

thinking or focusing on something delighted her. She loved how his face would light up when he talked about things he cared about.

"And what about the people fate has brought into *your* life outside your family, Aaron?" she asked.

He answered her question with a question of his own. "Would you like to hear the Socrates' quote I'm using to start the second section of the book?" Not waiting for her response and holding her mesmerized with his eyes , he recited, "Sometimes you put up walls not to keep people out, but to see who cares enough to break them down."

Jane barely heard the yowl from her cat as Henry tumbled unceremoniously from her lap. She stood and walked across the room, her eyes never leaving his. "I care enough, Aaron. I would love to break down those walls. Please ... let me in."

When she stepped into his arms, the world seemed to stop. Even though she knew it was too soon, she didn't care. She wanted him, and she knew he wanted her too. Still looking deeply into his eyes, Jane threaded her fingers lightly through his hair. She felt his hands clasp her hips possessively as he pulled her closer. When their lips met, she was lost. She felt his hand move up her spine, softly caressing every inch. Their mouths opened, and slowly he began stroking his tongue against hers.

Just the Way You Are

To Jane, kissing was always one of the most sensual and romantic aspects of making love. She could be content for hours enjoying every contour of his mouth … the texture and taste of his lips, his tongue. She heard her own moan of pleasure escape as he drew back his head to gently suck her lower lip and then give it a soft nip. Then his tongue was back in her mouth … invading … insisting. She responded in kind, tasting, sucking, and nibbling. Never before had she kissed or been kissed like this.

Chapter Eleven

Aaron was experiencing a kiss that was both sensual and sweet, passionate and playful. As their tongues and teeth tasted and nipped, sucked and soothed, he felt the softness of her breasts pressed against his chest and pulled her curvaceous hips even tighter against him. A shot of desire surged through him as soon as he touched her. It seemed as if he could feel the warmth of her skin right through the clothes she wore.

What would her skin feel like without all that fabric in between? I'll bet it's smoother than the finest silk.

He pulled her closer still, wanting the space between their bodies to be eliminated entirely. The powerful sexual magnetism he was feeling toward her was too intense to be denied. As his lips and tongue continued to explore hers,

Just the Way You Are

emotions he'd thought were locked away permanently rushed to the surface.

After his first disastrous marriage, he'd thought the one-night stands to which he'd become accustomed were enough. His travel schedule was often quite hectic, and not entirely conducive to a long-term relationship. He often spent two weeks or more a month on the road when promoting a new book. He also justified his solitary lifestyle by telling himself that being a writer required him to have plenty of time alone. Yet he'd accomplished more in the past few hours with Jane sitting in the room reading quietly, than he had in several months.

There was no denying it. Deep down, he *wanted* a successful marriage. He wanted children. As a psychologist, he knew that being part of a couple in a healthy marriage made for happier and healthier people, both physically and mentally. And he didn't need his doctorate to know how important it was to grow up in a happy home. Aaron and his siblings were living proof. Also, studies had proven that children with a happy home life were more likely to excel in their studies, enjoy more positive social interactions, and even tended to be more physically fit.

Writing about relationships was something his publisher had been encouraging him to do for quite some time, but he'd been avoiding the request. Was he really qualified to give advice on how to have a solid marriage or long-lasting

Anita Louise

relationship? After all, his own experiences had been either short term or ended badly.

He'd found the Socrates' quote while half-heartedly doing preliminary research for at least a section on relationships in his upcoming book to appease his publisher. As soon as he read the philosopher's words, he knew it applied to him personally. Undoubtedly, many other people who'd been in disappointing relationships would relate to it much like he did.

Meeting Jane and having her in his home these past several days, had given the words new meaning. Now, holding her in his arms, tasting the sweetness of her lips, feeling the softness of her breasts pressed against his chest, he felt the walls he'd built around his heart begin to crumble. He forced himself to pull his mouth away from hers and looked into her eyes which were glazed with passion.

"Jane, Jane, Jane. What are you doing to me? From the first moment I saw you, the first time we touched, I felt something. Something I've always wanted to feel, but thought it was impossible. I want you, Jane. I'm not ready to promise you anything right now. All I can say is you're making me *feel … really feel* for the first time in years. If you're willing to be patient, I'm willing to do my best to open up and let you in." He could see her hesitation. How could he ask her to give fully of herself, when he would not … could not do the same?

Just the Way You Are

She trembled slightly, took in a deep, sustaining breath and looked him squarely in the eye. "I want you too, Aaron, so very much. And I want *all of you* ... body, mind, heart and soul. I'm willing to start with this incredible connection that's happening between us. And I won't ever ask for more than you can give. I only want what you're ready and willing to share with me." With that, she cupped his face in her hands and kissed him, slowly and thoroughly. Then she clasped his hand and brought it to her breast. "Touch me, Aaron," she whispered.

The desire that hit him practically buckled his knees. He could feel her nipples, firm and erect beneath her clothes. He ached to feel her bare flesh, to flick his tongue over the stiff peaks of her breasts. His erection was rock hard, and he pressed his leg between her thighs to feel the heat of her arousal. He heard her gasp and felt her wrap her leg around his waist. He tilted his pelvis back and forth, rubbing himself against her willingness. The threads of what little control he had left snapped. As he lifted her into his arms, she nuzzled intimately into him and began kissing, licking and biting his neck. He groaned with pleasure as he walked quickly from his study across the living room to the master bedroom.

He needed to get her to his bed, needed to remove the articles of clothing from both of their bodies. He wanted ... needed skin to skin. Pushing the door to the master suite open the

Anita Louise

rest of the way with his shoulder, he strode across the carpeted floor. When he reached the king size bed, he sat on the edge for a moment with her on his lap. Then he took her with him as he lay back on top of the soft duvet cover and continued to roll until she was beneath him.

Sitting on his knees, he raised up slightly. She looked at him, smiled and reached toward his upper body and began unbuttoning his shirt. With every button, she exposed more of his chest and ran her fingers lightly over his skin. Once his shirt was fully open, she reached for his belt.

"Not yet," he said. "Now it's my turn." With that he took the hem of her sweater in his hands.

Aaron Adler was an accomplished and passionate lover. Eliciting a sensual response from women turned him on. The more he could see that his partner was enjoying herself, the more his own pleasure was increased. But somehow, being with Jane was different than any of his other sexual conquests. The connection between them seemed so much stronger and deeper than anything else he'd ever experienced.

She raised her arms as he pulled her sweater over her head, revealing a lacy and low-cut bra that barely contained her voluptuous breasts. He ran his fingers lightly over her collarbones to the thin straps over her shoulders. Her skin was so soft and her breasts were so perfect ... so full, so round. He could hardly wait to get his hands on them, to touch them, taste

Just the Way You Are

them. Their eyes locked as he pushed the straps of her bra from her shoulders. Her breasts were released from the thin lace, revealing dark and swollen nipples. He leaned forward and ran his tongue over her skin. A soft moan escaped from her lips. Cupping her supple flesh with his hands, his mouth found the hard peaks. He sucked on the stiff points, moving from one to the other, softly pinching and pulling with fingers and mouth.

"Aaron ... please."

He covered her mouth with his own, their kisses growing more intense ... hotter. She pushed his shirt from his shoulders and arched her back to close the gap between their upper bodies. She pressed and rubbed her breasts against his bare chest, and the sensations had him drowning in desire. When he pushed one of his legs between her thighs, she spread them to give him access. He quickly removed her slacks. She unclasped the thin lace below her beautiful breasts, and they moved sensuously with her every breath. When he stood to remove his own trousers, he stared at her body clothed only in small lace panties. The lust that hit him nearly knocked him over.

"Jane. What are you doing to me?" Lying down on the bed next to her, he reached out and touched her cheek. Then he trailed a finger slowly down her neck to the cleavage between her breasts. Once more, he leaned over and

Anita Louise

covered her breast with his mouth, hot yet gentle … sucking and licking while his hand moved down between her legs. "You're so beautiful."

"As much as I love hearing you say that, Aaron, I know it's not true. But, I don't mind being 'Plain Jane' when you look at me that way," she said shyly.

"Plain Jane?" he said incredulously. "You're the farthest from 'plain' there could ever be. I've never seen anyone as exquisite as you. You're like a rare and wonderful work of art." He could see by the look on her face she was not entirely convinced, but was certainly pleased by his declaration. It might take some time, but he'd make sure the day would come when she would know, without a doubt, that she was anything but plain.

"Show me, Aaron. Help me to see what you see," she pleaded.

When he pressed his lips to her as he lay down on the bed next to her, his kisses had turned from desperate to gentle sweetness. He kissed her forehead, her cheeks, the corners of her eyes. Then he covered her mouth with his own, savoring her lips. His tongue invaded her mouth … tasting her and allowing her to taste him too. He explored her mouth thoroughly, entwining his tongue with hers, then running it over her teeth, her lips … nibbling and sucking. Next he moved to her breasts once more. He kissed and licked the soft flesh of her beautifully round

Just the Way You Are

globes while caressing them. Taking his time, he teased and suckled each nipple. As he brought each of the peaks to firmness, he licked and nibbled until she was short of breath ... panting for more.

His erection was rock hard, and her passion showed she was clearly ready for him. It would be easy to simply take what he so desperately wanted, but he wanted to please her even more. He wanted to show her that she was far from "plain" ... she was extraordinary. As he continued to suckle, lick and play with her breasts, his hand moved down her stomach to the vee between her legs. With her panties still in place, he moved his fingers between her thighs. Immediately he felt the wetness seeping through the thin cloth. She trembled with need. Tossing her head back and forth, she moaned and whimpered for release. He then moved his hand to the top of her panties, and she raised her hips to allow him to more easily remove them.

"Yes!" she cried.

"What do you want? Tell me what you want, my beautiful Jane."

"You ... Aaron! I want you ... inside me .... Please," she begged.

"Not yet. I want you to know how perfectly exquisite you are. I want to taste your magnificent sweetness."

She stiffened slightly. "Are you sure? I'm so wet. It's ... I've... No one ..."

Anita Louise

He felt like he'd just won the lottery or been given the opportunity of a lifetime. He moved quickly. As he put his head between her thighs, he looked up at her. "Look at me, Jane," he said. "Watch as I enjoy your sweet nectar." As his tongue tasted her essence for the first time, he murmured his delight. He quickly found her firm bud and as he ran his tongue over its crest, she exploded ... crying out.

"Oh, my God!"

He inserted two of his fingers into her and felt her inner muscles squeeze spasmodically. "Ah, yes, Jane. I love watching you come for me. I love feeling your muscles grip my fingers and now I want to feel those muscles grip me." He came up to his knees on the bed so she could see his throbbing erection.

"Aaron, please ... now ... please!" she cried.

Reaching over to his bedside stand, he pulled out a condom and put it on as quickly as he possibly could. Then he positioned himself once more between her thighs and looked at the wet and willing opening he was about to enter. He spread her legs wide and lubricated the tip of his hard shaft by rubbing it up and down along her slippery outer surface. He watched the ecstasy on her face and moaned his own pleasure as he plunged swiftly and deeply into her core.

Just the Way You Are

She gasped … shouted, "Yes. That's it! Oh Aaron, it feels so good to have you inside me."

Their eyes were locked and she reached for him. He lifted her into his arms and continued to move in and out of her wetness. His lips found hers and they kissed hungrily. Now it was his turn to experience the ultimate pleasure. He felt himself explode, threw his head back and came with an animal like roar. At the same moment, he heard his name on her lips and felt rewarded as her inner muscles tightened around him once more.

Chapter Twelve

Jane awoke the next morning and stretched luxuriously. She considered herself a sensual woman, but last night was like nothing she'd ever experienced before. For once she allowed herself to completely let go, to feel not only sexual, but to feel wanted ... shamelessly sensual ... beautiful.

She could hardly believe that she was lying in bed next to Aaron Adler. If not for the fact the doctor told her to "get plenty of rest," they would probably have been awake all night, making mad, passionate ... *love*. Yes, for her it was love, but what was it to Aaron?

The past few days together in his fabulous home were better than anything she could remember. Just then, an unwanted, but realistic thought popped into Jane's mind. *As much as I love being here with Aaron, for all I know, he*

Just the Way You Are

could tire of me quickly. Sooner or later, I'll have to quit 'playing house' and get back to the real world.

She turned to her lover who was sleeping peacefully by her side. Shivering deliciously, she remembered how wonderful it felt when he brought her to one magnificent climax after another. A small smile curled the corners of her mouth as she looked at him. Jane wasn't sure if their lovemaking had completely relaxed him or completely exhausted him.

Might as well enjoy this while I can, she thought as she snuggled up to him.

She'd met Aaron less than a week ago. Beyond simply meeting him, fate had also given her time to get to know him. He'd been the object of her dreams and flights of fantasy for years. Now she was a guest in his home and was even sharing his bed. Aaron Adler was her friend *and* her lover. Not even in her wildest dreams did she think she'd find a man with all the qualities she was looking for in a life mate. Yet the more she got to know Aaron in real life, the more she saw her dreams becoming reality.

She'd not only given him her body, but had fallen head over heels in love with him. However, this was not a fairy tale or the plot from a thoroughly romantic Julia Roberts' movie. This was real life and while it was clear that Aaron was happy to have her in his bed, she'd yet to see proof he was ready to trust her with his heart.

Anita Louise

Aaron lifted his arm and brought it around her naked shoulders. As he drew her closer, he mumbled something unintelligible in his state of semi-sleep. Nestled comfortably in his arms, she allowed her mind to drift. Her dreams of the future included waking up every morning in this bed ... with this man. She could hear the sounds of children ... their children stirring in the other rooms. Their days would be spent working together, blending their careers to complement a lifestyle that included raising a happy, healthy family. She sighed with the pure joy those visions brought.

He stirred, and Jane felt his fingers gently smooth her hair away from her face.

"Good morning, beautiful," he said just above a whisper.

Opening her eyes, she smiled and gazed at the man she loved. "Good morning, you handsome hunk," she replied with a teasing grin.

They leaned toward each other almost simultaneously for a sweet morning kiss. The next several minutes were spent lying comfortably on the soft sheets, limbs entwined ... no words needed, each lost in their own thoughts.

Several minutes later Aaron was snoring quietly. Evidently he'd drifted back to sleep. Since she knew this was, most likely, only a temporary arrangement, it only made sense to make the most of it while she could. When he stirred next to her Jane nuzzled closer into the warm,

Just the Way You Are

muscular arms that held her throughout the night. She was a little surprised when she felt his erection, hot and hard against her, and was even more surprised by her own body's reaction. There was no denying the tingle between her thighs as her own juices began to flow once more.

She nuzzled into his neck and placed a soft kiss just below his chin. The morning stubble of his beard felt so different than his smooth shaven skin of the evening before. Her hand found its way to the other side of his face, and she felt a thrill of excitement as her fingers stroked and smoothed the rugged planes of his handsome countenance.

With Aaron still apparently asleep, she decided to explore further. She moved her hand down his body to touch the firmness of his chest. This was obviously a man who took the time to work out. His chest was sculpted, even at rest.

Without consciously thinking about what she was doing, her head followed her hand. She proceeded to place soft kisses on his firm pectoral muscles. Wanting to feel even closer, she turned her head and laid her cheek against his chest. Jane took pleasure in simply listening to the steady beat of the heart she wanted to steal.

Her hands moved even lower. She felt the thin line of hair that led her down, over his abs and to his groin. She felt the strength of his abdominal muscles and traced the lines of his

Anita Louise

pelvic bones. Lightly skimming her fingers down his legs and up his inner thighs, she could hear his breathing begin to accelerate.

As she shifted her attention to the center of his body, she lightly caressed the sensitive sacs between his legs with one hand before wrapping her other hand firmly around his erection. His skin was like silk … satin over steel. Just as it had seemed to be impossible for him to resist wanting to taste her the night before, her mouth watered with the desire to explore with her tongue what her hands had just encountered. Her heart was beating a rapid staccato in her chest, and she trembled with anticipation.

Slowly and deliberately her mouth followed the path her hands had recently taken. Kissing and tasting his skin with her tongue, she moved further down his body. Timidly at first, she touched the tip of her tongue to the end of his shaft. He groaned and shifted his body to more easily accommodate her. The boldness she felt increased. She licked around the end, and then sucked lightly on the tip. Without even being aware of it, she moaned softly in delight. She found the sensation of licking and tasting the firm length of him to be thoroughly intoxicating.

It was obvious to her that Aaron was wide awake by this time. He appeared to be doing his best to leave his hips motionless so as not to disturb her activity. However, he must have wanted to watch her as she licked and sucked his

Just the Way You Are

maleness, because seconds later he threw the blankets on the floor that had been partially covering their naked bodies and stared at her in amazement.

"Oh, God, Jane," he sighed.

She loved the look on his face and the almost strangled sound of his voice. Watching him as he watched her gave her a sense of power she had never felt before. With her hand wrapped firmly around his erection, she moved her fist up and down while her tongue ran circles around the head of his shaft. Then she took him into the depths of her warm, wet mouth, licking and sucking as her hand continued to stroke his throbbing member.

He groaned again ... making almost unintelligible sounds of indescribable ecstasy.

She could feel the dampness between her legs, and her own need became almost more than she could bear.

"Oh, *Jane*, that feels sooo good, but you've got to quit doing that," he said as he pulled himself from her mouth.

As much as she was enjoying herself, she knew even a man like Aaron could only control himself for so long. She'd just given him what she hoped was one of the best sexual experiences he'd ever had, and she really didn't want him to come just yet. When he reached into the bedside table for a condom, she took it from him.

Anita Louise

"Let me," she said as her deep blue eyes locked with his.

Quickly tearing open the foil package, she rolled it onto him and immediately straddled his hips with her naked thighs ... impaling her slick heat on his rigid shaft.

"Ahhhh," they moaned in unison.

She felt like a sensual goddess, as if she'd reached a higher plane of existence. Her eyes locked with his as she lifted and lowered herself on his hardness over and over ... up and down ... up and down. The way he moved his hips to match her, made her feel as if she were riding a wild stallion. She closed her eyes and held her own breasts, pulling on her hardened nipples. Lost to everything except the erotic excitement of the moment, her level of arousal grew higher and higher with every rise and fall of her hips.

His hands joined hers on her breasts as she continued to ride him. She could feel his erection grow and pulse as her inner muscles tightened on him. When he dropped his hand to the space where their bodies met in the most intimate of ways, he found the hard little bud between her thighs. Her eyes flew open, she threw her head back, arched and voiced her release as she cried, *"Oh Aaron! Yes!"*

At the same moment, she felt his climax explode inside of her. It was incredible ... the most amazing experience of her life ... almost beyond belief. Seconds later she collapsed against his chest, snuggling her head into the crook of his neck and planting small, sweet kisses.

It was impossible to hold back her thoughts. So, in the softest voice she could manage she whispered, "I love you, Aaron Adler."

He didn't say a word ... only pulled her snuggly to him and held her close.

Chapter Thirteen

"Well, looks like it's brunch instead of breakfast today," Aaron said. There was a mischievous grin on his face. With only a slight blush and a smile, Jane replied, "That's good. Brunch has always been a favorite of mine."

Growing up in an extra-large family, Aaron learned if he wanted to be one of the first to get a few nibbles before dinner, it was a good idea to help prepare the food. He always enjoyed being in the kitchen with his mother and one or two of his sisters, sharing talk of the events of the day while putting together a meal for the family. As a result, he found cooking to be a relaxing and pleasurable hobby.

The aroma of the delicious breakfast burritos he was preparing wafted through the air. The southwest rollups loaded with sausage, eggs and cheese were quick and easy to make, and today that was an important consideration. They'd stayed in bed much later than usual. Plus, they'd both expended a lot of energy and burned a ton of calories over the past evening and morning.

Thoughts of how enjoyable his lovemaking with Jane had been replayed in his mind. *Lovemaking? What an interesting choice of words,* he mused.

Aaron knew his words were a reflection of his thoughts. Why did he choose the word *lovemaking* instead of *sex* to describe his time with Jane? He knew she was looking for much more than sex. In fact, he was quite sure Jane must've thought there was at least a *chance* something more could come as a result of her giving herself to him. Otherwise, it was very likely the sensually satisfying hours he'd just experienced would've never happened.

She'd shown him there was a fun and playful side to her. He could also see she was clearly a woman who knew what she wanted. And she was willing to do whatever was necessary to accomplish her goals as well.

Aaron was not the kind of man to toy with a woman. He knew it was because of him Jane was still here in his home. She'd been willing to return to her pretty little condo yesterday after her doctor's appointment. In fact, she hadn't even gotten her physician's clearance when she began talking about getting her cat Henry back home. Aaron was the one who convinced her to stay a little longer. Using the excuse of not wanting to drive her back and forth to his brother Michael's party tonight had been his ploy to keep her with him.

Yes, he wanted Jane Barloc. His desire for her far surpassed anything he'd ever felt for another woman. Sure, he'd been with dozens of beautiful women since becoming a best-selling author. Most of the time, he'd meet someone while on a speaking or book signing tour. It wasn't uncommon for a buxom blonde, redhead or studious brunette with glasses to catch his eye. After conversing for a while, he'd ask her to join him for dinner or a local event to which he was invited. The woman almost always happily accompanied him. While not *all* of them ended up in his bed, many did.

It was common for him to give the woman assurances of returning or at least calling. However, experience proved he would rarely if ever, see or speak to her again after that one night. Occasionally, he'd spend an extra night or two with one of his conquests. But, most often it was only a couple of days before he was ready to move on. Although he would sometimes say the words *they* wanted to hear, *he* knew he had no intention of keeping those promises.

Somehow it was different with Jane. *She* was different. There was something special about her ... something unique. At times he had this uncanny feeling he'd met her before. Surely, if she was one of those nameless faces he'd encountered over the years he would remember. Yes, she mentioned she was at one of his events, but had he seen her in the front row, he'd have noticed her. Instinctively he knew Jane would've been impossible to forget. Knowing her as he did now, he knew if he'd tried to lure Jane Barloc back to his hotel room, he'd have ended up alone.

Aaron Adler had been with plenty of women ... beautiful women ... sexual women, yet being with Jane was poles apart from anything he'd ever experienced before. Being with her was even more thrilling than what he'd felt so many years ago when making love for the very first time. Was it possible that, in truth, his experience in bed with Jane *was* the first time he had ever really made *love?* After only one blissful evening that spilled over into an equally rapturous morning, he wasn't sure if he could *ever* let her go.

Where did those thoughts come from? He shook his head and smiled quizzically to himself as he finished up the burritos and put them on plates for himself and Jane.

I wonder what Jane's thought processes entailed before she decided that giving herself fully to me was a good idea? Lovemaking ... yes,

Anita Louise

I'm sure in Jane's mind, we were definitely making love.

He brought the plates over to the small table in the nook where Jane was sitting. She jumped slightly when he placed the delectable breakfast treat in front of her. It appeared she'd been lost in thought ... looking out at the mountains and sipping her coffee while Aaron was cooking breakfast.

"A penny for your thoughts, Ms. Barloc."

"Ah, Aaron, this smells and *looks* delicious. I'm *famished,*" she said.

"It's no wonder you're so hungry ... with all the activity you've been involved in since yesterday afternoon," he said with a lascivious grin. Once again, she blushed demurely. He reached across the table and took her hand in his, squeezing it gently. "You were wonderful, Jane. And I hope you know how utterly beautiful you are to me."

Looking deeply into his eyes, she returned the slight pressure of his tender touch and covered his hand with hers. "Thank you, Aaron. That means so much to me."

"I know it does, Jane, but *why?* How is it possible for you to look into a mirror and not see what I see? Please, help me to understand."

She pulled her hand away. It looked as if she might get up and leave the table. Obviously, she was experiencing some kind of an internal struggle. Finally, she said, "I wasn't exactly a

Just the Way You Are

'pretty little girl.' I was *extremely* skinny, had crooked teeth, and I was painfully shy. My parents thought it was wonderful that I had a high IQ, but it didn't make it any easier for me."

"Go on," he encouraged.

"I did my best to stay in the background as much as possible, because I just couldn't seem to blend in. I didn't have many friends. Oh, every once in a while someone would *pretend* to like me so I'd help them with a project or something, but as soon as it was finished, they'd conveniently disappear." She looked up, and he could almost feel her pain. "Kids can be cruel sometimes. I think it was about third grade that someone decided that 'Plain Jane' was a good nickname for me." Shrugging she went on, "When you hear it over and over, year after year, I guess you just get so you believe it."

He took her hand once more. "That was a long time ago, Jane. You're so far from plain it isn't even funny. Yes, you're smart, but you're also beautiful ... and kind ... and considerate. Oh, and did I mention *sexy as hell?"*

She blushed, then looked up and with a mischievous grin said, "You ain't seen nothing yet."

"I can hardly wait," he replied with his own lascivious grin in place.

As they sat there grinning foolishly at each other, he felt another significant part of the wall around his heart come tumbling down.

Anita Louise

After breakfast, they worked together to clear the dishes, clean the counters and put the kitchen back in order. It was one of those lazy weekend days. He'd thrown on a comfortable CU Buffs' sweatshirt and pants earlier that morning. Jane also looked comfy with her long tunic over warm leggings and thick socks.

With nothing special on the agenda, he asked, "Is there anything in particular you'd like to do today, Jane?"

"You said you were on a bit of a deadline with your current book. Would you like to spend a few hours on it again? I'd really enjoy reading more of what you've written, and if you don't mind, there are a couple of areas where I could use some clarification."

"Are you sure?" he asked. He was somewhat surprised she'd remembered his comment about his book deadline. It also pleased him to learn she was interested enough to not only want to read more, but to ask questions about parts on which she wasn't totally clear.

With a twinkle in her eye, she replied, "To be quite frank, there's only one other option I can think of that would be more enjoyable, but it wouldn't help you meet your deadline."

"You're tempting me mightily, Ms. Barloc," he replied, giving her a knowing grin. "There's nothing that says we can't do both. Not at the same time, of course. Why don't we first follow your suggestion of working on my book. When we tire of that, I'm sure we can find something even more exciting to do with our time."

"Sounds good to me, Mr. Adler. Shall I lead the way?"

He nodded and then watched the sway of her hips appreciatively as she walked out of the kitchen and into his study. Was it his imagination or was she leading him in more ways than simply to his office?

Once they were in his home office, she again settled comfortably into the reading chair next to the window. It seemed like only seconds before Henry appeared out of nowhere and found his way to her lap, sending his loud "purrrr" of contentment into the air.

Aaron positioned himself behind the computer at his desk and smiled to himself as he looked toward the windows. As far as he was concerned, even the view of the mountains was not as beautiful as the woman who sat in front of them.

Within moments, they were both involved in their work. As much as he'd been dreading the idea of devoting a section of his newest book to relationships, Aaron was finding his writing to be progressing much more easily than he'd anticipated. There was no doubt Jane had a *lot* to do with it.

Spending time with her over these past few days was helping him to experience something that previously had only been a

Anita Louise

concept in his mind. He was learning that a relationship tended to blossom more quickly and develop more easily when both parties share the same or similar values.

As Aaron explained in the section he was writing on relationships, there are many reasons why two people are initially attracted to one another. Often a couple comes together because of shared interests. They might both be fans of the same sports team. At the stadium or sports bar, they catch each other's eye while shouting "Go Team Go," and their relationship blossoms from there. Or perhaps they meet in a museum while carefully considering the merits of one painter or sculptor over another. Their love of the arts and the art world then brings them together. Still others are drawn together because of political persuasions or because they both support a charity or cause for which they care deeply.

He went on to explain that while shared interests may be the reason a couple becomes attracted to one another in the beginning, it takes more than just having a few things in common for a relationship to last. To stay together over an extended period of time, the couple needs shared *values.* Mutual respect, taking personal responsibility and keeping lines of communication open are principles adhered to by both partners in a successful relationship. Each person makes it a habit to truly listen, because they sincerely

Just the Way You Are

want to understand the other person's point of view. Successful couples know it's more important to be kind than it is to be right. As he stated in his book, a lot of connections are sustained by taking a moment to pause and ask, "What's more important? Proving I'm right, or being kind to the person I care about most and keeping our relationship on solid ground?"

The last, and most important tenet of relationships that endure the test of time ... *love.* Love, he wrote, is the most powerful word in the English language and the glue that holds the most solid marriages together.

He was using all of these points as he wrote about not only finding a life partner, but *keeping* a mate. As his relationship with Jane continued to develop, it was giving him even more insight ... on a very personal level, and he wanted to share it with his readers.

As soon as he and Jane took the step to become lovers, they also opened the door to vulnerability. Even though Aaron was enjoying a physically intimate relationship with Jane, he was still hesitant to allow himself to totally let down his defenses. The protective walls around his damaged heart had not yet been completely obliterated.

It'd been years since his marriage to Sharon, yet the pain still lingered. The very intimacy that in the beginning brought him such happiness, had ultimately also caused him more hurt than he'd ever experienced previously. He understood the truth ... with intimacy comes power. When you give a lover the power to make you feel valued and special, there is a dark side. At the same time, you also give your lover the power to hurt you deeply ... unlike anyone else.

Will I ever be able to trust fully again? I <u>*want*</u> *what I've seen in my parents' marriage ... a faithful, undying love ... a happy family. And I know that what I want requires my full engagement.*

Aaron had erected almost impenetrable walls around his heart. His relationship with Jane was slowly breaking those barriers down. Before meeting Jane Barloc, he thought it might be impossible for him to see his dreams of love ever come to fruition. Now, for the first time in many years, he had *hope.*

What is it about you, Jane? What are you doing to me?

No other woman ... not even his ex-wife, ever made him feel the way he felt when he was with Jane. Yes, there was the thrill and excitement of incredibly hot sex, but it was more than that. He felt like he could be totally *himself* with her. There was no need for pretense. When he was with Jane, he was the best *Aaron* he'd ever been.

I love you ... <u>just</u> <u>the</u> <u>way</u> <u>you</u> <u>are</u>. Those beautiful words drifted through his mind. To love and *be loved* without conditions ... to accept and be accepted ... that was the kind of love he sought.

He didn't want to change Jane. He didn't want her to be anything or anyone other than the wonderful woman he was getting to know and beginning to open his heart to. He really liked the fact that Jane obviously enjoyed her work as a counselor. Consequently, she was exceptionally *good* at her job. Her career also meant she'd studied and shared many of the same philosophies he embraced and embodied as a successful psychologist and now as a writer.

So many of the women he had dated over the years seemed to have no concept at all of the wonderfully potent and amazing power of the human mind. That was certainly not true of Jane Barloc! She understood more than most that a person's thinking ultimately determines what transpires in their lives.

Thinking back to the evening he first met Jane brought his youngest brother to mind. If there was one person in his extra-large family that might be considered somewhat of a "black sheep," it was Connor Adler. For as long as Aaron could remember, Connor was the one sibling to consistently make questionable choices ... the one that just didn't seem to live up to the expectations the Adler family had come to expect.

Now that Aaron knew Connor had been working with Jane for several months, he felt

Anita Louise

certain Jane had a lot to do with many of the positive changes he'd noticed in his brother recently. His youngest sibling always had a tendency to be somewhat irresponsible, and then when he'd get into trouble, it was never his fault. He was always quick to blame other people for his problems. Connor could never seem to hold a job, and his employment history was sketchy at best over the years. Of course, there was always an excuse ... the boss was too demanding, the job was a lot harder than he expected, they didn't give him enough hours or they gave him too many hours. Connor *never* claimed responsibility. But he'd started working at a landscaping company over three months ago now, and not only was he still there, he'd recently been given the position of crew supervisor.

It was Connor's use of "recreational" drugs that had everyone in the family more worried than anything else. He'd started *experimenting* when he was barely into high school. When the State of Colorado made it legal to possess and use marijuana, several of the Adler children shuddered at what might happen with the youngest of the Adler children as a result. Just as they'd expected, it hadn't taken long before Connor was in trouble for having *well over* the one ounce limit.

Thinking back to his conversation a few days earlier with his youngest brother, that court case must have been the reason Jane Barloc had

Just the Way You Are

been brought into the picture. Aaron wasn't a particularly religious person, but he couldn't help thinking that God certainly worked in mysterious ways. Who'd have thought that Connor's court case would bring to Aaron Adler the woman of his dreams?

"You ready for a break?" Jane's question broke Aaron from his reverie.

Rolling his shoulders and stretching his arms, he looked at the clock and was surprised to see it was almost two hours since they'd stepped into his office.

Pushing back his chair and walking across the room, he extended his hands to the woman who'd been consuming most of his thoughts. She put down his manuscript, and placed her fingers lightly into his palms. As he gently pulled her up from the chair, their eyes met. It seemed only natural to take her into his arms. He then covered her mouth with his own for one of the sweetest, most tender kisses he'd ever experienced.

It didn't take long before the tenor of their kisses changed from sweet to spicy ... from warm to hot. Instead of gently pressing his lips to hers, he found himself running his tongue over her lips and teeth, nipping softly ... encouraging her to open for him. As soon as her lips parted, his tongue invaded her sinfully seductive mouth. Her response was immediate, and their tongues were soon doing a delightful dance, weaving around

Anita Louise

one another and alternately advancing and retreating.

As their kiss continued, his desire grew in intensity. The fingers of one of her hands were entwined in his hair while her other hand moved sensually up and down his back. She was rubbing and pressing her breasts against his chest. He pulled her hips tightly to his so she could feel his throbbing erection.

"I've got an idea," he managed to say between kisses, "why don't you let me live out a fantasy I've had ever since I built this house?" Kissing her along the side of her neck he continued. "Have you taken a close look at the shower you've been enjoying *all by yourself* since you've been here, Ms. Barloc? If you have, then you know there's plenty of room for two people. In fact, it was *designed* with two in mind. I'm sure you've been enjoying the rain showerheads, but did you notice the multiple body jets and *hand* showers?"

"Hand showers? Hmmm. That sounds very interesting, Mr. Adler."

Moving his hands up to her breasts and kneading them while gently nibbling on her earlobe, he went on. "Did you know that showers like mine ... with no doors are called 'wet rooms?' And we know there's more than one way you get *wet,* isn't there, Ms. Barloc?" His voice was husky and his words meant to be tantalizing. "As soon as I saw your beautiful form lying there in the tub,

Just the Way You Are

I've had a fantasy. I want to experience what it would be like to stand next to you with streams of hot water flowing across your skin as I soap up every inch of that gorgeous body. And I have wonderful ideas as to what we could do with those *hand* showers." He paused to let his words sink in. Nuzzling her neck, he then planted kisses down to her collarbone. He continued to fondle her breasts while he allowed the vision of the two of them, wet and naked to develop in her imagination.

"That sounds *really* good, as long as turnabout is fair play, and I get to soap you up too." She fairly panted as her hand slipped between them, and she moved it slowly up and down the firm bulge in the front of his sweat pants.

"What are we waiting for?" He grinned as he took her hand and tugged her impatiently toward the master bedroom and bath.

"*Beautiful.* Absolutely beautiful." He seemed to be delighted to find her totally naked when she stripped off her tunic and leggings.

She still wasn't completely used to him looking at her as if she actually *was* beautiful, but her self-image was gradually improving the longer she was with him. The way he looked at her made her feel as if she was *special*. Even though she knew he'd been with plenty of others, he was looking at her like she was the most extraordinary woman he'd ever seen.

And when he revealed his own nude body as he threw his sweats on the pile of clothes just outside the "wet room," she knew she'd never been with another man who was anything like Aaron Adler. After adjusting the temperature they stepped under the soft spray of the water hitting them from all angles.

She leaned back under the rivulets of water cascading down over her breasts, leaving droplets on her nipples and then sliding over her stomach. He seemed almost mesmerized as he watched the water flow across her body. After flowing over her breasts and down her abdomen, it disappeared between her legs where there was as much wetness coming from inside her as from the shower.

Through a lust filled haze she heard him say, "Soap." She watched as he took the scented bar and rubbed it between his hands. He stepped in front of her and began to move his soapy hands from the base of her neck to her shoulders. From there he went down her arms, caressing and stroking every muscle along the way. Retracing his path back up her arms, he massaged her shoulders before sliding his hands down her back. Taking the soap from his hands she lathered his back as he had hers. Their bodies were slippery with heat and wet and wanting.

Just the Way You Are

He continued to move his hands across her body, and she felt her nipples come to attention. Moments later he took both of her breasts in his hands and stroked his large thumbs slowly across her taut peaks. She stared in wonder as she watched his hands, big and bronzed, move slowly, almost reverently across her pale skin.

"*Aaron*," she moaned as he replaced one of his hands with his mouth, licking the water from the peak of her breast and then placing his lips fully around the dusky rose of her areola. She pushed her chest forward to move more fully into his mouth and pulled his wet head to her with both hands. He continued to lave her breast with his tongue. After giving his full attention to the first, he moved his mouth to her other breast and repeated his thorough onslaught.

As he stepped even closer to her, she felt the firmness of his erection against her thigh. Now, it was her turn to drive him crazy just as he'd done to her. Once more filling her hand with fragrant lather, she began to wash the most sensitive areas of his body. He groaned with pleasure as she carefully caressed the large sacs between his legs with one hand while sliding her soap filled palm up and down his stiff shaft.

She maneuvered him over to the bench along the back wall of the shower. Because of the multiple shower heads, they both continued to be covered from head to toe with warm water.

Anita Louise

Pushing down on his shoulders, she got him to sit on the bench and then kneeled in front of him. Continuing her ministrations until the soap was completely washed away, she then replaced her hands with her mouth, just as he had done earlier to her breasts.

"Oh, my God, *Jane.*" Hearing her name on his lips as he groaned his bliss emboldened her even more. With Aaron it pleased her to make him happy. Because she knew how much he enjoyed it, she found herself enjoying it too. Slowly and sensuously, she moved her tongue up and down his swollen member and then put as much of it in her mouth as possible ... sucking and licking. He reached between her legs, and she could feel the slick wetness of her juices mixed with the water from the shower. He stroked her moist heat as she continued to slide him in and out of her mouth. Her own release was getting closer, and she knew his was too.

"Jane? Are you sure?" he asked. She continued to stroke him up and down while holding him firmly in place between her lips.

"Yes!" she cried. As she tasted his release, her own climax was spectacular in a way she'd never experienced before.

Chapter Fourteen

Fresh from her gloriously sexy shower with the most gorgeous, sensual man she'd ever known, Jane was absolutely sure she could never get enough of Aaron Adler. The first time she'd seen him, she knew he was special. With each and every one of his books she'd read, she learned more about becoming a better person and living a happier life. Now, she was also getting to know *him* on a very personal level.

It only made sense to her that in order to write a book on personal development, the writer would've had to go through experiences to help him bring the concepts to life. She remembered reading in one of his books, "Life's most *challenging* events are often the ones that ultimately lead to the most growth and to a person's highest good."

Anita Louise

Of course, sex with Aaron was by far the best she'd ever known. Yet it was more than just two bodies learning how to please one another. She felt a closeness to Aaron she was sure would never happen again in her life.

She'd now spent a full week with him, and he'd taken all she was happy to give ... her body, heart, and soul. So far, it was clear Aaron's *body* was hers ... at least for now. If she wanted a lifetime of happiness with the man of her dreams, she needed to capture his heart as well. It seemed he was gradually opening up to her more and more, but she knew the barriers between them hadn't *yet* been completely eliminated.

Well, tonight's party at Michael's house will be a real opportunity for me. I'll have a chance to get to know Aaron's family a little better. And it might also be my chance to get some 'inside information' to help me understand why Aaron has closed his heart to long lasting intimacy.

In true male fashion, Aaron took all of ten minutes to get ready for the party. Then he considerately left her alone to finish doing her hair and make-up. She smiled as she remembered his comment of, "I think you look perfect just the way you are." When he said it there was a look of hunger in his eyes. At the time, she was standing with clean skin, wet hair and only a white fluffy towel wrapped around her. His comment, along with the magnetic pull of his

Just the Way You Are

gaze, almost had her leaping across the room to cover him with kisses once again. However, she knew if she did, they'd *definitely* be late for the Adler family gathering.

Leaning over, she dried her shoulder length golden hair. The color of freshly mown hay, it was thick, and she thought it was one of her best assets. As much as she tried, it would never hang straight ... there was invariably a slight wave. Therefore, most of the time she pulled it up into a pony tail, chignon or some other easy up-do. But tonight she wanted to wear it down. Even though he hadn't said so directly, she knew Aaron liked to thread his fingers through her hair when they made love. Tonight, as much as possible, she wanted to hold a place in his thoughts even when they were across the room from each other.

Never one to over-do it when it came to make-up, she carefully applied a light powder and blush along with a little eye shadow and mascara. She applied a red wine stain to her full lips. Jane wasn't one to fuss with her looks once she had done her face and hair. It was likely she wouldn't bother to look at herself in a mirror again for the rest of the evening.

Standing in her lacy undergarments, Jane looked once more at her clothing options for the gathering with Aaron's family and friends. Since she didn't want to be overdressed, she opted for the lavender silk blouse and skinny jeans. She

Anita Louise

went back to the mirror once more and applied another layer of mascara in an attempt to put more emphasis on her blue eyes. Not being especially tall, she decided her heeled boots would give her the extra height she felt she needed. As she walked out of the bedroom, she took one final look over her shoulder into the mirror. The jeans she wore hugged her hips perfectly and as her hair moved across her silk blouse, she thought to herself, *Not bad, Jane Barloc ... not bad at all.*

When she entered the living room, Aaron was struck once more by her beauty. Even though she seemed to exude an air of quiet confidence, her brow wrinkled as she asked, "Do I look all right?"

How in the world could she not know how stunning she is? Rather than voicing his thoughts, he simply smiled and said, "Jane, you look lovely ... absolutely perfect. In fact, if you're ready to go, I'm ready to show you off to all my family and friends."

He helped her with her coat, opened and then followed her through the door leading to the garage. First helping her into the passenger seat, he then settled himself behind the wheel of his Jeep. Aaron was surprised to hear the music and words, "I love you just the way you are," coming from the speakers as he backed out of the garage. As surreptitiously as possible, he looked across at Jane to see her smiling contentedly.

There was little conversation during the first part of their drive to his brother's house. He couldn't help but notice his passenger smelled good, sultry and intoxicating. His mind flashed back to the erotic picture of her in the shower with him. The look of pure ecstasy on her face when they'd both climaxed had his erection beginning to grow again. *Now is not the time to be thinking about sex, and besides that, there's so much more to Jane Barloc.* Aaron recognized he was beginning to fall for Jane, but that didn't mean he was ready to completely open his heart ... to allow himself to be vulnerable once more.

He glanced discretely at Jane again and wondered what she was thinking. Sometimes it seemed as if she could almost read his mind. How did she get to know him so well so quickly? Somehow, she'd found a way into his carefully guarded heart at the same time as she'd been sharing with him the most glorious and passionate lovemaking of his life. He shook his head slightly and did his best to direct his thoughts away from the feelings he was developing for Jane. He put his attention back to the familiar route he was on. He'd safely driven to the two magnificent homes owned by Michael and his parents many times over. It'd been his intention to tell her earlier that Michael's house sat next door to his parents' home on High View

Anita Louise

Drive. However, other much more pleasurable, and thus more important things had "come up," so to speak, and he'd forgotten. Now they were approaching the base of the mountain and would soon be traveling the road where she'd had her accident.

Aaron decided to break the news by sharing with Jane the story behind his parents and his oldest brother becoming next-door neighbors. "I did tell you that my brother Michael was the architect and builder of my house, didn't I?" he began.

Tilting her head in a thoughtful pose, she said, "You told me your sister-in-law helped you a little with the decorating, but I don't remember you saying Michael was the designer and builder. When Connor and I were on the way to the party where I met you, he told me Michael designed and built your parents' house. Having seen both your home and your parents', it's clear your brother is a very talented architect."

"Yes, he is. My folks' place was Mike's first big design/build job in Boulder. Of course, they had faith in him and, as you know, he did a fantastic job. Once he had their house as the showpiece of his portfolio, his business grew by leaps and bounds from there."

"How long ago was that?" Jane asked.

"Over ten years now, but my folks bought the land more than twenty years ago. In fact, they got such a good deal on the property, they

Just the Way You Are

bought twice as much acreage as they needed to build on ... more than enough to build another home near them without infringing on their privacy." Wondering if Jane was reading between the lines, he continued. "It's a pretty good drive up and down those winding roads to Mom and Dad's place."

"That's for sure. My poor little Volkswagen is testimony to that fact."

"When Dad turned sixty, two years ago, we had a little family meeting, and we all agreed it'd be best if the folks had family closer ... just in case."

"Yeesss, and ...?"

"Well, Mike built his house on the land next to Mom and Dad."

Aaron heard her intake of breath. She sat quietly for a moment, apparently thinking of how she wanted to respond. Finally she stated in a calm and rather matter-of-fact manner, "Oh, so this is going to be my first opportunity to travel on the road that made it possible for me to not only *meet* you and get to know you better, but to fall in love with you."

Now it was Aaron's turn to gasp for air. *Fall in LOVE?* What was he supposed to do with that information?

There! I said it. The cat's out of the bag, she thought.

Anita Louise

She'd dropped a bombshell, but Aaron remained silent. They'd just approached the beginning of the twisting and turning road she now knew led not only to the Adler parents' home, but to Michael's as well. Apparently keeping his focus on driving was his excuse for not responding. She hadn't really expected him to. Oh sure, it would've been great to hear Aaron say, "I've fallen in love with you too," but that was entirely too much to hope for ... at least for now.

As far as she was concerned, *not* falling in love with Aaron would've been virtually impossible. Of course, he *was* one of the most handsome men she'd ever had the pleasure to meet, but he was also amazing on the *inside* too. Not many men would've done what he did after her accident last weekend. He could've called the police, given his report and walked away. Instead he came to the hospital and stayed by her side for *days*. Then when he learned she had no family in the area, he'd opened his home to her and her pet. She smiled to herself at the thought.

And then of course, there was the very *hot*, very pleasurable sexual part of their relationship. Whenever her mind drifted back to their lovemaking, like it was now, she found herself heating up all over again. She could feel the tingle starting between her thighs once more. Just thinking about his mouth and his hands on her had her hormones raging. Right now, she wished the party was over and they were on their

Just the Way You Are

way back to his house ... to his bed. She had to change her train of thought, or they'd never make it to the party. Not knowing what else to say, she asked, "Who else besides your family will be there tonight, Aaron?"

He hadn't said a word since her confession of love. She could almost feel his sense of relief. She wasn't going to push him to make a comment, or even acknowledge her admission.

"Mostly family, as you might guess. Of course, Phillip's wife Rachel will be there with him. A few of Mom and Dad's friends might show up too. Some of the other brothers and sisters may have dates as well. But as far as I know, there's nothing serious going on with anyone, so I can't give you any names or backgrounds."

"Well, I'm definitely looking forward to getting to know everyone. Even though I got a chance to meet most of them when I brought Connor to the last party, I wasn't an invited guest. That's a big part of the reason I left so quickly." *That and the fact that even standing in the same room with you was having a very powerful effect on me.*

"You're going to love everyone, and they're going to love you too!"

Oh, how thrilled she would've been if he'd added just a few more words. "Just like *I* do." Jane was pretty sure Aaron had been married before, and it had ended badly. However, she certainly didn't know the details. The old adage of "once bitten, twice shy" seemed to apply.

Her best friend Sheila was married for ten years ... and it wasn't good. Sheila told Jane she knew she shouldn't have gone through with the marriage even before the wedding. Sheila chuckled as she told the story of being late for her own wedding. In addition, her fiancé's family dog, who weighed approximately fifty pounds, sat firmly on the train of her wedding dress as she attempted to walk down the aisle for their backyard ceremony.

"I should've known right then and there I was making a *huge* mistake, but I just didn't have the courage to leave him at the altar," Sheila confessed.

Last year Sheila was dating a guy who seemed *perfect* for her. He was good looking, super nice, and from what Jane could tell, totally in love with Sheila. She'd even told Jane she thought he could be her soul mate. All of Sheila's friends were shocked when she suddenly broke it off after about a year into the relationship.

It took a while for Jane to get her to talk about it, but when she finally did, Sheila said there was no concrete reason for ending the relationship. Nothing happened. The guy didn't do anything wrong at all. Sheila just got worried that things *might* go sour, and the *thought* of getting hurt again scared her too much. Her fear was the cause of the break up.

Just the Way You Are

Jane did her best to talk to her friend about it. Even though Sheila's ex was an idiot, that didn't mean all guys were. But, Sheila had to figure it out for herself, and until she was ready there was nothing Jane or anyone else could say or do to change her mind.

Of course, Jane understood the same thing applied to Aaron. She knew it was going to require a lot of loving patience on her part if she wanted to have a lasting relationship with him. She was ready to do whatever was necessary to make her dreams come true.

Jane tensed only slightly when they approached the curve where she'd wrecked her car. Aaron was so in tune with her, he immediately reassured her. "My folks, Michael, and all the rest of the family have been up and down this road a countless number of times. Heck, I've driven it so many times I could practically do it with my eyes closed." His hands were firmly at nine and three, the new steering wheel hand placement recommended because of air bags. He didn't take his eyes off the road for even a second when her breath hitched, and she turned her head to make sure he was only joking. However, he did chuckle slightly and comment, "Of course, I'd never even *think* of doing something as foolish as that."

"Very funny, Aaron Adler, but you notice I'm *not* laughing," she said in as stern a tone as she could manage. "Okay, so you had me going for a second ... brat!"

"Uh-oh, I must be in trouble. The only time my mother ever used my first and last name was when she was less than pleased with me. I'm sorry if I scared you, Jane, but anyone who's going to be part of this family has to be comfortable with driving this road on a regular basis."

Does he realize what he just implied? she wondered. Instead of putting him on the spot by voicing her question, she put a smile on her face and said, "Well, then I guess I'm just going to have to get used to driving this well maintained and perfectly beautiful stretch of pavement."

It really was quite a lovely drive. She knew Colorado had several scenic roads for tourists to explore. Although this wasn't designated as one of them, it certainly was an example of mountainous beauty. Only a few homes were nestled among the thousands of aspen, pine, spruce and other trees covering the slopes. The footprints of deer, rabbits and other animals native to the area dotted the snow blanketing the hillsides. Although she hadn't taken time to look when she was previously at Aaron's parents' home, she was sure the view from theirs and Michael Adler's home would be spectacular.

It was only a few minutes later when they pulled into Michael's driveway. Jane stared at the structure. *This home is an architectural masterpiece,* she thought. She turned to Aaron. "I see some similarities to your home. I'm not sure which one is more beautiful."

"I know what you mean. Michael graduated from the Frank Lloyd Wright School of Architecture about ten years ago. He loved it there and learned so much."

"I've heard a lot of great things about Frank Lloyd Wright," she replied.

"I remember Michael saying that architecture should harmonize with its surroundings. He even quoted Wright, who said 'House and hill should live together each happier for the other.'"

Jane nodded and smiled as she admired Michael's home. If Aaron hadn't told her his parents lived next door to Michael, Jane would've never known there was another house close by. Since there was still some daylight, she wanted to take the opportunity and see the panoramic views. Impulsively, she grabbed Aaron's hand. "Would you mind giving me a mini tour outside before we go in? It'll be dark by the time we leave, and I'd really like to take a quick peak." Aaron squeezed her hand and gave her one of his heart melting smiles. She felt the now familiar zing of attraction move through her body. Standing with their hands clasped, looking over the spectacular view made it impossible for her to

Anita Louise

resist. She turned her body to face his, reached up and gently pulled his mouth to hers. "Please."

His response was immediate. Within seconds, gentleness was replaced with hot, urgent need. Dropping her hand his arms went possessively around her. He pulled her hips to his and began moving his pelvis rhythmically against hers. Flames of desire shot through her with amazing speed. She was almost ready to beg him to take her home or to simply take her right there. Fortunately, the sound of tires crunching on the loose gravel in the driveway, indicating the arrival of another guest, brought them back to their senses.

He turned his back to the arriving vehicle to hide the erection stretching the fabric of his trousers. With his arm around her waist, he took a calming breath and hugged her to his side. "See what you do to me, woman," he said, nodding toward the front of his pants.

"Wait and see what I do to you later when I get you alone," she whispered seductively.

He gave her another smile and a tiny hug as he said, "Stop that now, or we'll never make it to this party."

While they waited for his clothing to return to its normal appearance, they stood together with arms around each other admiring the snow-capped peaks of the Continental Divide as well as the views of both the Boulder and the Denver skylines below.

Chapter Fifteen

The party seemed to be in full swing by the time Aaron and Jane made their way inside. This wasn't the first time Jane had been to an Adler family gathering, but this *was* the first time she'd actually attended as an invited guest. And this time she was here with Aaron ... as his date.

Connor and Michael both knew Jane was in an accident after the last party. They were also aware that Aaron had been kind enough to open his home to her while she recuperated. When Michael last saw Jane, Aaron had been carrying her in his arms. And when Connor arrived at Aaron's house, she and Aaron were fresh from their first kiss. However, Jane was almost certain no one knew she and Aaron were now lovers. *Our secret should be safe if I can keep myself from appearing to be a love struck teenager every time I look at Aaron,* she mused.

After they entered the house, Aaron helped her with her coat before going to get drinks for them. Jane was feeling surprisingly comfortable in her surroundings, and she looked around the room. The atmosphere of Michael's house was one of openness and warmth. She took in the wall of glass across the rear of the home. The view of the now setting Colorado sun was spectacular. One by one, the city lights of Boulder in the valley below began to blink on. If it'd been summer, the humongous deck would likely have been filled with guests enjoying the sites from Michael's veranda in the sky.

Much like his parents' home, the room was spacious and open. A large island was the only separation between the kitchen and the rest of the living areas, and the furnishings looked very comfortable. Everything was arranged in such a way as to accommodate both large and small groups. The oversized L-shaped sofa in front of the fireplace was already filled with laughing and smiling people.

Michael appeared to be a fantastic host. He moved easily around the room taking time to listen to and speak with each of his guests. Jane could see that he also checked to be sure everyone had whatever food or drink they desired.

Just the Way You Are

When she saw Aaron walking across the room toward her, their eyes met and she felt herself relax.

"Here you go." He handed her a large goblet filled with sparkling water along with slices of lemon and lime.

She smiled and took a refreshing sip. "Thank you, that's just what the doctor ordered."

"As you can see, I'm having the same. I wouldn't want you worried in the least about getting home safely."

"Aaron, don't worry about me. If you'd like to have a cocktail or a glass of wine, please feel free. I'd have one myself, but Dr. Carter still has me on a couple of meds that don't mix well with alcohol."

"Honestly, Jane, I'm not much of a drinker anyway. And considering what happened the last time you drove down this mountain, I figured you'd relax and have a lot more fun if you knew your driver was completely sober."

She raised her glass in a toast and said, "In that case, here's to good times."

"I seem to always have a good time when I'm with you," he replied as he touched his glass to hers.

Just then, Michael walked up. "What are we toasting?" he asked.

Jane's smile was warm and genuine as she extended her hand to her host. "We were just acknowledging the fact we're already having a wonderful time. Thank you so much for including me. Your home is absolutely amazing."

She was pleasantly surprised when, instead of shaking her hand, Aaron's brother wrapped her in a big bear hug. When she stepped out of Michael's arms, she couldn't quite understand what happened to cause the look of distress on Aaron's face.

Aaron didn't think he had a jealous bone in his body. But when he saw Jane engulfed in his brother's arms, the emotion hit him like a ton of bricks.

"Is everything all right?" Jane asked.

Aaron thought he heard his brother chuckle. "Yeah, you okay?" Michael queried.

Being a psychologist had its advantages. He knew exactly what Michael was doing and *why* he was doing it. Aaron also understood the only reason he was experiencing feelings of jealousy was because he'd developed a strong attachment to Jane. As much as he didn't want to admit it, he recognized he was falling in love with her. Not wanting to take too close a look at his discovery right now, he decided to tuck that little piece of information away for further examination at a later date.

Looking from Jane to Michael and back to Jane, Aaron smiled slightly and said, "I'm fine ... just fine. Come on, Jane, let me introduce you to

Just the Way You Are

the rest of my family. We'll catch up with you later, Mike." With that he took Jane's hand to escort her over to the group seated on the sofa.

Aaron was having a difficult time ignoring the intense feelings he was experiencing. It stopped him in his tracks. His eyes found Jane's, and emotions he'd thought were locked away permanently rushed to the surface. Looking into her clear blue eyes, the only thing he could do was lose himself in their depths for a few seconds. She swallowed hard and licked her lips. As he followed the path of her tongue with his gaze, he found himself wanting her once again. He wanted her all to himself ... only her.

Forcing himself to remember where he was and what he was doing, Aaron pushed his desire down. Squeezing her hand softly, he whispered, "If it wouldn't be totally impolite, I'd take you home right now, but we'll have to put that off until later." Her smile was the only response he needed. With her hand in his, they continued across the room. Aaron put his hand on the shoulder of a handsome silver haired man. "Dad, you remember Jane Barloc, don't you? She helped Connor out when his car broke down and gave him a ride to your anniversary party."

John Adler stood and took Jane's hand into his much larger one. "Of course I do," he boomed in his signature baritone voice. "I never forget a pretty face, do I, Jules?" He smiled affectionately at his wife. "It's a pleasure to see you again, Miss Barloc."

"Oh please, Mr. Adler, call me Jane," she replied as she covered his hand with her own.

"That's a deal Jane, as long as you call me John. All right?" His warm smile went all the way to the same gray-green eyes she loved in his son.

"Of course ... John," she said with a grin.

Juliette Adler stood next to the big man she'd loved since the moment she laid eyes on him over forty years ago. As far as Aaron was concerned, they could put a picture of his mother next to the definition of "unconditional love." From broken bones to broken hearts, from tears of joy to tears of pain, Juliette Adler always had a way of being there for her family and friends.

Without waiting for Aaron to re-introduce her, Juliette placed her hands on Jane's shoulders and asked, "May I?" as she leaned in and gave her an affectionate hug. "I've always heard that a hug is a handshake from the heart, so I hope you don't mind," she said as she released Jane from her embrace.

"Mind? Of course not. Thank you for the hug, Mrs. Adler. I'll remember to share what you said every time I'm lucky enough to give or receive one of those 'handshakes from the heart.'"

Just the Way You Are

"Now Jane, you know you don't have to call me Mrs. Adler. Juliette, Julie, Jules ... whatever you prefer."

"Thank you, Juliette. What a wonderful, romantic name. I love it," Jane replied.

"I've always enjoyed my name too. I like to say I found my Romeo that fateful day he was brought into the emergency room where I was on duty as a nurse." She turned and gave her husband a loving squeeze. "But Johnnie likes to call me Jules or Julie, and I've always loved the sound of his voice no matter what he's saying."

Aaron stood back and watched as Jane interacted with his father and mother. As they chatted, Jane's genuine warmth and caring showed through like a beacon. He'd been pretty sure his parents would like her even before he witnessed their meeting again this evening, but now there was no doubt in his mind. Jane was the kind of person everyone in his family would love. Everyone ... including him. He smiled to himself at his subconscious confession. Once again, he decided to file it away for future consideration. Then he continued to introduce Jane to the rest of the congenial group on the sofa. "Jane, this is my baby sister, Whitney." He knew his youngest sister would not be pleased with his comment, but could never seem to resist riling her up.

As she rose to a height of six-foot four including her three inch heels, Whitney replied

Anita Louise

frostily, "I don't know why you always insist on calling me that, Aaron. You *know* I'm not a 'baby' and haven't been one for a very long time." Her tone softened immensely when she took Jane's hand warmly and said, "Hello, Jane. I'm glad to see my brother is finally making better choices when it comes to women. I've been watching you. Not only are you lovely, but there's a warmth and grace about you that's absolutely charismatic. If you're ever interested in exploring modeling as a part-time gig, give me a call. I'm sure I could find work for you. You've got a face the camera would love."

"Why, thank you, Whitney," Jane almost stammered.

Aaron watched Jane's face blush prettily at the compliment from his sister. Whitney Adler's face and figure had graced the covers of everything from Sports Illustrated to Vogue and Cosmopolitan. An astute business woman, she'd moved from modeling to becoming the owner of an agency destined to be one of the industry's most powerful. Aaron knew Whitney was one hundred percent sincere in her comments. He hoped Jane would finally believe it was time to permanently remove the label of "Plain Jane" she'd placed on herself so many years ago.

"Seriously," Whitney said as she pressed her business card into Jane's hand, "call me some time."

Just the Way You Are

Aaron didn't want to look like the hovering boyfriend. Consequently, he excused himself and left Jane seated on the sofa after making sure she was at ease sitting with Olivia, Gabriella and Brooke. He was certain Jane would be perfectly comfortable with his sisters while he went down to the lower level. A couple of his brothers and some of the other guests were down there taking advantage of the pool table in the game room.

"Hey, Aaron," his brother Luke shouted as soon as he stepped into the room, "how about taking my place for a few minutes so I can grab a few brewskis?" The brothers embraced each other fondly. At six foot six and two hundred twenty-five pounds, Luke definitely stood out in a crowd. The tallest of the Adler sons, he towered above most men. He'd seriously considered the option of making the Navy a career, but found being away from family and old friends just wasn't for him. Luke's discipline and integrity made him the perfect candidate for becoming a police officer, and a job offer was his almost immediately after putting in his application. Now he'd been with the Boulder PD for over three years. Being with family was always something he enjoyed, and tonight Luke was in high spirits.

"Sure, Bro, happy to help you out. But I don't know how the rest of these folks will like it. I used to be quite the pool shark in my younger days," Aaron said.

Anita Louise

Connor scoffed loudly, "Yeah, right. You're so busy being a big deal writer it's probably been years since you've even held a pool cue in your hands. You most likely won't be able to hit the broad side of a barn, let alone make some of the tricky bank shots you used to be so famous for."

The pool players teased each other and made good-natured comments back and forth as Luke climbed the stairs, and Aaron took his first shot.

Jane was having a great time. Getting to know the Adler siblings was quite the enjoyable experience. Aaron's sister Olivia was so sweet, and she was just the cutest little thing! She was only about five foot three and couldn't weigh more than a hundred pounds soaking wet. With her blonde pixie haircut and petite stature, it was no wonder the family nicknamed her Tinker Bell. Jane listened intently as Olivia talked.

"I was always the smallest one in the family. When I was eight years old, I took up martial arts." She smiled. "I think my size had a lot to do with it. That and the fact I was the seventh of nine children." She went on to explain that the more she got into the disciplines, the more she loved them. "Jiu-jitsu and Tai Chi are my two favorites. Jiu-jitsu is a combat sport. As a smaller person, it allows me to use leverage and proper technique to defend myself from larger adversaries. I've never had to use it outside the Dojo, but you never know."

"Having those skills probably gives you more confidence," Jane said.

"Absolutely," Olivia responded. "Have you ever tried Tai Chi? I use it for meditation and relaxation."

"No, I haven't, but I'd really like to."

An attractive young man waved from across the room. Olivia smiled and waved back. Before excusing herself, she said, "Here's my card, Jane. Come on down to the studio some time. I'll give you a free lesson or two."

"That'd be great," Jane said. When she looked at the business card, Olivia was listed as the Sensei and owner.

Jane then turned to the twins. Watching and listening, it soon became clear that although Gabriella and Brooke were identical in appearance, their personalities were quite different. Gabriella's flamboyance contrasted with Brooke's quite manner.

Although Gabriella worked long hours as a veterinarian and horse trainer, she also had a very active social life. Jane observed with amusement how Gabriella's date, Marco, stuck to her like glue. However, much of the time it seemed Gabriella barely remembered he'd accompanied her to the party. When she finally noticed him, she rewarded him with a quick peck on the cheek and a somewhat breathy request. "Marco, sweetie, would you be a darling and get me another glass of wine?" She seemed relieved when he trotted off like an obedient pet to do her bidding.

Brooke was a middle school teacher who was also an avid bicyclist. Jane and Brooke hit it off right away.

"I've really gotten into bicycling since I've been living here in Boulder," Jane commented.

"Really?" Brooke asked. "Me too. I started biking several years ago. I love it."

"What kind of bike do you have? Which trails do you like? Oh ...there's just so much I don't know yet," Jane confessed.

"Why don't we get together for coffee or a glass of wine sometime. If you want to get more into the sport, I'll be happy to answer any questions I can."

"That'd be great!" It was clear to Jane if she really wanted to get more into the sport, Brooke would be an invaluable coach. The two women really enjoyed getting to know each other. They found it amusing when they discussed the fact that both of them were minivan owners, even though neither of them were mothers ... yet. The final word had been said in unison and caused them to laugh uproariously.

Just the Way You Are

When Aaron's brother Luke came up from the lower level, Jane noticed him right away. Of course, it would be difficult *not* to notice the biggest man in the room. Even though they were twins, Olivia and Luke were polar opposites. It was obvious Luke was a member of the Adler family as he was extremely good looking ... tall, dark and very handsome.

He'd walked straight over to Jane and the look in his eye was echoed by his flirtatious comment of, "Hello there, gorgeous. I'm Luke. Haven't we met somewhere before?" While she was flattered by the compliment, she felt none of the thrill she got from even the slightest glance from Aaron.

She thought back to the look on Aaron's face when his brother Michael gave her a hug upon their arrival, and wanted to set the record straight right away. Extending her hand while increasing the distance between them at the same time, she said, "Nice to meet you, Luke. I'm Jane Barloc, your brother Aaron's date."

"Oh my gosh. I'm so sorry," he sputtered. "I had no idea you were here with Aaron. Nice to meet you, Jane."

In an effort to ease his discomfort, Jane gave him her warmest smile and shook his hand courteously. "It's a pleasure to meet you too, Luke."

Anita Louise

From across the room, Aaron breathed a sigh of relief and felt another piece of his armor disappear. Luke was obviously putting his best moves on Jane. At first, Aaron started to see red and memories of Sharon's infidelities flooded his mind. Watching from the doorway, he saw Jane back up and move away from Luke's advances. Then she extended her hand. Luke turned beet red and became extremely flustered. It was clear Jane shot his brother down completely. Just as he was about to return to Jane's side, he felt his mother's hand upon his arm.

"I'm so glad you brought Jane with you this evening. Everyone really likes her. She's beautiful inside and out, isn't she, Aaron?"

"Yes she is, Mother. Indeed she is."

Chapter Sixteen

They were on their way back to Aaron's home when Jane spoke up from the passenger seat of his Jeep. "Your family is completely delightful. I wish Phillip and Rachel had been able to make it. Your mother told me that Rachel's due date is less than a month away so they decided a trip up the mountain might not be the best idea right now. But I sure would've loved the opportunity to get to know them better too."

"You will," Aaron replied. "With nine children, there are always plenty of things going on. It doesn't take much of an excuse for us to get together." *I'm beginning to think that you'll have a lifetime to get to know my family, Ms. Jane Barloc.* He was not ready to share his thoughts with her just yet. But he was rapidly coming to the conclusion that letting Jane go and returning to his life as a bachelor held less and less appeal with each passing moment.

"So my brother Luke was making a pass at you, was he?"

"Oh, Aaron, you know he never would have done it if he'd known I was with you," she stated matter-of-factly. "In fact, he practically tripped over his own feet trying to get away from me as soon as he found out." She chuckled, then looked at him curiously. "Hey, wait a minute. How did *you* know?"

"I saw you."

"You saw me?"

"Yes, I was coming upstairs and saw the whole thing. I saw you shut him down ... cold ... dead in his tracks. It was a beautiful thing," Aaron said with a smile on his face.

Jane was quiet for a few moments before she responded, "Like everyone else in your family, he's very nice and very attractive, but he isn't *you*. There's no one like you, Aaron. No one's ever made me feel the way you do."

Now it was his turn to sit in silence for a while. The sky was dark except for the stars. Maybe it was because it was a new moon. Legend said the new moon was the symbol of beginnings, a time to see your life more clearly. Maybe it was because they were in the car, and he didn't have to look at her directly. Whatever it was, he began to speak. "This isn't easy for me, Jane. It's been a long time since I've even

Just the Way You Are

thought about being in a long term relationship. But I'm thinking about it now ... with you." She didn't say a word, didn't move—just listened. "I know you have to go back to work on Monday, and I know Dr. Carter said you're fine to be back on your own again. But I don't want you to go, Jane. I want you to stay ... with me."

"Wow," she whispered, almost reverently.

He hadn't planned to ask her to stay, the words just seemed to spill out of their own volition. He heard her sniff and then rummage through her purse and extract a tissue.

"Are you *crying?"* he asked.

"Only a little," she croaked, "and these are *happy tears.* Oh, Aaron, there's nothing in the world I'd like more than to stay with you. If you weren't driving on this god-awful road, I'd wrap my arms around you and give you the biggest kiss you've ever had. You have no *idea* how happy you've just made me.*"*

And you have no idea how happy you've just made me, he thought. Out loud, he chuckled while keeping his eyes on the road and hands on the wheel. "Can I take a rain check on that kiss?"

"When we get home ... *home.*" Jane released a heartfelt sigh as she repeated the word, and it seemed to express her feelings more than anything else could. "When we get *home*, you're going to get waaay more than just a kiss. In fact, you may not get any sleep at all tonight." She reached over and laid her hand gently on his

Anita Louise

thigh. "I know you're not ready to say it, and you might not even be totally ready to hear it, but *I love you, Aaron Adler.* And I'm going to love you forever."

For some strange reason, his own throat was thick with emotion. It *almost* felt as if he was ready to shed a couple of joyful tears himself. So he didn't say a word, but he did take one hand off the steering wheel to place it atop hers.

True to her word, they were barely in the house before Jane threw her arms around his neck and gave him a kiss. It only took a few seconds before the kiss turned from happy and warm to hot and passionate. When they parted briefly, he looked into her eyes. There was so much emotion ... so much longing and urgency. He threw their coats across the back of the couch, and together they ran hand in hand to the bedroom.

Not even bothering to throw back the bed coverings, he pulled her with him onto the bed. He knew if anyone had seen them, they would likely have looked like a couple of teenagers whose parents had left them alone in the house for the first time. Fully clothed, they kissed and hugged, touched and tasted, laughed and moaned. The thrill of simply being together made it feel almost impossible to get enough of her.

Just the Way You Are

Moving his hand under her lavender silk blouse and feeling her erect nipples beneath the lace of her bra, he managed to say between kisses, "Got ... to get ... out ... of these ... clothes."

"Yes." Jane's breath was as ragged as his, and she began to open the buttons on his dress shirt as quickly as her fingers could move. As soon as she reached the last button, her hand continued downward and cupped his erection, rubbing up and down with firm strokes. "I ... need ... this ... need *you ... now,*" she whispered urgently.

He groaned as he felt the throb of his desire and ran his tongue along the skin of her neck. "Lift your arms." There was no time to undo the buttons of her blouse. He grabbed its hem and pulled it straight up over her head. "You're so beautiful," he murmured as his hands returned to her breasts and pushed down the lace to release them. "So beautiful," he repeated. Leaning forward he licked one of the hardened peaks while squeezing and pulling the other between his thumb and forefinger.

Her hands had undone his belt and were now working impatiently at the zipper of his pants. He felt his erection spring forward only to be stopped by the cloth of his boxers. She pushed down on the waistband of his clothing.

"Now ... I want you *now,*" she demanded. He adjusted his hips to allow her to slide the interfering garments out of the way, and before his trousers even hit the floor her mouth was on him—hot and wet. "Mmmm," she moaned as she licked and sucked. She ran her tongue around the tip of his shaft as her hand moved up and down its length.

He watched, mesmerized by the sight of her. Sounds of desire continued to emerge from her throat as she almost reverently worked his erection with hands and mouth. He had to slow her down or he wouldn't be able to hold out another minute.

"My turn," he said as he moved to stand and lifted her gently from her ministrations. She seemed almost dazed as he laid her back onto the bed. She whimpered and continued to reach for him. "My turn," he said again, more firmly this time. He quickly spread her legs and ran his fingers over the moist strip of material between her thighs. "So wet. I love how wet you get for me," he murmured as he slid his finger between the lace of her panties and the soft skin beneath.

"Oh, Aaron, that feels so good," she gasped as his finger moved up and down and then into the slick opening between her legs. Her hands were on her own breasts, kneading them, pinching and squeezing her nipples.

"That's it, baby, feel those beautiful breasts while I take care of you down here." Pushing the lace to the side, he replaced his finger with his tongue. "Ummm, you taste so good. These are in the way. Got to go. Close your legs for just a second, darling."

"Yes." She did as requested, and he slipped her panties off.

"Beautiful. So beautiful," he repeated as he looked into her eyes and then up and down the length of her body. He ran his fingers through the soft mound above the vee of her legs. "Open your legs for me, Jane. I want you to watch me when I taste you. I want you to see how much I love having my tongue filled with your sweetness."

"Ahh." Moaning softly, she did as he asked.

His eyes locked with hers as he dipped his head between her thighs and extended his tongue. Starting at the base of her opening he moved his tongue slowly up its length making sounds of pleasure as he did. Using his hands, he gently parted her lower lips and dipped his tongue as far as he could into the wetness of her most private space. "So sweet. So wet. So delicious," he murmured in delight. Finding the nub of her pleasure, he ran his thumb over and around it and then began flicking it gently with his tongue.

Her hips were moving up and down, and her head rolled from side to side as she repeated, "Oh, oh, oh," over and over. Continuing to flick her nub with his tongue he inserted two fingers into her dripping opening. "Oh, Aaron, I'm going

Anita Louise

to come ... soon. Yes. Please, I *need you. I need you inside me, **now***," she cried urgently.

"Watch with me, Jane," he managed to say ... his voice unsteady. He poised his erection at the entrance between her thighs. They both watched as their bodies joined, enthralled as he entered her. He pushed in ... inch by inch and then drew his length out slowly. With each stroke he went a little deeper and a little faster. Their hips moved in unison ... an ancient dance ... inexplicably beautiful. "I can't hold back any longer. Come with me, Jane."

Matching him stroke for stroke, she pulled him to her. *"Now, Aaron, now!"*

With a final plunge, deep and hard, they both went over the edge.

Hours later Aaron woke as if from being drugged. *Wow, that was some hot sex,* he thought with satisfaction. *Sex? Was it just sex?* He sighed as he pulled the woman sleeping quietly next to him a little closer. There was no denying it. Being with Jane was *much more* than just sex. There was something much bigger going on here, something inextricably connected to his heart. As much as he hadn't thought it was possible, he realized Jane Barloc had finally removed the last barrier he'd so carefully built around his heart. Softly kissing the top of her

Just the Way You Are

head as it lay gently on his chest, he whispered, "I love you, Jane."

With that he closed his eyes and drifted back to sleep.

Chapter Seventeen

Oh, my God! Jane awoke the next morning with a realization that had her practically sitting straight up in bed, and it wasn't because of her wanton behavior the night before. Never in her wildest imagination would she have dreamed she was capable of being so completely caught up in the moment that she didn't seem to possess a single shred of self-consciousness. Just thinking about their lovemaking had her heating up all over again, but now was *not* the time for that.

What woke her from a sound sleep was a sobering fact. She and Aaron were both so wrapped up in the sensual ecstasy they were experiencing, neither of them remembered a very important little piece of thin flexible material ... a condom. Jane hadn't been on birth control pills since her break up with William over a year ago.

Just the Way You Are

Ending up in Aaron Adler's bed was the furthest thing from her mind when she left the hospital with him at the beginning of the week.

What if I'm pregnant?

Aaron said he wanted her to stay. And there was no doubt, the two of them were fantastic in bed. Surely their sexual connection wasn't the only reason he wanted to be with her. Was it? She needed to think, and she wasn't ready to discuss it with Aaron. Careful not to disturb him, she slid silently from the bed and padded softly across the room. Her pajamas, robe and slippers were just inside the walk-in closet. She grabbed them, then closed the door softly behind her. Donning her nightwear, she then headed down the hallway to the kitchen and put on a pot of coffee.

Pacing back and forth across the kitchen floor waiting for the coffee to brew wasn't working. Maybe some fresh air would help. She quickly grabbed her coat and slid open the sliding glass door leading out to the back patio. The cold, crisp air hit her solidly, and she took a deep breath. Looking at the mountains in the distance, she felt like she had her own *huge* mountain to climb. Somewhat consoled by the scripture verse she'd memorized many years before, she spoke aloud, "Truly I tell you, if anyone says to this mountain, 'Go, throw yourself into the sea,' and does not doubt in their heart but believes that what they say will happen, it will be done for them."

Aaron told me he wants me to stay, but what if it's all about the sex? Amazing as it is, that's just not enough. I want more. I want to be with a man who wants to be with me for me ... for who I am inside and out. I don't want to have to change to please him, and I sure as heck don't want to try and change him. I want him to love me. If I'm pregnant and he finds out, I'll never know if we're together because he loves me or because I'm having his child. Of course, I might not be pregnant, but what if I am?

Back and forth, back and forth she went.

What if I'm pregnant? What if I'm not? Does he love me, or does he just want my body? If I'm pregnant and he asks me to marry him, will it be because of the baby or because he really wants us to be together ... to be a family?

She was so confused! Sitting down on the cold stone bench facing the mountains, she burst into tears. Somewhere in the back of her mind she heard a rustling in the shrubbery. The soft pat on her shoulder followed by a female arm around her waist brought her out of her daze.

"There, there, what's this all about?"

Jane looked at Mrs. Worthton through tear stained eyes.

"Nu ... nu ... nothing," she managed to choke out.

Just the Way You Are

Mrs. Worthton pulled a soft cotton handkerchief monogrammed with the letter "W" and a pair of oversized woolen mittens out of her pocket. She handed them to Jane.

"Here, sweetie. Blow your nose and then put these on. Your hands look like their freezing. We don't want you to get frostbite now, do we?" Jane did as instructed. After a few moments of silence, Millie Worthton spoke again. "You've been here with Dr. Adler for quite a few days now. He certainly is a nice young man ... handsome too."

"Yes, I have and he is ... all of those things."

"You know, my Richard and I, we had one of those whirlwind romances. Of course, that was a long time ago."

"Oh, Mrs. Worthton, I'm just so confused, and I really don't have anybody to talk to. You have no idea how much I appreciate you coming over here." Jane sniffled and then blew her nose on the monogrammed hankie.

"You *must* call me Millie. All my friends do," she said as she gave Jane another motherly squeeze. When Jane didn't speak, Millie Worthton continued. "A lot of things were different back in my day, but some things never change. Do you mind if I ask you something, Jane?"

"No, I don't mind, but is it okay if I'm not comfortable answering you?"

Anita Louise

Millie patted Jane's hand reassuringly. "Yes, that's just fine. Besides, I think I already know the answer." After a brief pause she asked, "You love Dr. Adler, don't you?"

"Yes!" Jane blurted without hesitation. "So *much*. So very much!" The tears that'd stopped only moments before reappeared in her eyes, and she dropped her head into her hands.

"And you're not sure if he loves you back. Am I right?"

"I *wish* I knew. I think he *might*. I think he's *starting* to. If only I knew for sure," Jane said tearfully.

"My Richard was like a lot of men. He wasn't much when it came to talking about his feelings. Oh, but I knew. And do you know how I knew?" Jane shook her head and Millie continued. "I knew by what he *did*. I knew by the way he looked at me when he thought I wasn't looking. I knew by the little things he did for me ... how he watched out for me ... took care of me. And when he was ready, he finally got around to telling me, and *oh,* how wonderful it was to hear those three little words ... 'I love you.'" She sighed blissfully.

Jane looked thoughtfully at Aaron's mature neighbor, and said, "Thank you, Millie. Thank you very much. You've helped me a *lot*."

The two women gave each other a big hug. As Millie Worthton made her way back through the shrubbery dividing her property from

Just the Way You Are

Aaron's, she looked over her shoulder and winked at Jane. "You know more than you think you do, my dear. Listen to your heart. It always tells you the truth."

Wiping her eyes one last time, Jane squared her shoulders and walked back into Aaron's house.

When Aaron woke, he rolled over and reached out his arm expecting to find Jane sleeping next to him. He was surprised by how disappointed he was when he realized she wasn't there. It'd only been a couple of days and already he'd gotten used to how good it felt to wake up next to a beautiful woman and to cuddle up to her soft warmth.

Who am I trying to kid? It's not just waking up next to any *beautiful woman ... it's waking up next to Jane.*

Even though he'd admitted to himself the night before that he'd fallen in love with Jane Barloc, he wasn't sure if he was ready to admit it to *her.* He remembered the words he'd written earlier in the section on relationships of his new book.

"With intimacy comes power. And when you give a lover the power to make you feel valued and special, the dark side is, at the same time,

Anita Louise

you also give them the power to hurt you deeply ... unlike anyone else."

Was he ready to give Jane that kind of power over him? It'd been years since his relationship with Sharon fell apart. He was just *now* coming to a point where he could open himself up to even the *possibility* of being with someone for the long term.

Just the fact that it *bothered* him that Jane wasn't there next to him when he woke up ... *bothered* him. Was he already giving her the power to hurt him? He could almost feel the wall around his heart begin to go back up. Telling himself everything would be all right ... that Jane was nothing like Sharon, he pulled on some comfortable sweats and walked out into the main living area of the house.

Jane was sitting at the little table in the breakfast nook sipping a cup of coffee and staring out at the mountains.

"You're up early," he said with as much lightheartedness as he could manage. "Everything okay?"

Her reply was not the cheery Jane he'd come to expect. "Good morning, Aaron. Everything's fine. I just couldn't sleep. Coffee's ready."

Something *was* wrong. He could feel it. What was she hiding? Why wasn't she talking to

Just the Way You Are

him about it? He walked into the kitchen and poured himself a cup of coffee, took it over to the table and sat down next to her. When he looked at her, he noticed her eyes were puffy and a little red. It was apparent she'd been crying.

"Jane, everything's not okay. I can tell ... you've been crying. What's wrong? Do you want to talk about it?"

She kept her hands wrapped around her cup as she set it carefully on the table. "You're right. I *have* been crying, but I'm not really ready to talk about it, if that's okay with you."

"Well, I can't *make* you talk to me, but you know as well as I do that the happiest couples are the ones who *talk* to each other."

"Are we a couple, Aaron?" she asked. "Sure, we've been together almost constantly for over a week. You stayed with me at the hospital and then you brought me, and even Henry, to your house. And these past few days ... well, they've been wonderful." She hesitated and he could see the color creeping into her face as she said, "And then there's the sex ... the absolutely amazing sex, but does that make us a couple?"

He couldn't tell if it was hopefulness or sadness he heard in her voice. He ran his fingers through his hair, closed his eyes and took a deep breath. "Wow. I didn't see this coming." He remembered his earlier thoughts regarding his writing about relationships. Was he really ready to give her the power to hurt him? His guard was

Anita Louise

back up. He wasn't ready for this, this ... whatever this was. He blurted the next thing that popped into his mind. "Maybe you're right, Jane. I mean, this has all happened super-fast. I don't know. Maybe we should ..." *Should what? Break up? We aren't even officially together, are we?*

Lost in his own thoughts, he almost didn't notice her stand, but when her chair scraped against the floor he looked up. He could see the pain in her eyes ... the same pain he felt in his heart.

"I think it's time for me to go, Aaron," she said quietly. "It should only take me a few minutes to gather my things together. Would you mind taking me home?" She didn't wait for his answer ... simply turned her back and walked away.

The drive back to Jane's condo was almost completely silent except for a few loud "meows" from the disgruntled passenger in the back seat of the Jeep.

Aaron was totally miserable. *What happened?* he asked himself. *One minute I'm telling myself it's time to open back up ... that I'm ready to love again, and the next minute ... this. She's leaving, and I don't even know why. What happened?*

Just the Way You Are

She'd hardly said another word. She just walked out from the bedroom with her suitcase in her hand and said, "I'm ready to go."

He insisted on carrying her things to the car. While he did, she gathered up Henry's dishes and put the cat into his carrier. When he pulled up to her condo he gave it one last effort. "Jane, can we talk about this?"

She looked at him sadly and said, "Maybe later. Not now ... maybe later."

Once again, Aaron insisted on carrying her luggage into her condo. He couldn't understand it. It almost felt like she couldn't get away from him fast enough. Now he stood at the doorway of her home with his hand on the knob. She let Henry out of his carrier. The feline quickly climbed to the top of his cat tower, plopped down and fell asleep. Aaron glanced at Jane's luggage at the base of the stairs where he'd left it.

Jane was standing in the kitchen with the dining table positioned as a barrier between them, her arms wrapped around her midsection. She looked as miserable as he felt.

He didn't know what to say. The world famous psychologist, author, and speaker couldn't think of a single thing to say to change this unbelievably horrible, and totally unexplainable situation, so he just stood there ... with his hand on the doorknob.

"Thank you, Aaron," she whispered. "Thank you ... for everything."

"Uh, okay. You're welcome. Um, uh."

"Good bye."

"Yeah, uh. Good bye then." He gulped, raised his hand in a feeble wave and said, "G'bye," as he walked out of her door.

Jane broke into sobs almost immediately after she saw Aaron's Jeep drive away. "What have I done?" she practically screamed to the empty room.

She'd had absolutely no intention of walking out of Aaron's home or Aaron's life when she woke up that morning. Sure, she was concerned about what happened. In their overwhelming desire for each other, neither one of them remembered to use protection against potential pregnancy. But that didn't mean she didn't still want to *be* with him. In fact, if it turned out she *was* pregnant, it'd be even *more* important for them to stay together.

When she'd sat outside and talked to Millie Worthton, she'd actually felt a little better about her relationship with Aaron. Okay, so he hadn't told her he loved her yet. Like Millie said, he'd *shown* her in many ways how much he cared. After talking with Millie, Jane's heart was telling her that given a little more time, Aaron would come to realize he *did* love Jane, and he *would* say those three wonderful words she so desperately wanted to hear.

Just the Way You Are

But on the other hand, the first time there was even the slightest *hint* of everything not being absolutely *perfect* with their relationship, Aaron started talking about how *fast* everything happened and "maybe they *should ...*" Of course, Jane assumed the worst case scenario and figured he meant that they *should* ... should what? Cool it, slow down, take a break from seeing one another? That didn't mean that he wanted her to *leave* right then and there! She was in such an emotional state, her own self-preservation mechanisms must have kicked in. The words, "What was I thinking?" held more impact than she'd ever before believed possible.

Jane was half tempted to call Aaron's cell phone before he even got home and beg him to come back and pick her up. But when she'd told him she wasn't ready to talk about it, she'd been telling the truth. Her thoughts were a jumbled mess, and she needed to sort them out in her own mind before discussing them with Aaron.

This was the first time Jane wished she was the kind of gal who paid attention to her menstrual cycles. She tried to think back. When *was* her last one? She didn't tend to be a drama-queen, so it wasn't like her to make a big deal out of nothing. So why was she so freaked out about this?

Am I just being overly dramatic? There's no possible way to know if I'm pregnant or not since it only happened last night. Was I secretly *hoping that I <u>am</u> pregnant so Aaron would be <u>forced</u> into staying with me ... even marrying me?*

For the first time since she woke up to the shocking realization that she and Aaron had indulged in unprotected sex, Jane was finally starting to step back from her totally out of control emotions and put things into perspective. Had she been able to do this earlier, perhaps she wouldn't be sitting here in her condo, alone, with only her cat Henry to keep her company.

No doubt the Universe is unfolding as it should. Jane clearly recalled her childhood days before losing her Mom. She could remember hearing her mother quoting that particular passage from the Desiderata whenever something seemingly unexplainable would occur. Somehow those were the same words that comforted her and her sister when their mother died suddenly before they'd even reached their teens.

Maybe Aaron was right. This relationship had been moving at warp speed. Perhaps this is what needed to happen to slow the whole thing down.

Yes, she thought, *slowing down was probably a good thing, but totally going off the rails is something else entirely, and that is <u>not</u> something that's going to happen.*

As Jane stood looking out over the commons area behind her condo, she felt a little like she imagined Scarlett O'Hara must have felt at the end of *Gone With the Wind.* Jane squared her shoulders and paraphrased the indomitable southern belle. *Home ... to Aaron. I'll go home. I'll think of some way to get him back. After all ... tomorrow is another day.*

Sharon Demasi wasn't sure what was going on with her ex-husband and the woman who'd been staying at his house. All she knew for sure was she didn't like it one bit.

Over the last several months, she'd gotten into the habit of driving past Aaron's house fairly regularly. Ninety percent of the time there wasn't anything to see. But there'd been a new development recently. One day last week instead of pulling his Jeep into the garage as he usually did, he'd parked it in the driveway. At first she thought it might give her the opportunity to pull up to the curb and declare how shocked she was to see him.

Sharon had her story all figured out. She'd rehearsed it multiple times. "Oh, my gosh! Aaron? Is that you? I just *happened* to be driving through this neighborhood. I've got a client who's looking to buy in this vicinity."

However, her carefully thought out ploy didn't materialize. After Aaron got out, he walked around the vehicle and opened the passenger door. Then he helped a blonde out of the Jeep and took her into his house.

Anita Louise

Who the hell is that bitch? Sharon wondered. The really bad news was the blonde appeared to be *living* with Aaron. That is, until today.

This time when Sharon drove by she observed the bitch walking out, and Aaron was sending her baggage with her. *Good riddance.*

She'd followed the Jeep to a condo community near the CU-Boulder campus. *That's a good boy, Aaron. Take that little slut back to the crumby little dump where she belongs.*

After Aaron left, Sharon decided to keep an eye on Blondie for a while. *After all, you can't defeat your enemies until you know who they are,* she thought.

Chapter Eighteen

Aaron was totally miserable as he drove away from Jane's condo.

What the heck just happened? he asked himself. Last night was the most incredible night of his *life*, and now he was driving back to his empty house. It just didn't make any sense!

He needed to take some time and do what he did best ... analyze the situation. As soon as he got home, he walked into his study. Seating himself in the chair where Jane sat the last time they'd worked together so companionably felt right. It made him feel closer to her somehow by just sitting where she'd been only a short time ago.

He relaxed and reflected on everything that'd taken place in such a short period of time. Thinking back, he admitted he'd handled it badly

Anita Louise

when Jane said she wasn't ready to talk about it ... whatever "*it*" was.

If only I'd just given her some space ... some time to think about whatever it was that had her so upset. Why did I have to push her to talk to me right then and there?

Being a psychologist, one of the many subjects he'd studied was EQ, emotional intelligence. He thought he totally understood the importance of being self-aware and managing his own *emotions* intelligently. What he seemed to have forgotten this morning was the other part of EQ. He'd forgotten the importance of managing his *relationships* intelligently.

He could see Jane was acting with emotional intelligence and integrity by acknowledging her true feelings and sharing them with him. She'd told him, yes, she was upset, but she was not *yet* ready to discuss it with him. He, on the other hand, was only thinking about his *own* need to know what was troubling her. And, he wanted to know *now*, instead of giving her the time *she* needed before discussing whatever it was.

Looking back, he could see when she'd asked him the simple question, "Are we a couple?" he'd *totally blown it*. The old saying that hindsight is always twenty-twenty sure was the case here. Instead of whatever stupid comments he'd made, what he wished he would've said was, "Of course, we're a couple. Are you kidding me? This time we've spent together, has been the most incredible time of my life. Everything about it's been *wonderful*. *You're* wonderful. I've *loved* being with you. I love *you*, Jane Barloc. *I love you.*"

But instead of opening his heart and letting her know how he felt, he'd allowed his fear to speak. He thought back once more to the quote he'd been thinking of before he walked into the kitchen.

> **"With intimacy comes power. And when you give a lover the power to make you feel valued and special, the dark side is, at the same time, you also give them the power to hurt you deeply ... unlike anyone else."**

Because he didn't want to give her the power to hurt him, he'd done exactly that to *her* instead. Rather than making her feel valued and special, he'd used the power she gave him through their intimacy to hurt her deeply. It's no wonder she wanted to get away from him. Well, now that he understood the problem, it was time to work on a *solution*.

Even though, he admitted to himself, the whole thing was his own fault, the situation still left him feeling hurt, confused, and to a certain extent, emotionally drained. He knew if that's the way *he* was feeling, Jane was probably in the same boat. Now, the question was how to overcome this hurdle and get them back together. He needed a *plan* to give him a sense of direction ... and *hope.*

The last thing he wanted to do was push her further away by appearing too needy. Repeatedly calling, texting, and begging her to come back would only make him appear weak and insecure. *I need to give her the time and space now that I should have given her in the first place. If I'd done that, I probably wouldn't be sitting here ... alone and miserable.*

Since he'd been working on the section on relationships for his new book, he decided to bury himself in his work for a day or two. Writing was one of the ways he'd always used in the past to help him get through challenging situations in life. And this was certainly a challenging situation. He moved to his desk, fired up his computer, pulled out his notes and picked up where he'd left off. Soon he was lost in his work.

Jane was feeling a little better. She talked the dealership into delivering her new mini-van on Saturday instead of waiting until Monday. In fact, the guy who delivered it was quite flirtatious with her, and boy oh boy, did that feel good! She was still stinging over her abrupt "break up" with Aaron. The twenty-something, rather studly

Just the Way You Are

looking young man gave her an appreciative head-to-foot once over. Then he said, "You look like you should be driving a Corvette instead of a mini-van." His words made her feel like all was not lost.

Unpacking her bag was ... interesting. Every piece of clothing seemed to hold special meaning as she pulled each one from her suitcase. *This is what I was wearing when he first brought me home from the hospital,* she thought. Smiling to herself as she hung up her lavender silk blouse, she remembered the look of admiration in Aaron's eyes when he'd seen her wearing it, and then how he'd looked when he'd removed it. Her body tingled at the thought of how he'd held her and kissed her.

Shaking her head to keep her thoughts from going to a place she wasn't yet ready to explore, she decided she needed to keep busy. One look around her condo and she knew it was time for a bit of vacuuming and dusting. After being gone unexpectedly for an entire week, she also needed to clean out her refrigerator. By the time she was finished the fridge was glaringly empty. Now she needed to restock it with lots of healthy produce and a few lean cuts of meat.

It was a beautiful sunny afternoon. When she was finished with all her household chores, she still had energy to spare. Not wanting to end up brooding over the fact she was back at her condo instead of still with Aaron, she decided to

Anita Louise

take her new vehicle out for a drive. A visit to the gym for a light aerobic workout before going to the grocery store might be just what she needed.

After making a list of things to pick up at the store, Jane quickly changed into her workout clothes and tennis shoes and hopped in the mini-van. As she drove to the health club, her thoughts drifted back to the past week. It was almost hard to believe it'd only been the previous weekend when she'd ended up in the hospital. She smiled to herself when she remembered waking up and seeing Aaron sitting by her side ... holding her hand.

Dr. Carter assumed the man staying with her the whole time she was in the hospital *must* be someone significant in his patient's life. Even so, it was Aaron's *choice* to bring Jane back to his home. There were just too many unexplained coincidences. Surely fate didn't bring them together only to see them split apart so soon. They simply needed more time. Jane was certain this was not the end, there was more to their story.

I wonder where Blondie's off to now. Sharon was fairly positive this interloper and her ex were no longer a couple, but she needed to be sure. *There must be some way I can "accidentally" bump into this broad and find out a little more about what's going on.*

Just the Way You Are

A few minutes later the mini-van she was following pulled into the parking lot of the fitness center Sharon belonged to. *Well, isn't this just perfect? Sharon Demasi,* she said to herself, *you have got to be one of the luckiest people on the planet.* She chuckled to herself. *What are the odds?*

She watched her nemesis go inside the Lakeshore Athletic Club. *Take your time, sweetheart. Your new workout partner will be there shortly.* Sharon drove the short distance to the Flatirons Mall. She practically sprinted into Dick's Sporting Goods where she purchased leotards, a sports bra and a pair of athletic shoes.

Finding a parking place toward the back of the parking lot, Jane walked slowly toward the entrance of the gym. Keeping her thoughts somewhere other than on Aaron Adler was proving to be even more difficult than she'd imagined. Once inside, she found an elliptical trainer in front of a flat screen TV and got started. The television was tuned to some sort of nature show about bears, and Jane found it easy to ignore. She'd only been on the elliptical for about fifteen minutes when she heard a voice.

"Enjoying the show?" asked the woman from the adjacent machine.

Anita Louise

"What? Oh, it's fine. I'm not really watching it, to be perfectly honest. Change it to anything you like."

"Thanks," she said as she flipped the channel to a station showing local real estate listings. "I'm checking to make sure the homes I've got listed are showing up like they're supposed to. It costs a small fortune to advertise like this, but I think it's worth it." Without waiting for a response, she smiled broadly. "I'm Sharon. Sharon Demasi, realtor extraordinaire!"

Although she wasn't really in the mood to make conversation, Jane nodded and replied politely, "Hi, Sharon. I'm Jane."

"Nice to meet you, Jane. If you're ever thinking of listing or buying, give me a call. I've been one of the top realtors in Boulder for over ten years!" she said proudly. "Everything from helping a college student find a little condo to live in for a few years, to listing and selling multi-million dollar homes up in the mountains. You name it. I'm your gal!"

"Well, up until this morning, I thought I might be listing my condo at some point, but things have changed dramatically." The words seemed to pop out of her mouth before she could stop them. Jane wasn't even sure she *liked* this Sharon, "realtor extraordinaire" and sharing personal, private information with her was the last thing Jane was interested in doing.

Just the Way You Are

"Guy trouble? I know all about it ... been married ... and divorced ... twice. I'm a great listener if you want to talk about it."

"Not really," Jane said. The woman next to her had long hair tied up in a messy bun on top of her head. She wore a little too much make-up for the gym. By the looks of her figure, Sharon obviously took good care of herself. Although it looked like Sharon's workout clothes might be a size too small.

As much as she wanted to simply excuse herself and get away from her new "friend," Jane didn't have enough energy to think up a good excuse to leave. So she stayed put.

The woman continued. "So what happened? Did you and your boyfriend get in a fight? Do you think you'll patch things up?"

"I don't really know. It's too soon to tell."

"Are you *sure* you don't want to talk about it?" Sharon asked again.

"No. I don't think so," Jane replied. "I'm sorry, but you'll have to excuse me. I'm not feeling real well. I've got to go."

Sharon reached into her low-cut sports bra and pulled out a plastic card case from which she extracted her business card. Handing it to Jane, she said, "Call me if you change your mind. I'd be happy to help in any way I can. Do you have a card, Jane?"

"No. Sorry." Not giving the woman the opportunity to ask any more questions, Jane quickly exited the gym.

Damn! Sharon wanted to learn a whole lot more about the woman she'd dubbed Blondie, but the chick was pretty closed mouthed. Sharon now knew Blondie's real name was Jane. Although Jane didn't say much, she *did* say things changed *dramatically* with her and her boyfriend.

I better put my plan into action sooner rather than later. Looks like right now is my best chance to get Aaron back. She smiled at herself in the gym mirror. *You've still got it,* she said to her reflection. *With this body and the most enticing offer Aaron's ever had in his life, it's practically a done deal,* she thought.

Hmmm. Maybe this time I'll change my name. Nah. I've worked too hard to establish my Sharon Demasi brand. How about Sharon Demasi-Adler? Yeah, that's got a nice ring to it ... preferably at least three carats, please. She chuckled at her own quip.

Even though nothing had really changed, Jane felt a new sense of hope when she left the gym. She looked at the business card from the

Just the Way You Are

woman she'd met. "Sharon Demasi – Realtor Extraordinaire."

As far as Jane could see, there wasn't *anything* extraordinary about the woman. But if *that* person had managed to get married *twice*, surely the one solid marriage Jane craved was possible. Once she and Aaron vowed "till death do us part," they'd live by that commitment for the rest of their lives. She was absolutely positive.

Jane climbed into her vehicle with a new spring in her step. When she looked at it honestly, she had to admit leaving Aaron's house so abruptly was pretty much her own doing. Yes, she *was* less than pleased by his reaction when she asked whether or not they were really a couple. But, she *had* put him on the spot. No one likes to feel they're being pushed into a corner.

The idea of going straight back to Aaron's house and explaining everything was tempting. But, there was still the whole "we forgot to use a condom" situation to take into consideration. Talk about feeling pushed into a corner! If Jane told Aaron she was concerned about the possibility of being pregnant, he might feel even more pressured and pull back even further.

I need to look at this as objectively as possible. If one of my counseling clients came to me with a similar situation, what would I advise them to do?

The more she thought about it, the more sense it made to wait and see if she was

Anita Louise

pregnant or not. It was important to be as open and honest as possible with Aaron if they were going to have a long lasting relationship built on trust and faith. Until she knew for sure whether or not she and Aaron had a baby on the way, it would be difficult to communicate with complete honesty.

Just because we had unprotected sex doesn't mean I'm pregnant, and I don't want to be a drama queen. I could probably get one of those 'morning after' pills, but the truth is I don't want to. Even if Aaron and I don't end up getting back together, if I'm pregnant, I want this child.

She was almost shocked as she listened to her own thoughts. Having a family someday was something she'd always wanted. Of course, she'd assumed it would be after dating, getting engaged and being married for a year or two. Getting pregnant and having a baby with someone she'd only known for a very short time had never entered her mind.

I never thought I'd fall in love this quickly either. Besides, I know Aaron will make a wonderful father.

Before she knew it, she'd arrived at her local shopping center. As she strolled through the aisles of the grocery store, she picked up an early pregnancy test kit.

Chapter Nineteen

As much as he missed having her in the house, Aaron did the best he could to settle into his old "pre-Jane" routine. He had a fully equipped home gym in his basement. It hadn't gotten a lot of use recently, so he decided to put part of his energy into working out. From time to time he'd bring in a personal trainer to keep himself on track and learn the latest trends in workout techniques. In the absence of a trainer, he had a decent routine he stuck with, and today it was his fallback.

He hadn't slept well, so it was pretty easy for him to get up before dawn and lift some weights. After weightlifting he spent about fifteen minutes burning calories in front of the punching bag. The truth was, he was having a hard time just lying there without Jane in bed next to him. It was amazing how quickly he'd become

Anita Louise

accustomed to having her beside him. Even though he'd spent every night alone prior to Jane's arrival, it now felt unnatural without her there.

After finishing his indoor workout, Aaron decided he needed some fresh air. Taking a jog before hitting the shower sounded like a good idea. He stretched, layered up and pulled on a Gore-Tex jacket and pants to ward off the cold before heading out the rear of his home. Beginning at a slow lope, he then gradually picked up his pace. It felt good to physically push himself. By the time he turned and started back toward his home, he was feeling the best he had all morning.

Just as he was approaching the path to his back yard, he heard Mrs. Worthton calling his name. As nice as she was, he really didn't feel like talking to her or anyone else right now. Pretending he hadn't heard her, he stepped through the bushes into his yard. It didn't work. Millie Worthton was standing just in front of the shrubs separating their property.

"Dr. Adler? You must not have heard me. I was calling you, but you just kept going. Did you have those ear things in?" she asked.

Ignoring her question he said, "I'm sorry, Mrs. Worthton. Now's not really a good time for me."

Just the Way You Are

"This won't take but a minute. I just wanted to make sure that lovely young lady of yours was all right. Jane, isn't it?"

She had his attention now. "Yes, Mrs. Worthton, her name is Jane. What do you mean, you wanted to make sure she was 'all right?'"

"Well, yesterday morning, she was out here all by herself. Still had her slippers on and everything ... crying like the world had come to an end. Is she okay?"

"I'm not sure, Mrs. Worthton. Jane left late yesterday morning. She's not here. She's back at her condo."

"Oh ... I see," she said slowly.

"What is it, Mrs. Worthton? Is there something you're not telling me?"

"Well, first of all, you've got to stop calling me Mrs. Worthton. I'm Millie. Jane calls me Millie, so you should too," she insisted.

"Okay, what is it you're not telling me? What did Jane say to you?"

"Oh, I don't know." Millie seemed hesitant. "She didn't tell me *not* to say anything, but then again, she didn't give me permission either."

He walked over to where she stood, and placed a hand gently on her arm. Looking directly into her eyes, he said, "Millie, *please*. Tell me what Jane said. It's important ... to Jane and to me. I really need to know. Please."

"Ohhh, I just don't know." Talking to herself quietly he heard the name Richard. It almost sounded like she was having a conversation with someone. He didn't really care *who* she talked to if it helped him find out what Jane told her. Finally, she nodded her head as if she'd made up her mind. "She loves you. She said she loves you, Aaron."

That was apparently the end of the conversation, because once again Millie Worthton disappeared between the bushes separating their property. Aaron just stood there staring at the empty space where his neighbor had been only seconds before.

She loves me. Last night ... when we got home ... she told me she loved me.

He replayed her words in his mind. "I love you, Aaron Adler. And I'm going to love you forever."

Forever. She said she's going to love me forever.

He knew it took courage for her to say those words because once said, there'd be no turning back. She'd left it up to him to either accept what she said as true ... accept her love, or know that at some point in time, their relationship would have to come to an end.

He asked himself, *Am I willing to stick it out? Am I willing to make the effort to move past the pain I experienced the last time I opened my heart?*

Moving as if sleepwalking, Aaron went back into the house with his mind in turmoil. Was he ready to admit to himself ... to Jane that he'd fallen in love with her too?

When he stepped into the shower only a few minutes later, he was catapulted back to the erotic time he and Jane spent together in this very same space only the day before. In moments he felt his erection begin to grow. Never before had a woman affected him like Jane Barloc. He turned the cold water faucet on full blast and stood under the freezing stream as long as possible. Finally, he stepped out of the "wet room" and pulled the large, fluffy towel from the warmer. As he wrapped it around himself he thought, *Cold showers are completely overrated.*

After dressing in jeans, a casual shirt and sweater, he went into the kitchen. He caught himself looking around. He'd almost expected to hear a loud "meow" and feel a plump body rubbing against his legs. The room seemed empty without the oversized Garfield look alike begging for food and attention. Aaron looked toward the table in the breakfast nook. He couldn't force himself to even step foot into the space. The memory of sitting there with Jane was too strong. Even his morning cup of coffee seemed to have lost its flavor.

Moving into his office with the plan of working on his manuscript wasn't much better. As soon as he sat down behind his desk, he looked toward the chair where only yesterday Jane sat. She'd poured over the beginning chapters of his latest book and given him some insightful comments.

"Well, I'll certainly have some new observations and understanding to add to the section on relationships," he mumbled softly.

Doing his best to focus on being a positive resource to his readers helped him only slightly. He was finding it very difficult to forget about how much he missed having Jane with him. It was approaching noon, and he'd managed to work for a little over an hour. Researching how to best handle relationship challenges held his attention for a while, but visions of Jane kept distracting him as they appeared frequently in his mind.

He was surprised when his doorbell sounded. *"Who could that be?"* he wondered. Hopeful, but not really believing it was possible, he went to the door. There was only one person he wanted to see, and it certainly *wasn't* the person standing on his front steps. "Sharon? What in the world are you doing here?" he asked abruptly.

"Aren't you going to invite me in, handsome?" she asked as she walked past him through the open door. Looking around appreciatively she commented, "Nice place you have here, Aaron. A hell of a lot better than that dump we had when we were married."

"I didn't even know you were still in the area," he said, confused by her sudden appearance.

Just the Way You Are

"Are you kidding me? I've got for sale signs on houses all over Boulder County with my beautiful face proudly displayed on them. Yep, Sharon Demasi, Realtor Extraordinaire! That's me."

"What are you doing here, Sharon? We have absolutely nothing to say to each other."

"Oh come on, Aaron, you must miss me at least a *little bit*, don't you? We had a pretty good thing going there for a while, didn't we, honey?" she said in a low purr as she sidled up to him.

Moving away he replied flatly, "That was a very long time ago, Sharon. I'm sorry, but you're wasting your time."

"Maybe, maybe not. Give me five minutes. Just hear me out. Okay?"

Aaron didn't have the energy to fight. "Fine. Five minutes. After that I expect you to leave."

"You always were a sensible man." Sharon moved past him into the spacious living area running her finger across his jawline as she passed. She seated herself on the counter height stool next to the kitchen island. The already short skirt she was wearing rode up even higher on her thighs, but she made no move to adjust it. "You're a psychologist. All men have fantasies, right? You know, things they'd really *like* to do, but they're taboo or push the boundaries of social barriers a bit too far."

"I suppose."

Anita Louise

"Actually, I've done a little research. I'm prepared to give you the opportunity to live out the *one* fantasy most men will *never* get the chance to experience." When Aaron didn't respond, she continued. "You know I've always been a little more daring than the average female."

"Okay, so ...?"

"After you left for California ... well, let's just say things didn't work out for me and Lance." Aaron shrugged but didn't speak. "Anyway, I learned something about myself, something I think you'll find *very* interesting."

"Quite honestly, Sharon, I could care less what you learned about yourself. If you've got something to say, then just say it. Quit beating around the bush or leave. Either one's fine with me."

"Okay, here it is. I'm bisexual. I've already talked to my girlfriend Mia about you. You know the old saying, 'The only thing better than one woman is *two*.' A ménage à trois. You, me and Mia." Licking her lips she slid off the stool and walked slowly toward Aaron. "I'm getting wet just thinking about it." She slid her hands over her breasts and closed her eyes. "Ummmm. You can do me from behind while you watch me licking Mia. Or I can just watch and play with myself while you and Mia get it on. Oh, baby, I'd love to watch her suck you ..."

Just the Way You Are

"Enough!" Aaron shouted. Moving away from her and toward the door, his reply was directly to the point. "Whatever we had once is long over and will *never* happen again. Whatever you were thinking, you were wrong. And now *I think* it's time for you to go."

With that he opened the door and waited for her to exit.

Appearing unfazed, she replied, "Well, let me know if you change your mind." A business card appeared in her hand from out of nowhere. "And if you ever decide to put this place on the market, and you want to get it sold fast for top dollar, give me a call." She handed him her card. "Anything you need, Aaron, anything at all, just call me. Mia and I will be waiting." She looked at him seductively and winked as she walked out the door with her hips swaying to the max.

As soon as the door closed behind her, he tore her card in two and threw it in the trash.

Shaking his head and looking around, he spoke to the empty room, "What did I ever *see* in that woman?"

It was clear there was absolutely nothing about Sharon Demasi he found attractive. And what in the *world* made her even *dream* that he'd be the *least* bit interested in seeing her again ... let alone get involved with her? There must be something *wrong* with her thinking. But, in a way, seeing Sharon again was helping him a great deal. There was no way on God's green earth that Jane Barloc was *anything* like Sharon Demasi. Jane would never in a million years show up on his doorstep like that, especially after all this time and with such an outlandish proposition.

He thought of Jane's poise and beauty, her kindness and intelligence. He'd told himself he wanted someone who was open and honest. Yet when she'd shared her feelings with him he'd panicked and closed himself off. If he was truthful with himself, he'd have to admit he was utterly and completely in love with Jane. So much in love that even the *idea* of being with someone else was totally ludicrous.

Suddenly, he knew what he had to do. Aaron Adler was now a man with a mission. He threw on his coat, practically ran into the garage and backed the Jeep out almost before the door was completely open.

Jane thought about taking a mild sedative before going to bed, but seeing the early pregnancy test kit sitting on her bathroom counter changed her mind. It was still too soon to take the test with any degree of accuracy. But until she knew for sure, one way or the other, she'd do everything she could to take care of the potential unborn life inside her. Consequently, instead of a good night's sleep, it'd been a night of restlessness and dreams. She couldn't get Aaron

Just the Way You Are

out of her mind. Nor could she chase away the dream of laughing with joy while watching the happy little toddler with gray-green eyes run around the playground. Not wanting to face the day, she finally forced herself out of bed around ten o'clock in the morning.

Wandering into the kitchen, Henry immediately made his presence known. The feline was rubbing against her legs and making it clear with his loud "meow" that it was her duty to feed him without delay. Leaning over she stroked the soft fur and scratched his ears affectionately, and was rewarded with his rumbling "purr."

"I know, Henry. I miss him too." She spoke to the cat as if the animal totally understood. "Don't worry. Everything's going to be all right. I'm sure he misses us too," she said reassuringly. After his feeding, Henry retreated to his cat tower in front of the window to watch the birds. All the activity outside must have tired him because moments later his eyes were closed as he took a much deserved nap.

Jane smiled at her pet affectionately while she made herself some coffee and toasted a bagel. Taking her food to her kitchen table, she seated herself and closed her eyes. She pictured herself in the breakfast nook of Aaron's house. The Colorado mountains outside his window were covered with snow beneath the glorious blue sky. She could hear the sounds of her lover rattling around in the kitchen, doing whatever amateur cooks do when they're not preparing a meal. When she went to the store, she'd been sure to purchase the same brand of coffee Aaron served. Inhaling its aroma, each sip made her feel even closer to him.

Her visualization exercise gave her encouragement. After tidying up the kitchen, she went upstairs and took a quick shower. She washed her hair, dried and then brushed it to a lustrous shine. Next she dressed in a peach colored sweater and the skinny jeans she'd worn to Michael Adler's party. After carefully applying a small amount of makeup, she looked in the mirror approvingly.

"All set," she said aloud. *For what?* Oddly enough, she felt more at peace than she had since before she realized she and Aaron had, in the heat of their passion, forgotten to use protection. *No matter what happens, I'm going to be fine ... better than fine. I'm going to be happy and grateful. This past week with Aaron has been as close to perfect as anything I've ever experienced. And I'll always have that.*

Wandering into her spare bedroom/office, she smiled to herself as she ran her hand over her laptop computer. Only a few days earlier, Aaron sat here, in this very chair. His hands rested on this keyboard. His fingers typed the information to help her find the new vehicle now sitting in her assigned parking spot. Something kept trying to get her attention. She looked around, but Henry was nowhere to be seen. He was most likely still fast asleep on his cat tower in the window. Still, there was *something. What was it?*

As she gazed around the room, it suddenly hit her ... the bookshelf! She'd asked Aaron to autograph her copy of the first book he'd ever written, the bestseller that had brought him fame and fortune. She walked quickly across the room and took her well-worn copy off the shelf. *What did you write, Aaron?* Her hands were shaking. She needed to sit down. Holding the precious volume to her chest she moved quickly and descended the stairs. She sat in her favorite reading chair next to the sliding glass door overlooking the commons area. The book was in her lap. Somehow she just *knew* that whatever he'd written inside the front cover of this book was going to have a significant effect on the rest of her life.

She opened the book cover and instantly recognized his scrawling handwriting.

Dearest Jane,

How different my life is today after having met you such a short time ago. You're helping me break down the walls I've been hiding behind for so many years. Thank you for your patience and your love. You're teaching me how to love again.

Anita Louise

Sincerely,

Aaron

Thank you for your patience ... You're teaching me how to love again. She felt the tears moving slowly down her cheeks before she even realized she was crying.

I've made a terrible mistake. I never should have left. Oh why didn't I listen to Millie Worthton and accept his <u>actions</u> as proof of his love. Why did I feel the need to <u>push</u> him into expressing his feelings in words before he was ready? "Oh, Aaron, what have I done?" she said aloud.

She stood and held the book with Aaron's heartfelt inscription to her breast for a moment more. It wasn't too late. Carefully placing the book on the table next to her, she picked up her cell phone and dialed Aaron's number.

"Pick up, pick up, pick up!" she whispered almost desperately. But the phone just rang and rang until finally going to voicemail. "Aaron, it's me, Jane. I'm so sorry about this morning. Please. Call me. We need to talk." She paused before adding, "Aaron, I love you." She hung up the phone. *Where is he? What should I do? Should I go over there? Oh, Aaron, where are you?*

Chapter Twenty

Aaron knew he was driving faster than was probably wise, but he could hardly wait to get to Jane's house. He had to let her know. *I love you, Jane.* He wanted to shout it from the rooftops! Strangely enough, he was incredibly grateful to Sharon Demasi for showing up on his doorstep. Seeing her again made him realize Jane was *nothing* like his ex-wife. To compare the two would be like comparing a tiger to a house cat, a minnow to a whale, an angel to a ... well, not an angel. It was finally clear to him. Jane possessed every characteristic he was looking for in a lifetime companion, in a *wife,* in the mother of his children. He could hardly wait to get to Jane's house and tell her how very much he loved her.

He didn't care what caused her to be so upset this morning. Whatever it was, they'd work it out. The only thing that mattered was he loved her, and he *knew* she loved him. There was no longer even the *shadow* of a doubt in his mind.

He was happier than he'd ever been; ready to change his life for the better. Humming to himself and smiling broadly, he turned on the radio. Maybe he'd get lucky and they'd play that old Billy Joel tune that had somehow become "their song." When *Just the Way You Are* began playing only a few seconds later, he was singing joyfully at the top of his lungs. He picked up his ringing cell phone. It was his brother Michael.

"Hi, Mike. What's up?"

"You've got to get to the hospital right away," his brother said. There was an ominous tone to his voice.

"Hospital? Why? What's going on?"

It was devastating news. Aaron disconnected and immediately swung his car in the direction of Foothills Hospital.

Where is he? It'd been more than two hours since Jane's first call to Aaron's house. Since then she'd called both his home and cell phone over and over again. She'd left multiple messages on both, and he still hadn't called her back.

Jane paced the floor for several minutes, talking to herself, trying to figure out where Aaron could possibly be. Trying to figure out why he wasn't calling her back. She was trying to figure out the impossible.

Going back to her chair near the sliding glass door, she picked up Aaron's book once again. At first she simply held it to her breast, rocking back and forth while hugging the book as if some part of Aaron was inside. Finally, she opened it and reread the inscription.

"How different my life is today after having met you such a short time ago. You're helping me break down the walls I've been hiding behind for so many years. Thank you for your patience and your love. You're teaching me how to love again."

The tears were streaming down her cheeks.

Where are you, Aaron? I need to talk to you. I need to tell you how important you are to me. Our love is so new and fragile. We need time to nurture it and help it grow.

She was so grateful to read his words, telling her the walls he'd built around his heart were coming down. With time and love, she was sure he'd open up to her completely. Clutching the book to her chest, she climbed the stairs. She needed to rest as best as she could, but how could she possibly sleep until she found out why she hadn't yet heard from him?

It was after midnight when her phone rang. Since she'd been tossing and turning much more than sleeping, she immediately sat up and grabbed her cell phone. Thank God, it was Aaron.

"Aaron! Where are you? Are you all right? I've been trying to reach you for hours. What happened?"

"I'm sorry, Jane. I'm at the hospital."

"The hospital? Are you okay?"

"It's not me, it's Mom. She had a heart attack. Thank God, Dad got her to the hospital right away."

"Is she going to be all right?"

"We think so. I'm just now leaving the hospital. I should have called you sooner, but I had to turn my phone off and forgot to turn it back on until a few minutes ago. I called you as soon as I saw that you called several times. Jane, I'm really sorry ... about everything."

"Oh Aaron, there's nothing for you to be sorry about. I'm the one who should be apologizing. Besides, your Mom is most important now. You and I will talk. We'll work everything out. "

"I was on my way to see you," he said softly.

Her heart leapt. "You were?"

"Yes. In fact, I'd almost made it to your condo when I got the call from Michael that Mom was in the hospital. I was so worried about her I went straight there and ... well; I've pretty much told you the rest."

Just the Way You Are

"You were on your way to see me?" she repeated. "Really?"

"Jane, we do need to talk. There's a lot I want to tell you, but I don't want to do it over the phone. Would it be possible for you to meet me at the hospital tomorrow morning? I'd come to your house, but I really need to be there for Mom ... and Dad. He's a mess."

"Of course. Why don't I meet you in the cafeteria? Would nine o'clock be good?"

"Perfect. Nine would be perfect. Thanks for understanding, Jane. That's one of the things I love about you."

"It's no problem, Aaron. You just go home and get some rest. I'll meet you in the hospital cafeteria at nine tomorrow morning."

"Okay, you get some rest too. Sorry for calling so late. See you in the morning."

"I'll be there. Sweet dreams," she whispered gently before they hung up. *Did he just say what I think he said? 'That's one of the things I love about you'?* With that thought in her mind, she had her own "sweet dreams."

Jane was dressed and ready to go to the hospital by seven o'clock in the morning. She'd taken extra care with her make up to try and hide the dark circles under her eyes from lack of sleep. Of course, Henry demanded his breakfast and mandatory attention before retiring to his tower. Jane managed to down a light breakfast even though she didn't have much of an appetite.

By eight-thirty, she simply couldn't wait any longer. She thought of the last time she'd been at Foothills Hospital. She was the patient, and Aaron had taken time out of his day to be with her. He'd met her only a short time before. In fact, he barely even knew her. How kind he'd been. How considerate to open his home to her. She smiled as she thought about how sweet it was for Aaron to bring her cat Henry to his house.

It only took about ten minutes for her to get to the hospital. When she entered the lobby, she looked around to try and figure out where the cafeteria was located. Just then Jane felt a gentle hand on her shoulder. She looked at his name tag and then into the face of Dr. Zackary Carter who'd been her physician the previous week.

"Ms. Barloc? Didn't you have enough of this place last week? What's going on?"

"Oh Dr. Carter, you remember Aaron Adler, the man who was with me the whole time I was in the hospital, don't you?"

He smiled as he replied, "Of course I do. You two make a very memorable couple."

"Well, Aaron's mother was admitted yesterday. I'm supposed to meet him in the cafeteria, but I have no idea where it is. Would you please point me in the right direction?"

"Well, Ms. Barloc, I'll do better than that. Follow me."

Just the Way You Are

"Thank you so much, Dr. Carter. I appreciate the escort." She smiled as she fell into step next to him.

"You're very welcome, Ms. Barloc. I'm sorry to hear about Mr. Adler's mother. I'll stop by and check in with Mr. Adler myself later today after I finish my rounds. I know the staff will take good care of her." Once they reached their destination, he nodded politely and disappeared down the hallway.

When Jane entered the hospital cafeteria, she saw a table full of several members of the Adler family. Michael noticed her and waved her over to join them. It looked as if the entire family had very little sleep the night before.

"Aaron must have called you," Michael stated matter-of-factly.

"Yes, I'm supposed to meet him here at nine. As you can see, I'm a little early. He didn't mention you were all here, but I guess that's to be expected under the circumstances."

"We'll be taking shifts most of the day. Of course, everyone's concerned. Mom's the glue that holds this family together. It's funny, I always thought of Dad as being the strong one." He looked at Jane and shrugged. "But I think if it were him in the hospital instead of Mom, she'd be handling it a lot better than he is." In spite of the circumstances, the eldest Adler son chuckled a bit.

Brooke Adler scooted over to make room for Jane and gave her shoulders a sisterly squeeze as soon as she sat down.

"You okay, Brooke?" Jane asked solicitously.

"Yeah, I'm okay, just worried about Mom, like everyone else."

"She'll be fine." Jane comforted her friend. "Your mother's a strong woman. Look at what a great job she's done raising all of you. My guess is she's planning on being around to watch each and every one of her children learn what it's like to be a parent. As I recall, she was pretty adamant about you kids making her a proud grandmother. She's not going anywhere until you've done your job in that regard."

Brooke managed a small grin. "That's true. Mom's got a real stubborn streak. When she wants something, you can pretty much bet on her getting it. Thanks, Jane. I needed that."

Now it was Brooke's turn to return the hug. The two women held on to each other as if drawing strength. They'd quickly bonded when they first met. It seemed they had lots in common ... bicycling, mini-vans and not-yet-born children. The bond they'd formed was being strengthened and deepened through this adversity.

Jane sat quietly in their midst and listened as the family swapped stories about their mother. There were plenty of smiles and lots of laughter. It was clear this was a loving and congenial

Just the Way You Are

group. Although she didn't contribute too much, Jane felt accepted as part of the collection of people with shared concern for a loved one.

When Aaron entered the room, Jane got up from her seat next to Brooke and went to his side. She stood silently and held his hand as he acknowledged each of his family members and listened as they shared the latest information on their mother's status.

A short time later, John Adler walked into the cafeteria. Immediately everyone stopped talking and looked at him expectantly. Closely regarding each of his children he said, "The doctor says she's holding her own. Right now what your mother really needs is lots of rest. If you children want to stay, it's up to you. I was thinking we could make some sort of a schedule. Of course, I want to be with your mother as much as possible."

It took a little while, but the Adler family came up with a plan that would allow all the family members to visit with Juliette throughout the day. It also gave John time to grab a bite to eat or consult with his business associates and clients when necessary.

In spite of the circumstances, Jane was enjoying continuing to get to know everyone in the family better. She especially looked forward to the times when she had the opportunity to visit with Brooke, who'd become a dear friend.

Anita Louise

Later that afternoon, Juliette's doctor gave the family good news. The Adler matriarch would be able to go home soon. Tests showed there was very little damage to her heart, and she was recovering even faster than expected. Jane joined the family members who were present at the hospital as they hugged each other vigorously and jumped up and down in joyous celebration.

Chapter Twenty-One

I t was a good thing Juliette Adler had a private room, because Aaron and other members of the Adler family were in and out of her room on a regular basis. Tables and window sills were filled with flowers and cards. Colorful balloons wishing "Speedy Recovery" and "Get Well Soon" floated jauntily in the air. It was also clear to everyone that Aaron and Jane's relationship was more than just a fling. She was right by Aaron's side the whole time.

Juliette seemed to improve almost by the hour, steadily growing stronger and more alert. When first admitted, she'd slept most of the day. But only a couple of days later, Aaron noticed his mother remained awake for longer periods of time. Today the nurse helped her to stand next to her bed for a few moments before carefully assisting her to a chair near the window where she sat for a few hours. The next step would be for Juliette to go to the rehabilitation unit where physical therapists would work with her to regain her strength. All in all, it was anticipated she'd be ready to go home by the end of the week.

Jane was sitting next to Aaron when he learned his mother would soon be released from the hospital. She could almost feel the positive shift in his energy after hearing the good news. When Aaron sighed with relief, Jane reached out and took his hand in hers.

"It's wonderful, isn't it? She's going to be just fine. How about you? Anything you need?" she asked solicitously.

He squeezed her hands and looked directly into her eyes. "I need you to move back in with me. I know we agreed Mom's health was most important, but it's driving me crazy not having you in my bed."

"You know I want that too. It's not only your mother's health I'm concerned about, it's yours as well. You're stressed enough with worry, and as much as you hate to admit it, getting the rest you need is important. We both know the amount of sleep we'll get will be greatly reduced as soon as we're in the same bed."

"You're right about that," he said looking at her lasciviously. His demeanor quickly changed to one of regret. "I just wish I wouldn't have been so stupid in the first place. Then you never would've left. You know last Sunday when

Just the Way You Are

they admitted Mom to the hospital I was on my way to see you. Jane, I'm so sorry about messing things up with us. I wanted to apologize and ask you to come back."

She shook her head. "There's nothing you need to apologize for, Aaron. If anything, I'm the one who should be saying I'm sorry. You probably heard the message I left on your phone. I tried calling your mobile phone too, but I didn't want to look like a stalker by leaving message after message everywhere. The whole thing was all my fault. I'm the one who should be apologizing, not you."

"Jane," he said, "I know this isn't the best setting, but I have to let you know why I was on my way to see you on Sunday." It looked to him as if she was holding her breath. He knew for sure she continued to hold his hands and his heart. "I love you, Jane Barloc. I love you and I want you back home with me, where you belong. I love you, Jane, and I want you to marry me. I don't have a ring, but I want to get one for you as soon as possible. You can have whatever you want. I don't care what it costs. You're worth more to me than anything money can buy. Please Jane, come home ... marry me."

Jane was crying and laughing at the same time. "Yes, yes! Of course, I'll marry you, Aaron. I never imagined I'd be proposed to in a *hospital*, but it'll certainly be a great story to tell our children and grandchildren, won't it? You do want children, don't you?"

"Absolutely! I'm not sure if you want to have as many as Mom did, but we can have as many or as few as you like." Her hands stilled and she lowered her head. "Is something wrong?" he asked.

"No. Nothing's wrong," she whispered. "I'd like to tell you why I was so upset on Saturday morning."

"Okay." He nodded and waited for her to continue.

"You remember what happened after we got home from Michael's party, don't you?"

In spite of his concern about his mother, he could feel the sexual energy begin to move through his body from only the *mention* of their love making that evening. "Jane, that night with you was the most incredible experience of my life. That was when I realized I'd fallen head over heels in love with you."

Her head jerked up suddenly. She looked more shocked now than she had only a few minutes earlier when he'd told her he loved her for the first time. "You realized you'd fallen in love with me that night? But, when I asked you if we were a couple, you ... you ..."

He interrupted. "I was a fool. I was scared. Admitting to myself that I loved you threw me for a loop. All of a sudden it was like I was right back to where I was when I got divorced. That's why I

Just the Way You Are

acted like such a jerk on Saturday morning. And then, the strangest thing happened. On Sunday, my ex shows up. Right on my doorstep."

"Really? Your ex-wife came to your *house?*"

"Yep. She had some hair-brained idea. It's too bizarre to even repeat. Somehow she seemed to think I might be interested in getting back together with her ... *NOT!*" He shook his head, rolled his eyes and shrugged. "Pretty unbelievable, huh? Anyway, I'd been thinking about you and then when I saw Sharon ... well, it was *obvious* there wasn't a single thing you have in common with my ex-wife. Seeing her made me realize that comparing what you and I have with anything or anyone else was just impossible."

"Sharon? Your ex-wife's name is Sharon?"

"Yes, it is. Why?"

"Does she happen to be a realtor?"

He looked at Jane incredulously. "How did you know that?" Jane shook her head and laughed softly. "Jane? What's going on?"

"I met her."

"You met her? What are you talking about?"

"Sharon Demasi, Realtor Extraordinaire. Right?"

He stared at Jane curiously. "How did you know?"

"The gym. She started talking to me at the gym. There's no way she'd know about you and me, is there? It seemed like she was pumping me for information. I don't know. Anyway, I got away from her as fast as I could." Jane reached out to him. Looking directly into his eyes and placing her hands over his, she said, "Aaron, I had no idea she was your ex-wife until just now. Quite honestly, she's nothing like I would've imagined your ex to be."

He relaxed and let out the breath he hadn't even realized he was holding. "I can understand that. After seeing her again, it's hard for *me* to believe I was once married to her."

Jane chuckled. "It's funny, isn't it? If I hadn't accidentally met and talked with your ex, maybe she wouldn't have shown up on your doorstep. And if she hadn't shown up on your doorstep, who knows how long it might've taken us to get back together. Even though I was going to call you, you might not have been ready to hear me if it hadn't been for Sharon. It really is quite extraordinary."

"Humph! I never thought I'd be saying 'thank you' to my ex-wife for *anything*, but ..." He tilted his head thoughtfully, "This doesn't mean we have to invite her to the wedding, does it?"

They both laughed uproariously.

Just the Way You Are

"I can't wait till Mom gets out of here so we can get back to normal," Aaron complained. The rest of Juliette Adler's hospital stay had been filled with physical therapy, tests, and doctors followed by more physical therapy, more doctors, and even more tests.

"It won't be long now." Jane grinned. "Her heart specialist Dr. Schaefer said everything looks good for her release tomorrow. I'm sure *both* your Mom and Dad are ready to get back home. You're not going to miss this place too much, are you?"

"Not in the least. With everything that's been going on with Mom, getting you moved back into my place ... I mean, *our place,* has gotten pushed to the back burner. Finally, having you back in my bed, sleeping next to me will give me the best night's rest I've had in over a week. How're you coming on getting your clothes and stuff back home?"

"Pretty good. I've been moving a few things at a time while you've been at the hospital with your mom. Almost everything's there except a few things in storage and my day-to-day items ... and Henry, of course. You were so preoccupied with what's been going on with your mother, it just seemed like a better idea for me to stay at the condo until Juliette was back home and things settled down."

"I know," he grumbled, "but Mom's getting out of here tomorrow, so let's stop by your place after we leave the hospital. We can pick up Henry and whatever else you need. Plus I want to go shopping for your ring as soon as possible. I know you didn't want to share the news of our engagement until we were sure Mom was going to be okay. But I'm lousy at keeping secrets from my family. Besides, I think they've all got a pretty good idea of what's coming anyway."

Jane smiled and nodded her agreement. She was ready to go shopping for her ring and announce their engagement as much or more than Aaron.

A few hours later, Aaron kissed his mother on the cheek as was his habit before leaving. "I'll see you tomorrow, Mom. Just let me know if there's anything you need me to do."

"Aaron, you've done *more* than enough," Juliette said, "all you children have, and you too, Jane. I almost feel as if you're part of the family now." There was a twinkle in her eye.

"Thank you so much, Julie," Jane replied. "You've done such a great job of raising this beautiful family of yours. It would certainly be my pleasure to be part of it." She looked from Aaron to his mother as she spoke.

Winking conspiratorially, Aaron whispered, "I promised I wouldn't tell yet, Mom, but I think you're going to like the news Jane and I are going to share with you all ... soon."

"I'm sure I will, son. I'm absolutely certain I will."

Just the Way You Are

"Okay. Do you want to meet me at the condo and pick up Henry?" Jane asked. "I think we can fit him and most of the things I have left in my van ... unless you want to go home. If I can't fit everything I need right now in my car, I can always come back and get the rest later."

"Uh-uh. No way. There's no need for you to make two trips. Your condo's right on the way. I'll follow you in the Jeep. Let's get that big, old ball of fur and go home," Aaron said emphatically.

A few minutes later they pulled up in front of her unit. Jane quickly hopped out of her van and called to him as she looked back over her shoulder. "I'll get the door opened and you can come on in and give me a hand," she said.

"I'm right behind you. Besides that I need to use the restroom. I should have done it before we left the hospital. But I was so ready to get out of there, I didn't want to take the time."

Leaving his vehicle at the curb, they walked hand in hand to her front door. Henry greeted them both with a loud "meow" and proceeded to rub himself against Aaron's legs. When Aaron reached down to scratch the cat's ears, Henry's "meow" turned to a "purr."

Jane was busy emptying the pet food dishes and stowing everything into bags while Aaron made his way to her half bath on the first floor. He looked around the bathroom aimlessly while doing what he needed to do. His eyes lit on a purple box lying next to the sink with the letters "**e.p.t.**" on the front. Taking a little closer look as he washed his hands, he read the words, "Early Pregnancy Test."

"Early Pregnancy Test?" Aaron zipped up and grabbed the box. He was moving faster than he'd moved since before his mother was admitted to the hospital. "Jane?" He called her name anxiously when he got back in the main living area. "What's this?"

She turned from what she was doing and looked at the box he was holding up. The room was silent for several seconds. A blush covered her face.

"I, uh, started to tell you about that the other day, but I got distracted and then totally forgot. It was when you first told me you realized you were falling in love with me. Remember? Then you *asked me to* _marry_ you! After that there was that whole thing about your ex showing up at your house. Somehow that little box you're holding in your hands got lost in the shuffle."

She stood there, apparently waiting to see what he was going to do or say next.

"You think you might be *pregnant? How? When?"*

"After Michael's party. We were so wrapped up in each other that neither of us remembered to use protection."

He took a moment to think back to that amazing night and realized she was right. "Wow," he said quietly. "So that Saturday morning when

Just the Way You Are

you were so upset. You were thinking it was possible you might've gotten pregnant because we'd forgotten to use a condom. Right?" She didn't say a word ... just nodded her head affirmatively and continued to stare at him. "Are you? Are you pregnant?"

"I don't know," she whispered. "I haven't done the test yet."

He walked slowly and deliberately to her. "Do the test, Jane. Do the test and tell me it's positive. Make me the happiest man in the world, and tell me that *we're* going to have a baby." He pulled her into his arms and hugged her as tightly as he possibly could. Then looked steadily into her eyes as he held her at arm's length and repeated. "Do the test, Jane."

Her hand shook slightly as she took the box from him. "Okay. Here goes." She stopped and turned to look at him before she went into the bathroom. "Aaron, I'm glad I waited. I'm glad you're here with me for this."

He smiled and said, "Me too. Now hurry up ... go." Using hand motions, he shooed her away. He found himself pacing back and forth in her kitchen while she was gone. Time seemed to have stopped. *"A father ... me. I could be a father!"* Pictures formed in his head ... pictures of him as a young boy playing catch with his dad ... pictures of him in the future, playing catch with his own son.

Anita Louise

When Jane finally walked back into the room he looked at her expectantly. She had a funny, sad look on her face. She shook her head and said, "No. It says I'm not."

"Are you okay?" he asked as they walked toward one another.

"I'm fine. It's just ... all this drama over nothing. I mean, my concern over the possibility of being pregnant is what started our quarrel. If that hadn't happened, all this moving out and moving back in stuff might never have happened." By this time she'd gotten herself so upset that tears were streaming down her cheeks.

He put his arms around her once more. "Jane, honey, it's all right. Everything happened just the way it was supposed to. Haven't you ever heard the quote from the Desiderata? 'No doubt the Universe is unfolding as it should.'"

Jane looked at him through her tears and managed to choke out, "Oh, Aaron, I can't believe you just *said* that. When I was growing up, anytime something happened that we couldn't understand, my Mom would quote that exact same line. If I didn't know it before, I *definitely* know now that you and I were *absolutely* _meant_ to be together. I love you so, so, so, so much."

Chapter Twenty-Two

By the time they got back to Aaron's house and got the car unloaded, they were both exhausted. There'd been more left to move than she thought. As it turned out, they had to make multiple trips to bring in everything from her condo. And, of course, there was Henry and all of his paraphernalia.

It was amazing how much the stress and worry of his mother's heart attack seemed to have worn Aaron out. He was sitting on the couch, almost zombie-like, just staring at the mountains in the distance.

She smiled as she walked over to him and touched his shoulder gently. "Aaron, sweetie? I'm a little tired. Would it be all right with you if we took a nap?"

Looking at her drowsily, he smiled and replied, "I think I was almost there already, but the bed sounds like it would be a bit more comfortable. Let's go." He got up, took her hand and led her to the master suite.

"I remember when you were here before. Even though I cleared space for you in the dresser, you didn't use it. Hopefully, that's not the case now. Right?" he asked.

She squeezed his hand. "Now that I'm moving *all* my things here, I think there might not be *enough* space. In addition to everything we brought over today, there're still a few things in the storage unit back at the condo."

"Not to worry. If need be, we'll buy new furniture. We'll do whatever it takes to accommodate you and make sure you're comfortable in your new home ... *our* home. We can make any changes you'd like. We can even get a different house, if you'd prefer. Although, you *are* the only woman, other than family, who's been here as my personally invited female guest."

"Aaron, I love your home ... our home," she said sincerely. "I didn't know I was the only woman you've ever had here. But now that I do, it makes me feel like you were just waiting for me."

"I think I *was*," he said thoughtfully. "Even though I didn't really know it ... I think I was."

After removing the bed cover and carefully folding back the sheets, they removed their shoes and laid down to rest. In moments Jane heard him snoring softly.

Just the Way You Are

I never thought I'd be so grateful to hear a man snoring, she thought sleepily.

Aaron was still sound asleep when Jane woke up less than an hour later. Feeling reinvigorated, she got up quietly. She didn't want to disturb him and wanted him to rest as long as he needed to. Since Aaron was out like a light, she decided to go online and do a little "research" on engagement rings and wedding sets. This was a totally new experience to her. The whole idea of getting engaged and planning a wedding was incredibly exciting.

She sat in the comfortable reading chair next to the window. Soon she was lost in page after page of wedding rings, men's wedding bands, wedding gowns and tips on planning the perfect wedding. Her research had her so engrossed, she didn't even hear Aaron walk into the room.

"Jane?"

"Oh, hi, Aaron," she acknowledged him, but was still mesmerized by all things wedding on the computer.

"Jane, look at me," he said. His intensity immediately captured her attention. She tilted her head up and locked her gaze with his. Just looking into his eyes made her heartbeat quicken, and she felt the stirrings of desire. "I love you,

Anita Louise

Jane. I love you with all my heart," he said passionately.

"And I love you too, Aaron. More than you could possibly know." Without hesitation, she put her computer aside and walked to where he stood.

Their lips met. The room was warm, yet she shivered when she felt his fingers entangle in her hair. He kissed her—long and slow, making her want him more with each passing second. She opened her mouth and was delighted when he moved his tongue sensuously across her lips. He then gently nibbled her lower lip before plundering her mouth with his tongue. She felt his hand move from her hip to her behind. Pulling her even closer, the hardness of his erection made her tingle with desire.

"Do you remember the first night you stayed here, my beautiful Jane?"

"Yes," she managed to respond.

"There's something I've been wanting to do ever since I saw you in the tub that first night. Take a bath with me. Let me bathe you." His hands moved softly, yet purposefully up and down the length of her back and lower torso as he spoke.

"Yes, oh yes, now ... please."

"Soon. First, I want you to strip for me. Remember, I've had a lot on my mind lately," he said with a wicked grin. "I need you to entice me." She started to move toward the bedroom, but he

Just the Way You Are

held her hand and stopped her. "Not in there. Here." He sat down in the chair she'd recently vacated.

"Here?" She looked through the open windows toward the mountains. "But, the windows."

"Yes, a nice view, don't you think?" he replied innocently.

"But there are no drapes. Someone could see me."

"I suppose that's possible, but there're no homes behind us. It's not really very likely that anyone will see you, is it? Haven't you ever wanted to live just a little dangerously ... to do something a little *naughty* ... something that maybe you *shouldn't* be doing, but makes you feel all quivery when you think about doing it?"

"Give me your feet," he ordered. She sat on the ottoman and put her foot between his legs, and he slowly removed her shoe and stocking. Ever so softly, he used his thumb and fingers to gently massage her heel, the ball of her foot and her toes. Then he pressed her foot firmly against his erection. Without direction she moved her foot up and down the rigid outline. "Now the other foot," he said. Once again he removed her foot coverings and performed an erotic foot massage. She then returned the favor and massaged his throbbing member once again with her foot. Next he pushed her foot to the floor and reached out to touch her breasts as he spoke, "Doesn't the idea

Anita Louise

of standing in front of this window, taking your clothes off for me, turn you on ... even just a little?"

He reached to tease the nipple of her breast to a hard peak with one hand. With his other hand he stroked her inner thighs, stopping just short of the vee between her legs. She could feel the tingle and the wetness begin to accumulate in that very spot. She blinked and swallowed. Closing her eyes she leaned her head back and sighed, "Ummmm."

"Here, let me help you," he said softly. Moving his hand from her thighs, he began to unbutton her blouse. He nuzzled her neck as he opened each button, running his tongue along her sensitive jawline. The words he murmured were indecipherable. She was mesmerized as she watched his hands open her shirt and caress her skin with his fingertips.

When all the buttons were undone, he pushed the lace down from the top of her bra to expose her breasts. Then he lowered his head and suckled her breast while teasing her thighs with his fingers once more.

"Ahhh, that feels good," she whispered.

Nudging her slightly, he said once again, "Strip for me, Jane. I want to see you naked. Right here ... please." He began to push her blouse from her shoulders. "Please?" She felt almost as if she were in a trance. Standing in front of him and the drapeless window, she shrugged out of her shirt. "Yes, that's it. Now your slacks, Jane. Let me see your beautiful legs."

Looking directly into his eyes she reached for the waistband of her slacks and undid the clasp and zipper. She let them fall to the floor and stepped out of them. "Like this?" she asked. Now she was clad in only her lacy bra and bikini panties. He reached out and traced the edge of her panties.

"Spread your legs for me, Jane." When she did, he rubbed his hand between her thighs over the damp cloth. She was trembling with desire and need. Then he slipped his finger beneath the thin fabric and felt her slick arousal. "Beautiful, oh so very beautiful," he murmured as he slipped two fingers in and out multiple times before stopping. "Now, Jane, let me see you naked."

She was at his mercy. "All right," she said and did as he asked. First she removed her bra, letting it drop to the floor. As she stood before him, she locked her eyes with his as she caressed her own breasts. Then she twisted and teased her nipples before moving to shimmy out of her panties.

"Perfect. You are absolutely perfect. Come here, Jane. Stand right here in front of me."

As she moved forward, he grasped her hips. She almost screamed with the intense pleasure she felt when he plunged his tongue

Anita Louise

between her legs. Standing naked in the living room, in front of the window with his tongue laving her most private parts almost caused her legs to collapse beneath her. She held on to his shoulders and moaned with pleasure. "Oh Aaron, that feels so incredibly good."

"And you *taste* so incredibly good," he replied between licks. He spread her lower lips, and suckled the edges returning his tongue to her sensitive nub. "Come for me, Jane. I want to make you come with my mouth."

"Oh my God, Aaron. I don't know if I can ... standing up ... in front of the window like this."

"Of course you can, my darling. Don't think about the window, just think about how good it feels to have my tongue between your legs." He inserted two fingers into her as he spoke. "How does that feel?" he asked. He pumped his fingers in and out as he returned his tongue to her most sensitive spot.

Her hips were moving rhythmically with the motion of his fingers. Her eyes were closed as her head fell back. She moved one of her hands to her breast, keeping the other on his shoulder for balance. "That feels sooo good. So very, very good." Her eyes flew open and she moaned in ecstasy, "Oh God! I'm coming. Yes, yes, that's it. Yes!" Her legs gave way and she collapsed on the ottoman with her inner muscles clenching his fingers.

Just the Way You Are

Jane felt Aaron move his hand and place his arm beneath her legs. "Put your arm around me, sweetheart," he whispered as he lifted her from the ottoman. She did as he asked and curled herself comfortably against his chest. He held her like a baby, kissing and nuzzling her neck as he carried her into the bedroom. Laying her across the bed, he then covered her with a soft throw. "Don't go falling asleep on me. I'm going to run a bath for us. I'll be right back."

She heard him turn on the water in the other room, and luxuriated in the glow of her recent pleasure. Life with Aaron would never be dull. Never would she have dreamed she could stand naked in front of a window and experience the kind of orgasm she just had.

A few minutes later Aaron walked back into the bedroom. Opening her eyes sleepily, she saw he'd removed his clothes. He could have been a model ... his body was so close to perfect. His shoulders were broad and his chest rippled with muscle that tapered down to his narrow waist. He looked into her eyes as he stroked his magnificent erection.

Just looking at him caused Jane's lethargy to leave her immediately. She threw off the cover from her body and walked purposefully toward him, watching his hand move slowly up and down his shaft.

"Let me help," she said as she knelt before him and replaced his hand with both of her own. She guided the tip of his member to her lips and licked the tip while continuing her firm and rhythmic stroke. "Now it's my turn," she whispered before taking him into her mouth fully.

"Ahhhh, yes. That's wonderful, Jane. I love seeing your mouth on me." He carefully lifted her hair away from her face and held it in his hand as he moved his hips in time with her motions.

Taking him from her mouth, she moved one hand to the tender sacs between his legs. Licking up and down his shaft with her tongue, she gently caressed and massaged with one hand while teasing his tip with her finger and thumb. When her tongue reached the base of his shaft she lowered her head and gently licked and then sucked one of his sacs into her mouth. She used her hand to continue the firm strokes up and down, up and down.

He moaned and she felt his knees give slightly.

"Ummm," she hummed as she continued to lick and suck. Moving her mouth back to his rigid shaft, once again she took him into her mouth. "Ummm." She knew the vibration of the sound added to his pleasure as he tightened his grip on her hair and pushed himself deeper into her mouth. Stopping only for a moment, she looked up at him and said, "Now *you're* going to see what it's like to come standing up."

Just the Way You Are

"Oh my God, Jane. What you do to me." It seemed like he could barely manage to speak as he watched his shaft move in and out of her mouth. "Yes, baby, yes. That's it. Oh yes, that feels so good." He moved his hips in time with her ministrations.

She pulled away slightly and licked the tip, dipping her tongue in the little cleft that was oozing slightly before taking him fully into her mouth again. Caressing his sac and stroking his shaft she continued to slide her lips and tongue up and down, again and again.

He roared her name as he exploded into her mouth. She swallowed and licked and swallowed some more. "Ummm," she moaned her delight as she continued to move his softening member in and out of her mouth. He stroked her cheek as she looked up with a satisfied grin. "How was that?" she asked.

"The best. The very best ever. I love you, Jane." He pulled her up to his chest and covered her mouth with his before saying, "Come on, now. The water's getting cold."

They moved languidly into the master bath and stepped into the oversized Jacuzzi. The size easily accommodated them both, and the faucet was positioned in such a way that they could lie back comfortably at opposite ends. Aaron had turned the jets on to a moderate speed that circulated the warm water pleasantly around them.

Anita Louise

"This is nice," Jane said softly while enjoying the jets massaging her back. She played with the water shooting out near her hand and ran her foot up and down Aaron's leg. "I could get used to this."

"Please do, my darling. This is the first of many Jacuzzis we're going to enjoy together. I want you to get used to being relaxed and happy. I'm going to do my best to make sure that's how you live the rest of your life ... relaxed and happy ... with me."

"I am happy, Aaron. Happier than I've ever been."

"You know, my original plan was to seduce you here in the tub."

"That sounds delightful. Right now, however, I'm thoroughly enjoying just lying here with you. If your libido flares up again, let me know. You obviously have what it takes to get me to do things I never dreamed I would ever do, so you could probably get me going again without a heck of a lot of effort."

"Hmmm," he mused as he too enjoyed the soothing massage of the water. "Maybe we'll take a raincheck on the tub seduction for now. How would you feel about going out and doing a little ring shopping after we get dried off and dressed."

Jane sat up so quickly that water splashed over the side of the tub and onto the floor. "Yes! Goodie, goodie, goodie. Yes, let's go ring shopping."

Just the Way You Are

Aaron grinned at her childish exuberance.

Sliding around to his end of the tub, she straddled him and put her arms around his neck. "Definite rain check on the Jacuzzi seduction, but now we've got to get out of this tub and get dressed. You, my handsome hunk, are going to take me ring shopping. I want to tell *everyone* I'm engaged and show off the gorgeous ring you're going to buy me." Standing up, she tugged on his arms. "Let's go. Let's go. Let's go!"

Chapter Twenty-Three

"Where are we going?" Jane asked once they were seated in Aaron's Jeep.

"Phillip got Rachel's rings at A.L. Brighton Designs on Pearl Street. They do great work and it's said to be one of the best places to get something beautiful and unique ... just like you. Besides, I want to make sure you'll be happy with your wedding set for at *least* the next fifty plus years."

Jane was beaming from ear to ear. "That sounds wonderful, Aaron. I'm not sure which part I like better, the beautiful and unique wedding rings or the fifty plus years. "

"I love you, Jane. You know, Mom's heart attack got me thinking. As much as I'm excited to move to the next phase of our relationship, I want to savor every moment along the way. To me, this is one of those 'red letter' days ... one for the memory books."

"I agree, this is a very special day, and we want to enjoy every minute of it. I also want to remember it as clearly as possible. This is the first day of the rest of our lives together, Aaron. I'm going to start documenting as much as I can. That way when we're old and gray, we can look back and remember all the details of the fifty plus years we'll have had together."

When they were in front of the jewelry store Aaron had chosen, Jane took a picture of Aaron standing in front with the store name in the background. They were trading places when a passerby noticed the happy couple taking pictures. Once the kind stranger snapped a few shots of the pair together, he handed Jane's phone back to her. The man was whistling cheerfully as he strolled down the sidewalk.

"You have a way of making people happy," Aaron said with a smile. "Not only do you have your first photo of our journey through life together, you've made my day and someone else's a little better too."

"Life's meant to be fun. I'm sooo happy right now, and happiness is contagious. I'm going to remember this day forever," Jane said with a sigh. "Now, my handsome husband-to-be, let's make some more memories."

Hand in hand they entered the jewelry store. Although he hadn't made an appointment, it wasn't crowded and they were given almost immediate attention.

"Think of it this way," the jeweler explained. "Once you're married, these rings will very likely be the only thing you'll both wear every day. You want to choose something you'll be comfortable wearing for the rest of your lives." He went on to explain the four C's: color, cut, clarity and carat. The budget Aaron set was very generous. Therefore, Jane was able to make her selection based on preference rather than price.

They took their time discussing what it was they were looking for and perusing several different settings. Ultimately, Jane settled on a flawless two carat oval diamond set in platinum with a vintage design. The diamonds on the wedding band were perfectly sized to complement the gorgeous engagement ring. Aaron chose a simple, eight millimeter platinum wedding band with a curved interior face for comfort.

"Oh, Aaron, it's sooo beautiful," she said as she admired what was soon to become her engagement ring.

"Not as beautiful as the woman wearing it," he responded sincerely.

"Thank you, darling, for the compliment and for the ring. I love you so, so much." She squeezed his hand lovingly and kissed him on the cheek.

Just the Way You Are

"How soon can we pick it up?" Aaron asked.

The jeweler responded, "Both the wedding and the engagement ring will be ready next week."

Aaron frowned. "Is there any way you can get it done sooner?"

Jane gave his knee another squeeze as if to say, *it's all right. I can wait until next week.* Understanding her message, Aaron said, "If, by any chance, you have the ring ready sooner, please give me a call. I'll come right over and pick it up."

Jane handed her cell phone to the proprietor. He was happy to grant her request, and took their picture while she once more admired the ring. That picture was followed by one of Aaron and Jane together, exchanging a loving embrace.

The next couple of days passed by quickly. Jane was excited to return to the jewelry store the next week so she could pick up and start wearing her engagement ring. However, she didn't want to appear too anxious, so she did her best to put it out of her mind.

She and Aaron settled into a comfortable routine. After breakfast together, she'd leave for her job at the college and her counseling appointments. Typically, they wouldn't see each

Anita Louise

other until she returned at the end of the day, although they spoke often on the phone. Sometimes she'd pick up something for dinner on her way home, but it wasn't unusual for her to walk into the aroma of something delicious simmering in the kitchen. Calling out the sing-song words, "Honey, I'm home," when she walked through the door always put a smile on her face. Sniffing the air brought no evidence of a home cooked meal today, however.

"Hi, sweetie pie," he said as he greeted her at the door with a welcome home kiss. Aaron was dressed nicely in slacks and a sweater as opposed to the jeans or sweats he usually wore. He'd gotten into the habit of helping her off with her coat and hanging it up for her at the end of her work day, and did so once again.

After exchanging her heels for the comfortable slippers she kept by the door, she went to the coffee maker where a fresh brewed pot stood waiting. Preparing a cup for both of them, she carried the beverages to the table where Aaron sat waiting.

"So how was your day? Anything special going on?" she asked after taking a sip.

"Not much today. I didn't feel like cooking so I thought we'd go out to dinner. Okay?"

"Sure. I'll freshen up after we relax with our coffee for a while. Do you have any place in mind?"

Just the Way You Are

"I thought we'd go to the Black Cat. Have you ever been there before?"

"Oh, that sounds nice," she exclaimed. "No, I haven't had the chance to dine there yet, but I've been wanting to. I heard the food's great ... all organic too."

"I think you'll like it. No rush, but whenever you're ready, we can get going."

They sat and chatted over their coffee, exchanging anecdotes about what happened during the day. After finishing her beverage, Jane changed from her business clothes into a teal sweater and gypsy print skirt. She washed her face, put on fresh make-up and brushed her golden hair to a glossy shine.

"Do I look all right?" she asked as she twirled around.

Aaron looked at her appreciatively. "You always look good, but you look especially gorgeous this evening, Miss Barloc."

"Why, thank you, Mr. Adler. I'm glad you approve. Ready?"

Aaron seemed a little jittery on the way to the restaurant, but Jane figured it was a case of "cabin fever." He'd been working diligently on his book ever since she'd moved in with him. They hadn't been out to eat since before his mother was released from the hospital.

"Do you want me to drop you off in front of the restaurant while I go find a parking spot?" he asked.

"No, but thanks for asking. It's really a beautiful evening, and I'll enjoy walking with you. Hopefully, we'll find something relatively close."

They were fortunate and found a spot less than a block away from the entrance to the Black Cat. Aaron had evidently made reservations as they were shown to a table as soon as he gave the hostess his name. He selected the tasting menu for them with premium wine pairings. The meal took over two hours, yet the time seemed to pass quickly due to the delicious food and outstanding wines. Jane had never before experienced such attentive service, and the creative dishes along with the superb wines made for a true culinary experience.

"Aaron, thank you so much. This place is remarkable. I'm so glad you chose to bring me here. It's almost too nice for just an ordinary evening," she sighed. Once again, Aaron appeared to be ... nervous? Why in the world would he be nervous?

"I got a little something special for you, Jane." He handed her a beautifully wrapped package.

"This is a surprise. Thank you." Taking the gift from his hands, she removed the bow before carefully unwrapping the unexpected present. It was a book of love poems. "How lovely, Aaron. You're so sweet." Jane opened the cover and perused the table of contents. Rumi, John Keats,

Just the Way You Are

Shakespeare, and Elizabeth Barrett Browning were among the authors.

"Would you mind reading one to me?" he asked. "I think you'll especially like the one on page ninety-five."

"Of course." Her pleasant smile turned to a cry of joy. Aaron had carved a small square through the back pages of the book just big enough for the engagement ring she'd chosen to fit.

He quickly moved out of his seat and took the ring from the book. The next thing she knew he was on one knee in front of her. "Jane Barloc, I love you. Will you marry me?"

"Yes! Absolutely yes, I'll marry you, Aaron Adler." She almost tipped over the table trying to get to him.

He slid the ring on her finger, and she gave him the biggest and best hug and kiss he'd ever had.

As they stood and embraced, everyone in the restaurant smiled and applauded. Jane barely noticed the flashes of cell phones and cameras snapping pictures of their special moment.

Epilogue

Brooke Adler was absolutely thrilled to learn her brother Aaron would be marrying Jane Barloc. He was only a couple of years younger than Brooke, and she and Aaron had always been close. As children he was the only one who'd been willing to "play school" with her at a very young age. Aaron was only about three years old when he became the first "student" in Brooke's pretend classroom.

The first time Brooke and Jane met they'd hit it off. The two women were at an impromptu party thrown by Michael, one of Brooke's older brothers. Jane's interest in bicycling prompted her to ask Brooke for advice. An avid bicyclist, Brooke was happy to chat with Jane about the abundance of hiking and biking trails available in the Boulder area. That little conversation led to a lot of laughter and a lasting friendship.

Just the Way You Are

Their bond was further solidified when Juliette Adler, the matriarch of the large Adler family was hospitalized with a heart attack. All nine of the Adler children were at the hospital every day. However, Brooke was pleasantly surprised to see Jane was also there with Aaron daily. Brooke knew Jane wasn't there just because she thought she'd win brownie points with the family, but because she *cared.* Jane's and Brooke's relationship developed to the point where both women considered the other to be one of their closest friends.

Brooke also had the pleasure of meeting Dr. Zackary Carter while chatting with Jane and Aaron in the cafeteria of the hospital. The trio had been asked to leave Juliette Adler's room while Mrs. Adler had some tests done. Brooke remembered it like it was yesterday.

Jane made some funny remark that had Brooke grinning happily. But when she'd looked up toward the door of the cafeteria, Brooke's mouth simply fell open. It was a good thing she was sitting down too because otherwise her knees might have buckled. The man who'd just walked in was wearing the iconic white lab coat of a physician, and he practically took her breath away.

Noticing Brooke's sudden change in facial expression, Jane turned a curious eye to see who'd entered the room. "Dr. Carter, hello!" Jane waved her arms and called him over to where she and Brooke were seated.

Anita Louise

In spite of her flailing arms, Dr. Zack Carter paid little attention to Jane. His eyes locked with Brooke's. He appeared to be as mesmerized as she was.

Jane made the introductions. "Dr. Zackary Carter, I'd like you to meet one of Aaron's sisters. This is Miss Brooke Adler.

"Dr. Carter." Brooke could barely speak. She nodded stiffly, and the knuckles of her hands turned white as she gripped the edge of the table for support.

"Nice to meet you, Miss Adler."

The sound of Dr. Carter's voice sent goosebumps up and down Brooke's spine, and tingles in other more private places.

Aaron joined the conversation at that point, but Brooke couldn't recall a word her brother said. The only thing she did remember hearing was Dr. McDreamy's voice saying, "Please, call me Zackary."

Through her lust fogged brain, Brooke heard Jane say, "Well, *Zackary*, after we get out of here, you'll have to come over so all of us can get to know each other in a more casual setting."

"Getting to know each other better sounds good to me," he replied as he looked directly at Brooke. He returned his gaze to Jane. "Glad to see you're doing better, Jane, and I know Aaron will continue to take good care of you. Just call my office when you get home, and we'll figure out where and when to get together."

Just the Way You Are

Nodding in Brooke's direction once more, he said, "Miss Adler."

"Brooke. You can call me Brooke," she replied just barely above a whisper.

"Brooke," he repeated as if savoring the sound of her name on his lips before he walked out of the room.

As soon as the doctor was out of hearing range, Brooke couldn't control herself any longer and squealed, "O ... M ... G!"

Jane grinned and said, "Uh-oh. Looks like *somebody* is smitten."

Even then, Aaron only had eyes for Jane. He looked at the woman who was now his fiancée and made the comment, "Somebody certainly is!"

Brooke just rolled her eyes and made an excuse to leave the two lovebirds alone. She made sure to give Jane's shoulder a squeeze before she left, reminding her, "You *better* have that little get together you just talked about. That's one guest I *definitely* want to spend some time with."

Dr. Zackary Carter spent the last eight years totally focused on his job, and he had zero time for women and relationships. Becoming a doctor had been his dream since he was a young boy, and he was totally dedicated to his career. Zack was only twelve years old when his own father had been hospitalized after being hit by a drunk driver while changing a flat tire at the side of the road. The

Anita Louise

emergency room physician saved his dad's life and left a lasting impression on the son.

However, the woman who sat next to Jane Adler in the cafeteria had a face so beautiful, it practically took his breath away. He could see she was tall and slender ... like a model without all the make-up and fancy hair-do's. In fact, there was an air of innocence about her. It made him wonder if there might be another side to her. A side he might persuade her to explore and see how good it could feel for her to be a "bad girl" every once in a while.

Not that he had any time to spare even now. During his residency, he'd spent over a hundred hours a week in the hospital. Now, as a relatively new physician, his hours still added up to between sixty and eighty a week.

He'd been engaged at one time to his high school sweetheart. She promised they'd always be together, "no matter what." However, it seemed when a fiancé had no time for his fiancée, she found other things and other *men* to spend time with.

He was in his second year of residency when he'd walked into their apartment unexpectedly. He was able to sneak away from the hospital for a couple of hours and wanted to surprise Miranda. As it turned out, he'd been the one who was in for a big surprise. As soon as he heard the high pitched sounds of her voice, he thought he recognized them as the sounds she made while in the throes of sexual ecstasy.

Just the Way You Are

She'd complained to him only the weekend before that his absence forced her to use her vibrator way more than she preferred. He was ready to replace her vibrator with his erection. Unfortunately, when he walked into the bedroom, he saw some other guy already had that taken care of. Her look of pleasure turned to horror as she exclaimed, "Oh, no! Zack! What are you doing here?"

Somehow, he was able to speak without showing one bit of emotion. "I'll sleep at the hospital for the next two days. Please be gone by the time I come back." He blocked all her calls and emails, and threw her letters into the trash unopened. The image she'd left in his mind was indelible. He was never going to forget it.

Since then, he'd put all his energy into his career and had no time whatsoever for women or sex. Nevertheless, the idea of a brief affair with the gorgeous Brooke Adler had him thinking. There were a lot of deliciously naughty things he could do with her in a relatively short period of time.

Later that same day, he was standing near the nurse's station reviewing some charts. In his peripheral vision, he noticed the unmistakable form of the woman who'd been occupying his thoughts. She was walking down the hall toward the elevators. He hurried to finish up his notes and handed the chart back to the nurse at the desk. Then he walked swiftly toward where she was standing.

Anita Louise

"Miss Adler, so nice to see you again ... and so soon." He used the smile he usually reserved strictly for his family and close friends.

She'd been looking up at the lights and tapping her foot impatiently. She hadn't noticed him as he approached. "Dr. Carter!"

"It's Zackary, remember? Or Zack, whichever you prefer."

She felt herself blushing. "Yes, Zackary. I remember, and please, do call me Brooke. Only my students call me Miss Adler."

"You're a teacher?"

"Yes. Summit Middle School. English and Language Arts."

"Lucky kids. I never had a teacher who looked like you when I was in middle school. All my teachers were either bald men or matronly women. I think it was a rule, no teachers under the age of fifty."

"Are you flirting with me, Dr. Carter?"

"Zack, remember? And, yes, I'm flirting with you, Brooke. How am I doing?"

"You're doing just fine, Zack. Just fine."

Their eyes met. She touched his arm as she spoke, and he felt an undeniable bolt of energy. All he could think about was how soft her skin would feel next to his. He wished he could drag her into the nearest call room with the hope that no other overworked staffer was occupying the bed. He could still feel the heat from her touch even after she pulled her hand away.

Just the Way You Are

Just then a voice came over the hospital's loudspeaker. "Dr. Zackary Carter. Emergency. STAT."

Immediately he nodded, turned and rushed off.

Brooke watched Dr. Zackary Carter as he hurried away to whatever dire emergency was waiting for him. Never before had she experienced the kind of instant attraction she felt to this man. When he'd walked into the cafeteria, she'd practically melted.

He had the darkest brown eyes she'd ever seen. When she looked into them, it almost felt like she was drowning. She'd dated a few guys over the years, and had a fairly significant relationship in college. But when that ended in disaster, she'd put the idea of having a serious relationship on the back burner indefinitely.

Since she'd met Zackary, it was crystal clear to her there were some people you simply couldn't walk away from. Sometimes you didn't even *care* if you were drowning, you just wanted to go deeper and find out what was down there in those depths.

When the elevator doors had opened, she'd stepped in and pressed the button for the floor where her mother's room was located. She found herself singing the old Richard Palmer tune ... something about a doctor and a bad case of lovin'.

Anita Louise

After that, although Brooke visited the hospital as frequently as her duties as a middle school teacher would allow, she hadn't run into Dr. Carter again. Every time she saw either Jane or Aaron she'd mention, as casually as possible, "If you see Dr. Carter please tell him I said 'hello.'" They told Brooke the good doctor also sent "hello's" back to her. Unfortunately, this news didn't make her feel any better.

Now Brooke was going to help Jane out with the plans for her engagement party. Brooke had just arrived at the home Jane and Aaron shared. When she rang the doorbell, Jane quickly opened the door.

"Brooke," Jane exclaimed when she saw who was standing on the porch. "Please, come in."

The two women hugged each other affectionately.

"I'm so thrilled you and Aaron are getting married. That means you and I will be *sisters!* Of course, I love Gabriella, Olivia and Whitney too, but you're different. We already chose to be friends, and now we get to be sisters by marriage."

"Brooke, you have no idea how much it means to me to have you as my friend, and as my sister. My Dad and my sister Patty will be coming to the wedding, but it's too much to expect them to come for the engagement party too. Having your help means a great deal to me."

Brooke returned Jane's heartfelt hug. "That's what friends and *sisters* are for."

Just the Way You Are

"You know, Brooke, I really love the fact your family is so close and supportive. I was just trying to figure out where to have the party. Come on in the kitchen. I'll fix us some coffee. You've lived in Boulder most of your life, and you know what your family prefers. Having your help is going to make it much easier for me."

They chatted companionably while Jane put on a pot of coffee to brew.

"I know this is primarily a family affair," Brooke said in as casual a manner as possible, "but is Dr. Carter invited by any chance?"

Jane laughed out loud. "You are soooo funny! Do you really think everyone can't see how attracted you and Zack are to one another?"

"I guess it *is* pretty obvious." She lowered her voice to a whisper. "It's *weird!* I've *never* felt like this before. Gabriella was always the 'boy crazy' one, not me. I mean, I'm not a prude or anything, but no guy *ever* did to me what that hunka, hunka doctor does." She sighed and a dreamy look came across her face.

Jane walked over and hugged her friend's shoulders. "I know what you mean. It was like that for me the first time I saw Aaron. I haven't told anyone this, but I had a crush on your brother for *years.* Even before I actually met him."

"Really? I thought you and Aaron met for the first time when you came to Mom and Dad's house with Connor."

"That was the first time we were *introduced,* but it wasn't the first time we'd seen each other. I was at one of his first speaking engagements, front row center. I took one look at him and fell ... hook, line and sinker. As silly as it sounds, I was *sure* we made eye contact when he was on the stage. And I was also sure there was *something* there. I even went to the reception they had for him afterward to see if what I felt was real. But he was with some skinny, model type, so I didn't stay."

"Huh? Who knows?" said Brooke. "I guess the timing just wasn't right back then."

"You're probably right. Anyway, back to your question about your own personal 'Doctor McDreamy.' Yes, he's been invited. And since he knows *you're* going to be there, my prediction is he's *definitely* going to show up."

"Well, in *that* case, not only do we have to get the plans together for your engagement party, I have to figure out what I'm going to wear. I want to make sure I catch the eye of that fine looking doctor friend of yours. Of course, I'll make it look like I didn't spend a single minute thinking about *him* while I was making my remarkable transformation from 'drab to fab.'"

There were many amazing places in Boulder to choose from. However, after considering several wonderful options, they finally decided to have the celebration at Tom's Tavern/SALT. Brooke's enthusiasm for the venue was apparent. "They have a private dining and event room they call the SALT cellar. I've been there for other events, and it's really nice. It's cozy and unique. Plus the food is fantastic. You're going to love it!"

Soon after, Brooke and Jane hugged, said their good-byes, and Brooke rushed out the door. After leaving Jane's, Brooke decided to go down to Pearl Street, the area where the engagement party would be held, and wander around. Her thoughts were filled with a tall, dark and handsome doctor.

~ THE END ~

Anita Louise

Look for other books in the Adler Family Series — available now!

BAD CASE OF LOVIN' YOU
Brooke & Zack

A HOUSE IS NOT A HOME
Michael & Analese

SHOULD I STAY OR SHOULD I GO
Connor & Gina

YOU LIGHT UP MY LIFE
Olivia & Tyler

Just the Way You Are

Connect with Anita Louise:

Author Blog:
http://www.anitalouiseromance.com

Amazon Author Page:
http://www.amazon.com/Anita-Louise/e/B018UGM56C/

Author Smashwords Interview:
https://www.smashwords.com/interview/CandlelitePublishing

Facebook:
https://www.facebook.com/AnitaLouiseRomance

Twitter:
https://twitter.com/anitaromance

Instagram
htttp://www.instagram.com/anita.louise.romance

Google Plus
https://plus.google.com/111029186791103969418

Pinterest
https://www.pinterest.com/romanticanita/